The Stench Struck Nora
Like a Blow—

that too familiar, dead smell—and she saw the tall, weirdly draped figure again.

Nora sat up quickly, trying not to breathe in, and the effort made her dizzy. The figure did not move. There was more light in the room this time, and she could see him clearly.

The strange cloak ended in blackened tatters that hung over his hands and feet, and the hood had ragged holes torn for eyes and mouth—with a sudden rush of horror, Nora realized what she was seeing. The figure was dressed in a human skin. The gutted shell of some other human being flapped grotesquely against his own . . .

—from "Sun City" by Lisa Tuttle

Books by Ramsey Campbell

Dark Companions
New Terrors (editor)
New Terrors II (editor)

Published by POCKET BOOKS

Most Pocket Books are available at special quantity discounts for bulk purchases for sales promotions, premiums or fund raising. Special books or book excerpts can also be created to fit specific needs.

For details write the office of the Vice President of Special Markets, Pocket Books, 1230 Avenue of the Americas, New York, New York 10020.

NEW TERRORS II

RAMSEY CAMPBELL

PUBLISHED BY POCKET BOOKS NEW YORK

POCKET BOOKS, a division of Simon & Schuster, Inc.
1230 Avenue of the Americas, New York, N.Y. 10020

Acknowledgments

"Sun City" by Lisa Tuttle, copyright © 1980 by Lisa Tuttle and reprinted with her permission.

"Time to Laugh" by Joan Aiken, copyright © 1980 by Joan Aiken Enterprises Ltd. and reprinted with her permission.

"Bridal Suite" by Graham Masterton, copyright © 1980 by Graham Masterton and reprinted with his permission.

"The Miraculous Cairn" by Christopher Priest, copyright © 1980 by Christopher Priest and reprinted with the permission of the author and his agent, A. P. Watt, Ltd.

"The Rubber Room" by Robert Bloch, copyright © 1980 by Robert Bloch and reprinted with his permission.

"Drama in Five Acts" by Giles Gordon, copyright © 1980 by Giles Gordon and reprinted with the permission of the author and his agent, Elaine Greene, Ltd.

"The Initiation" by Jack Sullivan, copyright © 1980 by Jack Sullivan and reprinted with his permission.

"Lucille Would Have Known" by John Burke, copyright © 1980 by John Burke and reprinted with the permission of the author and his agent, David Higham Associates.

Contents

Lisa Tuttle

Sun City

LISA TUTTLE WAS BORN IN 1952. SHE RECEIVED A BA IN *English from Syracuse University in 1973, and the John W. Campbell Award for the best new science fiction writer of the year (in conjunction with Spider Robinson) in 1974. She is a television columnist and critic for Austin's daily newspaper (Texas), and her stories have appeared in just about all the major science fiction magazines being published as I write. But it was her horror fiction I encountered first, and I was impressed by its ruthlessness. Even her optimism is disturbing.*

It was three a.m., the dead, silent middle of the night. Except for the humming of the soft-drink machine in one corner, and the irregular, rumbling cough of the ice machine hidden in an alcove just beyond it, the lobby was quiet. There weren't likely to be any more check-ins until after dawn—all the weary cross-country drivers would be settled elsewhere by now, or grimly determined to push on without a rest.

Clerking the 11 p.m. to 7 a.m. shift was a dull, lonely job, but usually Nora Theale didn't mind it. She preferred working at night, and the solitude didn't bother her. But tonight, for the third night in

9

a row, she was jumpy. It was an irrational nervousness, and it annoyed Nora that she couldn't pin it down. There was always the possibility of robbery, of course, but the Posada del Norte hadn't been hit in the year she had worked there, and Nora didn't think the motel made a very enticing target.

Seeking a cause for her unease, Nora often glanced around the empty lobby and through the glass doors at the parking lot and the highway beyond. She never saw anything out of place—except a shadow which might have been cast by someone moving swiftly through the bluish light of the parking lot. But it was gone in an instant, and she couldn't be sure she had seen it.

Nora picked up the evening paper and tried to concentrate. She read about plans to build a huge fence along the border, to keep illegal aliens out. It was an idea she liked—the constant flow back and forth between Mexico and the United States was one of the things she hated most about El Paso—but she didn't imagine it would work. After a few more minutes of scanning state and national news, Nora tossed the paper into the garbage can. She didn't want to read about El Paso; El Paso bored and depressed and disturbed her. She couldn't wait to leave it.

Casting another uneasy glance around the unchanged lobby, Nora leaned over to the file cabinet and pulled open the drawer where she kept her books. She picked out a mystery by Josephine Tey and settled down to it, determined to win over her nerves.

She read, undisturbed except for a few twinges of unease, until six a.m. when she had to let the man with the newspapers in and make the first wake-up call. The day clerk arrived a few minutes after seven, and that meant it was time for Nora to leave. She gathered her things together into a shoulderbag. She had a lot with her because she had spent the past two days in one of the motel's free rooms rather than go home. But the rooms were all booked up for that night, so she had to clear out. Since her husband had moved out, Nora hadn't felt like spending much time in the apartment that was now hers alone. She meant to move, but since she didn't want to stay in El Paso, it seemed more sensible simply to let the lease run out rather than go to the expense and trouble of finding another temporary home. She meant to leave El Paso just as soon as she got a little money together and decided on a place to go.

She didn't like the apartment, but it was large and cheap. Larry had picked it out because it was close to his office, and he liked to ride his bicycle to work. It wasn't anywhere near the motel where Nora worked, but Nora didn't care. She had her car.

She parked it now in the space behind the small, one-storey apartment complex. It was a hideous place; Nora winced every time she came home to it. It was made of an ugly pink fake-adobe, and had a red-tiled roof. There were some diseased-looking cactuses planted along the concrete walkway, but no grass or trees: water was scarce.

The stench of something long-dead and richly rotting struck Nora as she opened the door to her apartment. She stepped back immediately, gagging. Her heart raced; she felt, oddly, afraid. But she recovered in a moment—it was just a smell, after all, and in her apartment. She had to do something about it. Breathing through her mouth, she stepped forward again.

The kitchen was clean, the garbage pail empty, and the refrigerator nearly bare. She found nothing there, or in the bedroom or bathroom, that seemed to be the cause of the odour. In the bedroom, she cautiously breathed in through her nose to test the air. It was clean. She walked slowly back to the living room, but there was nothing there, either. The whiff of foulness had gone as if it had never been.

Nora shrugged, and locked the door. It might have been something outside. If she smelled it again, she'd talk to the landlord about it.

There was nothing in the kitchen she could bear the thought of eating, so, after she had showered and changed, Nora walked down to Seven-Eleven, three blocks away, and bought a few essentials: milk, eggs, bread, Dr Pepper and a package of sugared doughnuts.

The sun was already blazing and the dry wind abraded her skin. It would be another hot, dry, windy day—a day like every other day in El Paso. Nora was glad she slept through most of them. She thought about North Carolina, where she had gone to college, reflecting wistfully that up there the leaves would be starting to turn now. As she walked back to her apartment with the bag of groceries in her arms, Nora thought about moving east to North Carolina.

The telephone was ringing as Nora walked in.

"I've been trying to get in touch with you for the past three days!"

It was her husband, Larry.

"I've been out a lot." She began to peel the cellophane wrapping off the doughnuts.

"Do tell. Look, Nora, I've got some papers for you to sign."

"Aw, and I thought maybe you'd called to say happy anniversary."

He was silent. One side of Nora's mouth twitched upwards: she'd scored.

Then he sighed. "What do you want, Nora? Am I supposed to think that today means something to you? That you still care? That you want me back?"

"God forbid."

"Then cut the crap, all right? So we didn't make it to our third wedding anniversary—all right, so *legally* we're still married—but what's the big deal?"

"I was joking, Larry. You never could recognize a joke."

"I didn't call to fight with you, Nora. Or to joke. I'd just like you to sign these papers so we can get this whole thing over with. You won't even have to show up in court."

Nora bit into a doughnut and brushed off the spray of sugar that powdered her shirt.

"Nora? When should I bring the papers by?"

She set the half-eaten doughnut down on the counter and reflected. "Um, come this evening, if you want. Not too early, or I'll still be asleep. Say . . . seven-thirty?"

"Seven-thirty."

"That won't cut into your dinner plans with what's-her-name?"

"Seven-thirty will be fine, Nora. I'll see you then. Just be there." And he hung up before she could get in another dig.

Nora grimaced, then shrugged as she hung up. She finished the doughnut, feeling depressed. Despite herself, she'd started thinking about Larry again, and their marriage which had seemed to go bad before it had properly started. She thought about their brief honeymoon. She remembered Mexico.

It had been Larry's idea to drive down to Mexico—Nora had always thought of Mexico as a poor and dirty place, filled with undesirables who were always sneaking into the United States. But Larry had wanted to go, and Nora had wanted to make Larry happy.

It was their *luna de miel,* moon of honey, Larry said, and the Spanish words sounded almost sweet to her, coming from his mouth. Even Mexico, in his company, had seemed freshly promising, especially after they escaped the dusty borderlands and reached the ocean.

One afternoon they had parked on an empty beach and made love. Larry had fallen asleep, and Nora had left him to walk up the beach and explore.

She walked along in a daze of happiness, her body tingling, climbing over rocks and searching for shells to bring back to her husband. She didn't realize how far she had travelled until she was shocked out of her pleasant haze by a sharp cry, whether human or animal she could not be certain. She heard some indistinct words, then, tossed to her by the wind.

Nora was frightened. She didn't want to know what the sounds meant or where they came from. She wanted to get back to Larry and forget that she had heard anything. She turned around immediately, and began to weave her way back among the white boulders. But she must have mistaken her way, for as she clambered back over a rock she was certain she had just climbed, she saw them below her, posed like some sacrificial tableau.

At the centre was a girl, spread out on a low, flat rock. The victim. Crouching over her, doing something, was a young man. Another young man stared at them greedily. Nora gazed at the girl's face, which was contorted in pain. She heard her whimper. It was only then that she realized, with a cold flash of dread, what she was seeing. The girl was being raped.

Nora was frozen with fear and indecision, and then the girl opened her eyes, and gazed straight up at Nora. Her brown eyes were eloquent with agony. Was there a glimmer of hope there at the sight of Nora? Nora couldn't be sure. She stared into those eyes for what seemed like a very long time, trying desperately to think of what to do. She wanted to help this girl, to chase away the men. But there were *two* men, and she, Nora, had no particular strengths. They would probably be pleased to have two victims. And at any time one of them might look up and see her watching.

Trying to make no noise, Nora slipped backwards off the rock. The scene vanished from her sight; the pleading brown eyes could no longer accuse her. Nora began to run as best she could over the uneven ground. She hoped she was running in the right direction, and that she would soon come upon Larry. Larry would help her—she would tell him what she had seen, and he would know what to do. He might be able to frighten away the men, or, speaking Spanish, he could at least tell the police what she had seen. She would be safe with Larry.

The minutes passed and Nora still, blindly, ran. She couldn't see their car, and knew the horrifying possibility that she was running in the wrong direction—but she didn't dare go back. A cramp in her side and ragged pains when she drew breath forced her to walk: she felt the moment when she might have been of some help, when she could have reached Larry in time, drain inexorably away. She never knew how long she had walked and run before she finally caught sight of their car, but, even allowing for her panic, Nora judged it had been at the very least a half an hour. She felt as if she had been running desperately all day. And she was too late. Much too late. By now, they would have finished with the girl. They might have killed her, they might have let her go. In either case, Nora and Larry would be too late to help her.

"There you are! Where'd you go? I was worried," Larry said, slipping off the hood of the car and coming to embrace her. He sounded not worried but lazily contented.

It was too late. She did not tell him, after all, what she had witnessed. She never told him.

Nora became deathly ill that night in a clean, American-style hotel near Acapulco. Two days later, still shaking and unable to keep anything in her stomach, Nora flew back to her mother and the family doctor in Dallas, leaving Larry to drive back by himself.

It was the stench that woke her. Nora lurched out of sleep, sitting up on the bed, gagging and clutching the sheet to her mouth, trying not to breath in the smell. It was the smell of something dead.

Groggy with sleep, she needed another moment to realize something much more frightening than the smell: there was someone else in the room.

A tall figure stood, motionless, not far from the foot of her bed. The immediate fear Nora felt at the sight was quickly pushed out of the way by a coldly rational, self-preserving consciousness. In the dim light Nora could not tell much about the intruder except that he was oddly dressed in some sort of cloak, and that his features were masked by some sort of head mask. The most important thing she noticed was that he did not block her path to the door, and if she moved quickly . . .

Nora bolted, running through the apartment like a rabbit, and bursting out through the front door into the courtyard.

It was late afternoon, the sun low in the sky but not yet gone. One of her neighbours, a Mexican, was grilling hamburgers on a little *hibachi*. He stared at her sudden appearance, then grinned. Nora realized she was wearing only an old t-shirt of Larry's and a pair of brightly coloured bikini pants, and she scowled at the man.

"Someone broke into my apartment," she said sharply, cutting into his grin.

"Want to use our phone? Call the police?"

Nora thought of Larry and felt a sudden fierce hatred of him: he had left her to this, abandoned her to the mercy of burglars, potential rapists, and the leers of this Mexican.

"No, thanks," she said, her tone still harsh. "But I think he's still inside. Do you think you could . . ."

"You want me to see if he still there? Sure, sure, I'll check. You don't have to worry." He sprang forward. Nora hated his eagerness to help, but she needed him right now.

There was no one in her apartment. The back door was still locked, and the screens on all the windows were undisturbed.

Nora didn't ask her neighbour to check behind every piece of furniture after he had looked into the closets: she was feeling the loathing she always felt for hysterical, over-emotional reactions. Only this time the loathing was directed at herself.

Although one part of her persisted in believing she had seen an intruder, reason told her she had been mistaken. She had been tricked by a nightmare into running for help like a terrified child.

She was rude to the man who had helped her, dismissing him as

15

sharply as if he were an erring servant. She didn't want to see the smug, masculine concern on his face; didn't want him around knowing he must be chuckling inwardly at a typical hysterical female.

Nora intended to forget about it, as she had forgotten other embarrassing incidents, other disturbing dreams, but she was not allowed.

She had a hard time falling asleep the next day. Children were playing in the parking lot, and her doze was broken time and again by their shouts, meaningless fragments of talk, and the clamour of a bicycle bell.

When, at last, she did sleep in the afternoon, it was to dream that she and Larry were having one of their interminable, pointless, low-voiced arguments. She woke from the frustrating dream with the impression that someone had come into the room and, certain it was Larry and ready to resume the argument in real life, she opened her eyes.

Before she could speak his name, the stench struck her like a blow—that too familiar, dead smell—and she saw the tall, weirdly draped figure again.

Nora sat up quickly, trying not to breathe in, and the effort made her dizzy. The figure did not move. There was more light in the room this time, and she could see him clearly.

The strange cloak ended in blackened tatters that hung over his hands and feet, and the hood had ragged holes torn for eyes and mouth—with a rush of horror, Nora realized what she was seeing. The figure was dressed in a human skin. The gutted shell of some other human being flapped grotesquely against his own.

Nora's mouth dropped open, and she breathed in the smell of the rotting skin, and, for one horrible moment, she feared she was about to vomit, that she would be immobilized, sick and at the monster's mercy.

Fear tightened her throat and gut, and she managed to stumble out of the room and down the hall.

She didn't go outside. She remembered, as she reached the front door, that she had seen that figure before. That it was only a nightmarish hallucination. Only a dream. She could scarcely accept it, but she knew it was true. Only a dream. Her fingers clutched the cool metal doorknob, but she did not turn it. She leaned against the door, feeling her stomach muscles contract spasmodically, aware of the weakness in her legs and the bitter taste in her mouth.

She tried to think of something calming, but could not chase the visions from her mind: knives, blood, putrefaction. What someone who had been skinned must look like. And what was he, beneath that rotten skin? What could that ghastly disguise hide?

When at last she bullied and cajoled herself into returning to the bedroom, the thing, of course, was gone. Not even the cadaverine smell remained.

Nightmare or hallucination, whatever it was, it came again on the third day. She was ready for it—had lain rigidly awake for hours in the sunlit room knowing he would come—but the stench and the sight were scarcely any easier to endure the third time. No matter how much she told herself she was dreaming, no matter how hard she tried to believe that what she saw (and smelled?) was mere hallucination, Nora had not the cold-bloodedness to remain on her bed until it vanished.

Once again she ran from the room in fear, hating herself for such irrational behaviour. And, again, the thing had gone when she calmed herself and returned to look.

On the fourth day Nora stayed at the motel.

If someone else had suggested escaping a nightmare by sleeping somewhere else, Nora would have been scornful. But she justified her action to herself: this dream was different. There was the smell, for one thing. Perhaps there was some real source to the smell, and it was triggering the nightmare. In that case, a change of air should cure her.

The room she moved into when she got off work that morning was like all the other rooms in the Posada del Norte. It was clean and uninspired, the decor hovering between the merely bland and the aggressively ugly. The carpet was a stubby, mottled gold; the bedspread and chair cushions were dark orange. The walls were covered in white, textured vinyl with a mural painted above the bed. The murals differed from room to room—in this room, it was a picture of a stepped Aztec pyramid, rendered in shades of orange and brown.

Nora turned on the air conditioning, and a blast of air came out

17

in a frozen rush. She took a few toilet articles into the bathroom, but left everything else packed in the overnight bag which she had dropped on to a chair. She had no desire to ''settle in'' or to intrude herself on the bland anonymity of the room.

She turned on the television and lay back on the bed to observe the meaningless interactions of the guests on a morning talk show. She had nothing better to do. After the network show was a talk show of the local variety, with a plain, overly made-up hostess who smiled, blinked and nodded a lot. Her guests were a red-faced, middle-aged man who talked about the problems caused by illegal aliens; and a woman who discussed the ancient beauties of Mexico. Nora turned off the set halfway through her slide show featuring pyramids and other monuments in Mexico.

The television silent, she heard the sound of people moving in next door. There seemed to be a lot of them, and they were noisy. A radio clicked on, bringing in music and commercials from Mexico. There was a lot of laughter from the room, and Nora caught an occasional Spanish-sounding word.

Nora swore, not softly. Why couldn't they party on their own side of the border? And who ever carried on in such a way at ten o'clock in the morning? But she hesitated to pound on the wall: that would only draw attention to herself, and she didn't imagine it would deter them.

Instead, to shield herself, she turned on the television set again. It was game-show time, and the sounds of hysteria, clanging bells and idiotic laughter filled the room. Nora sighed, turned the volume down a bit, and pulled off her clothes. Then she climbed under the blankets and gazed blankly at the flickering images.

She was tired, but too keyed-up to sleep. Her mind kept circling until she deliberately thought about what was bothering her: the man in the skin. What did it mean? Why was it haunting her?

It seemed more a hallucination than an ordinary dream, and that made Nora doubly uneasy. It was too *real*. When she saw, and smelled, the nightmarish figure, she could never quite convince herself she was only dreaming.

And what did the hideous figure itself mean? It must have come crawling out of her subconscious for some reason, thought Nora. But she didn't really think she had just made it up herself—the idea of a man draped in another's skin stirred some deep memory. Somewhere, long before, she had read about, or seen a picture of, a figure who wore the stripped-off skin of another. Was it something from Mexico? Some ancient, pre-Columbian god?

Yet whenever she strained to recall it, the memory moved perversely away.

And why did the dream figure haunt her now? Because she was alone? But that was absurd. Nora shifted uncomfortably in bed. She had no regrets about the separation or the impending divorce; she was glad Larry was gone. They should have had the sense to call it quits years before. She didn't want him back under any circumstances.

And yet—Larry was gone, and old two-skins was haunting her.

Finally, worn out by the useless excavations of her memory, Nora turned off the television and went to sleep.

She woke feeling sick. She didn't need to turn her head or open her eyes to know, but she did. And, of course, he was in the room. He would come to her wherever she fled. The stench came from the rotting skin he wore, not from a neighbour's garbage or something dead between the walls. He didn't look like something hallucinated—he seemed perfectly substantial standing there beside the television set and in front of the draperies.

Staring at him, Nora willed herself to wake up. She willed him to melt and vanish. Nothing happened. She saw the dark gleam of his eyes through ragged eye holes, and she was suddenly more frightened than she had ever been in her life.

She closed her eyes. The blood pounding in her ears was the sound of fear. She would not be able to hear him if he moved closer. Unable to bear the thought of what he might be doing, unseen by her, Nora opened her eyes. He was still there. He did not seem to have moved.

She had to get out, Nora thought. She had to give him the chance to vanish—he always had, before. But she was naked—she couldn't go out as she was, and all her clothes were on the chair beside the window, much too close to him. In a moment, Nora knew, she might start screaming. Already she was shaking—she had to do *something*.

On fear-weakened legs, Nora climbed out of bed and stumbled

towards the bathroom. She slammed the door shut behind her, hearing the comforting snick of the lock as she pressed the button in.

Then she stood with palms pressed on the Formica surface surrounding the basin, head hanging down, breathing shallowly in and out, waiting for the fear to leave her. When she had calmed herself, she raised her head and looked in the mirror.

There she was, the same old Nora. Lost her husband, driven out of her apartment by nerves, surrounded by the grey and white sterility of a hotel bathroom. There was no reason for her to be here—not in this building, not in El Paso, not in Texas, not in this *life*. But here she was, going on as if it all had some purpose. And for no better reason than that she didn't know what else to do—she had no notion of how to start over.

Nora caught a glimpse of motion in the mirror, and then the clear reflection of the one who had come for her: the lumpish head with the mask of another's face stretched crudely over his own. She looked calmly into the mirror, right into the reflections of his eyes. They were brown, she realized, very much like a pair of eyes she remembered from Mexico.

Feeling a kind of relief because there was no longer anywhere else to run, Nora turned away from the mirror to face him, to see this man in his dead skin for the first time in a fully lighted room. "She sent you to me," Nora said, and realized she was no longer afraid.

The skin was horrible—a streaky grey with ragged, black edges. But what of the man underneath? She had seen his eyes. Suddenly, as she gazed steadily at the figure, his name came into her mind, as clearly as if he had written it on the mirror for her: Xipe, the Flayed One. She had been right in thinking him some ancient Mexican god, Nora thought. But she knew nothing else about him, nor did she need to know. He was not a dream to be interpreted—he was here, now.

She saw that he carried a curved knife; watched without fear as he tore seams in the skin he wore, and it fell away, a discarded husk.

Revealed without the disfiguring, concealing outer skin, Xipe was a dark young man with a pure, handsome face. Not a Mexican,

Nora thought, but an Indian, of noble and ancient blood. He smiled at her. Nora smiled back, realizing now that there had never been any reason to fear him.

He offered her the knife. So easy, his dark eyes promised her. No fear, no question in their brown depths. Shed the old skin, the old life, as I have done, and be reborn.

When she hesitated, he reached out with his empty hand and traced a line along her skin. The touch of his hand seared like ice. Her skin was too tight. Xipe, smooth, clean and new, watched her, offering the ritual blade.

At last she took the knife and made the first incision.

Joan Aiken

Time to Laugh

JOAN AIKEN IS THE DAUGHTER OF CONRAD AIKEN, AUTHOR *of at least two minor classics of the macabre* (Mr. Arcularis *and* Silent Snow, Secret Snow). *Her mother educated her at home until she was twelve, when she went to a small progressive boarding school in Oxford. She worked for the BBC and the United Nations, and was features editor for* Argosy *for five years before, in the early sixties, she began to write full time. By now she has written about fifty books, three of which won the Guardian Award for children's literature; one* (The Wolves of Willoughby Chase) *also won the Lewis Carroll Award, while* Nightfall *was honoured by the Mystery Writers of America. She is married to the American painter Julius Goldstein.*

Does she also get an award for the greatest number of title changes? In America, Trouble with Product X *became* Beware of the Bouquet; Hate Begins at Home *became* Dark Interval; The Ribs of Death *turned into* The Crystal Crow; The Butterfly Picnic *ended up as* A Cluster of Separate Sparks, *and yet some of us would be content to invent just one title as striking. Here is more of her originality.*

When Matt climbed in at the open window of The Croft, it had been raining steadily for three days—August rain, flattening the bronze-green plains of wheat, making dim green jungles of the little woods round Wentby, turning the motorway which cut across the small town's southern tip into a greasy nightmare on which traffic skidded and piled into crunching heaps; all the county police were desperately busy trying to clear up one disaster after another.

If there had been a river at Wentby, Matt might have gone fishing instead, on that Saturday afternoon . . . but the town's full name was Wentby Waterless, the nearest brook was twenty miles away, the rain lay about in scummy pools on the clay, or sank into the lighter soil and vanished. And if the police had not been so manifestly engaged and distracted by the motorway chaos, it might never have occurred to Matt that now would be the perfect time to explore The Croft; after all, by the end of three days' rain, what else was there to do? It had been ten years since the Regent Cinema closed its doors for the last time and went into liquidation.

A grammar-school duffelcoat would be too conspicuous and recognizable; Matt wore his black plastic jacket, although it was not particularly rainproof. But it was at least some protection against the brambles which barred his way.

He had long ago worked out an entry into The Croft grounds, having noticed that they ended in a little triangle of land which bit into the corner of a builder's yard where his father had once briefly worked; Matt had a keen visual memory, never forgot anything he had once observed and, after a single visit two years ago to tell his father that Mum had been taken off to hospital, was able to pick his way without hesitation through cement mixers, stacks of two-by-two, and concrete slabs, to the exact corner, the wattle palings and tangle of elderberry bushes. Kelly never troubled to lock his yard, and, in any case, on a Saturday afternoon, no one was about; all snug at home, watching telly.

He bored his way through the wet greenery and, as he had reckoned, came to the weed-smothered terrace at the foot of a flight of steps; overgrown shoots of rambler rose half blocked them, but it was just possible to battle upwards, and at the top he was rewarded by a dusky, triangular vista of lawn stretching away on the left towards the house, on the right towards untended vegetable gardens.

Amazingly—in the very middle of Wentby—there were rabbits feeding on the lawn, who scattered at his appearance. And between him and the house two aged, enormous apple trees towered, massive against the murky sky, loaded down with fruit. He had seen them in the aerial photograph of the town, recently exhibited on a school noticeboard; that was what had given him the notion of exploring The Croft; you could find out a few things at school if you kept your eyes open and used your wits. And he had heard of The Croft before that, of course, but it was nowhere to be seen from any of the town streets: a big house, built in the mid nineteenth century on an inaccessible plot of land, bought subsequently, after World War Two, by a rich retired actress and her company director husband, Lieutenant-Colonel and Mrs. Jordan. They were hardly ever seen; never came out, or went anywhere; Matt had a vague idea that one of them—maybe both?—had died. There was a general belief that the house was haunted; also full of treasures; also defended by any number of burglar alarms inside the building, gongs that would start clanging, bells that would ring up at the police station, not to mention mantraps, spring guns, and savage alsatians outside in the grounds.

However the alsatians did not seem to be in evidence—if they had been, surely the rabbits would not have been feeding so peacefully? So, beginning to disbelieve these tales, Matt picked his way, quietly but with some confidence, over the sodden tussocky grass to the apple trees. The fruit, to his chagrin, was far from ripe. Also they were wretched little apples, codlins possibly, lumpy and misshapen, not worth the bother of scrumping. Even the birds appeared to have neglected them; numbers of undersized windfalls lay rotting already on the ground. Angrily, Matt flung a couple against the wall of the house, taking some satisfaction from the squashy thump with which they spattered the stone.

The house had not been built of local brick like the rest of Wentby, but from massive chunks of sombre, liver-coloured rock, imported, no doubt at great expense, from farther north; the effect was powerful and ugly; dark as blood, many-gabled and frowning, the building kept guard over its tangled grounds. It seemed deserted; all the windows were lightless, even on such a pouring wet afternoon; and, prowling round to the front of the house, over a carriage sweep pocked with grass and weeds, Matt found that the front doorstep had a thin skin of moss over it, as if no foot had trodden there for months. Perhaps the back—? but that was some distance away, and behind a screen of trellis work and yellow-flecked ornamental laurels. Working on towards it, Matt came to a stop, badly startled at the sight of a half-open window, which, until he reached it, had been concealed from him by a great sagging swatch of untrimmed winter jasmine, whose tiny dark-green leaves were almost black with wet. The coffin-shaped oblong of the open window was black too; Matt stared at it, hypnotized, for almost five minutes, unable to decide whether to go in or not.

Was there somebody inside, there, in the dark? Or had the house been burgled, maybe weeks ago, and the burglar had left the window like that, not troubling to conceal evidence of his entry, because nobody ever came to the place? Or?—unnerving thought—was there a burglar inside now, at this minute?

Revolving all these different possibilities, Matt found that he had been moving slowly nearer and nearer to the wall with the window in it; the window was about six feet above ground, but so thickly sleeved around with creeper that climbing in would present no problem at all. The creeper seemed untouched; showed no sign of damage.

Almost without realizing that he had come to a decision, Matt found himself digging toes into the wet mass and pulling himself up—showers of drops flew into his face—until he was able to lean across the windowsill, bracing his elbows against the inner edge of the frame. As might have been expected, the sill inside was swimming with rainwater, the paint starting to crack; evidently the window had been open for hours, maybe days.

Matt stared into the dusky interior, waiting for his eyes to adjust to the dimness. At first, all he could see was vague masses of furniture. Slowly these began to resolve into recognizable forms: tapestried chairs with high backs and bulbous curving legs, side tables covered in ornaments, a standard lamp with an elaborate pleated shade, dripping tassels, a huge china pot, a flower-patterned carpet, a black shaggy hearthrug, a gold-framed portrait over the mantel. The hearth was fireless, the chair beside it empty, the room sunk in silence. Listening with all his concentration, Matt could hear no sound from anywhere about the house. Encouraged, he swung a knee over the sill, ducked his head and shoulders under the sash, and levered himself in; then, with instinctive caution, he slid the sash down behind him, so that, in the unlikely event of another intruder visiting the garden, the way indoors would not be so enticingly visible.

Matt did not intend to close the window completely, but the sash cord had perished and the heavy frame, once in motion, shot right down before he could stop it; somewhat to his consternation, a little catch clicked across; evidently it was a burglar-proof lock, for he was unable to pull it open again; there was a keyhole in the catch, and he guessed that it could not now be opened again without the key.

Swearing under his breath, Matt turned to survey the room. How would it ever be possible to find the right key in this cluttered, dusky place? It might be in a bowl of odds and ends on the mantelpiece—or in a desk drawer—or hanging on a nail—or in a box—no casual intruder could hope to come across it. Nor—he turned back to inspect the window again—could he hope to smash his way out. The windowpanes were too small, the bars too thick. Still, there would be other ways of leaving the house, perhaps he could simply unlock an outside door. He decided that before exploring any farther he had better establish his means of exit, and so took a couple of steps towards a doorway that he could now see on his right. This led through to a large chilly dining room where a cobwebbed chandelier hung over a massive mahogany dining table, corralled by eight chairs, and reflecting ghostly grey light from a window beyond. The dining room window, to Matt's relief, was a casement; easy enough to break out of that, he thought, his spirits rising; but perhaps there would be no need, perhaps the burglar catch was not fastened; and he was about to cross the dining room and examine it closely when the sound of silvery laughter behind him nearly shocked him out of his wits.

"Aha! Aha! Ha-ha-ha-ha-ha-ha!" trilled the mocking voice, not six feet away. Matt spun round, his heart almost bursting out through his rib cage. He would have been ready to swear there wasn't a soul in the house. Was it a spook? Were the stories true, after all?

The room he had first entered still seemed empty, but the laughter had certainly come from that direction, and as he stood in the doorway, staring frantically about him, he heard it again, a long mocking trill, repeated in exactly the same cadence.

"Jeeez!" whispered Matt.

And then, as he honestly thought he was on the point of fainting from fright, the explanation was supplied: at exactly the same point from which the laughter had come, a clock began to chime in a thin silvery note obviously intended to match the laughter: *ting, tong, ting, tong.* Four o'clock.

"Jeez," breathed Matt again. "What do you know about that? A laughing clock!"

He moved over to inspect the clock. It was a large, elaborate affair, stood on a kind of bureau with brass handles, under a glass dome. The structure of the clock, outworks, whatever you call it, was all gilded and ornamented with gold cherubs who were falling about laughing, throwing their fat little heads back, or doubled up with amusement.

"Very funny," muttered Matt sourly. "Almost had me dead of heart failure, you can laugh!"

Over the clock, he now saw, a big tapestry hung on the wall, which echoed the theme of laughter: girls in frilly tunics this time, and a fat old guy sitting on a barrel squashing grapes into his mouth while he hugged a girl to him with the other arm, all of them, too, splitting themselves over some joke, probably a rude one to judge from the old chap's appearance.

Matt wished very much that the clock would strike again, but presumably it would not do that till five o'clock—unless it chimed the quarters; he had better case the rest of the house in the meantime, and reckon to be back in this room by five. Would it be possible to pinch the clock? he wondered. But it looked dauntingly heavy—and probably its mechanism was complicated and delicate, might go wrong if shifted; how could he ever hope to carry it through all those bushes and over the paling fence? And then there would be the problem of explaining its appearance in his father's council flat; he could hardly say that he had found it lying on a rubbish dump. Still he longed to possess it—think what the other guys in the gang would say when they heard it! Maybe he could keep it in Kip Butterworth's house—old Kip, lucky fellow, had a room of his own and such a lot of electronic junk all over it that one clock more or less would never be noticed.

But first he would bring Kip here, at a time just before the clock was due to strike, and let *him* have the fright of his life . . .

Sniggering to himself at this agreeable thought, Matt turned back towards the dining room, intending to carry out his original plan of unfastening one of the casement windows, when for the second time he was stopped dead by terror.

A voice behind him said, "Since you are here, you may as well wind the clock." And added drily, "Saturday is its day for winding, so it is just as well you came."

This time the voice was unmistakably human; trembling like a leaf, Matt was obliged to admit to himself that there was no chance of its being some kind of electronic device—or even a spook—it was an old woman's voice, harsh, dry, a little shaky, but resonant; only, where the devil *was* she?

Then he saw that what he had taken for wall beyond the fireplace was, in fact, one of those dangling bamboo curtains, and beyond it—another bad moment for Matt—was this motionless figure sitting on a chair, watching him; had been watching him—must have—all the time, ever since he had climbed in, for the part of the room beyond the curtain was just a kind of alcove, a big bay window really, leading nowhere. She must have been there all the time . . .

"Go on," she repeated, watching Matt steadily from out of her black triangles of eyes, "wind the clock."

He found his voice and said hoarsely, "Where's the key, then?"

"In the round bowl on the left side."

His heart leapt; perhaps the window key would be there too. But it was not; there was only one key: a long heavy brass shaft with a cross-piece at one end and a lot of fluting at the other.

"Lift the dome off; carefully," she said. "You'll find two keyholes in the face. Wind them both. One's for the clock, the other for the chime."

And, as he lifted off the dome and began winding, she added thoughtfully, "My husband made that clock for me, on my thirtieth birthday. It's a recording of my own voice—the laugh. Uncommon, isn't it? He was an electrical engineer, you see. Clocks were his hobby. All kinds of unusual ones he invented—there was a Shakespeare clock, and a barking dog, and one that sang hymns—my voice again. I had a beautiful singing voice in those days—and my laugh was famous of course. 'Miss Langdale's crystalline laugh,' the critics used to call it . . . My husband was making a skull clock just before he died. There's the skull.''

There it was, to be sure, a real skull, perched on top of the big china jar to the right of the clock.

Vaguely now, Matt remembered reports of her husband's death; wasn't there something a bit odd about it? Found dead of heart failure in the underpass below the motorway, at least a mile from his house; what had he been *doing* there, in the middle of the night? Why walk through the underpass, which was not intended for pedestrians anyway?

"He was going to get me some cigarettes when he died," she went on, and Matt jumped; had she read his thought? How could she know so uncannily what was going through his head?

"I've given up smoking since then," she went on. "Had to, really . . . They won't deliver, you see. Some things you can get delivered, so I make do with what I can get. I don't like people coming to the house too often, because they scare the birds. I'm a great bird person, you know—"

Unless she has a servant, then, she's alone in the house, Matt thought, as she talked on, in her sharp, dry old voice. He began to feel less terrified—perhaps he could just scare her into letting him leave. Perhaps, anyway, she was mad?

"Are you going to phone the police?" he asked boldly. "I wasn't going to pinch anything, you know—just came in to have a look-see."

"My dear boy, I don't care *why* you came in. As you *are* here, you might as well make yourself useful. Go into the dining room, will you, and bring back some of those bottles."

The rain had abated, just a little, and the dining room was some degrees lighter when he walked through it. All along the window wall Matt was amazed to see wooden wine racks filled with bottles and half-bottles of champagne. There must be hundreds. There were also, in two large log baskets beside the empty grate, dozens of empties. An armchair was drawn close to an electric bar fire, not switched on; a half-empty glass and bottle stood on a silver tray on the floor beside the armchair.

"Bring a glass too," Mrs. Jordan called.

And when he returned with the glass, the tray, and several bottles under his arm, she said,

"Now, open one of them. You know how to, I hope?"

He had seen it done on television; he managed it without difficulty.

"Ought to be chilled, of course," she remarked, receiving the glass from him. One of her hands lay limply on the arm of her chair—she hitched it up from time to time with the other hand when it slipped off; and, now that he came near to her for the first time, he noticed that she smelt very bad; a strange, fetid smell of dry unwashed old age and something worse. He began to suspect that perhaps she was *unable* to move from her chair. Curiously enough, instead of this making him fear her less, it made him fear her more. Although she seemed a skinny, frail old creature, her face was quite full in shape, pale and puffy like underdone pastry. It must have been a handsome one long ago—like a wicked fairy pretending to be a princess in a fairy-tale illustration; now she just looked spiteful and secretive, grinning down at her glass of bubbly. Her hair, the colour of old dry straw, was done very fancy, piled up on top of her head. Perhaps it was a wig.

"Get a glass for yourself, if you want," she said. "There are some more in the dining-room cupboard."

He half thought of zipping out through the dining-room window while he was in there; but still, he was curious to try the fizz, and there didn't seem to be any hurry, really; it was pretty plain the old girl wasn't going anywhere, couldn't be any actual danger to him, although she did rather give him the "gooeys." Also he did want to hear that chime again.

As he was taking a glass out from the shimmering ranks in the cupboard, a marvellous thought struck him: why not bring all the gang here for a banquet? Look at those hundreds and hundreds of bottles of champagne—what a waste, not to make use of them! Plainly *she* was never going to get through them all—not in the state she was in. Maybe he could find some tinned stuff in the house too—but anyway, they could bring their own grub with them, hamburgers and crisps or stuff from the Chinese Takeaway; if the old girl was actually paralysed in her chair, she couldn't stop them; in fact it would add to the fun, the excitement, having her there. They could fetch her in from the next room, drink her health in her own bubbly; better not leave it too long, though, didn't seem likely she could last more than a few days.

Candles, he thought, we'd have to bring candles; and at that point her voice cut into his thoughts, calling,

"Bring the two candles that are standing on the cupboard."

He started violently—but it was only a coincidence, after all; picked up the candles in their tall cut-glass sticks and carried them next door with a tumbler for himself.

"Matches on the mantel," she said.

The matches were in a fancy enamel box. He lit the candles and put them on the little table beside her. Now he could see more plainly that there was something extremely queer about her: her face was all drawn down one side, and half of it didn't seem to work very well.

"Electricity cut off," she said. "Forgot to pay bill."

Her left hand was still working all right, and she had swallowed down two glasses in quick succession, refilling them herself each time from the opened bottle at her elbow. "Fill your glass," she said, slurring the words a little.

He was very thirsty—kippers and baked beans they always had for Saturday midday dinner, and the fright had dried up his mouth too. Like Mrs. Jordan he tossed down two glasses one after the other. They fizzed a bit—otherwise didn't have much taste.

"Better open another bottle," she said. "One doesn't go anywhere between two. Fetch in a few more while you're up, why don't you."

She's planning, he thought to himself; knows she can't move from that chair, so she wants to be stocked up for when I've gone. He wondered if in fact there was a phone in the house. Ought he to ring for doctor, police, ambulance? But then he would have to account for his presence. And then he and the gang would never get to have their banquet; the windows would be boarded up for sure, she'd be carted off to the Royal West Midland geriatric ward, like Auntie Glad after her stroke.

"There isn't a phone in the house," said Mrs. Jordan calmly. "I had it taken out after Jock died; the bell disturbed the birds. That's right, put them all down by my chair, where I can reach them."

He opened another bottle, filled both their glasses, then went back to the other room for a third load.

"You like the clock, don't you," she said, as he paused by it, coming back.

"Yeah. It's uncommon."

"It'll strike the quarter in a minute," she said, and soon it did—a low, rather malicious chuckle, just a brief spurt of sound. It made the hair prickle on the back of Matt's neck, but he thought again— Just wait till the rest of the gang hear that! A real spooky sound.

"I don't want you making off with it, though," she said. "No, no, that would never do. I like to sit here and listen to it."

"I wasn't going to take it!"

"No, well, that's as maybe." Her triangular black eyes in their hollows laughed down at him—he was squatting on the carpet near her chair, easing out a particularly obstinate cork. "I'm not taking any chances. Eight days—that clock goes for eight days. Did you wind up the chime too?"

"Yeah, yeah," he said impatiently, tipping more straw-coloured fizz into their glasses. Through the pale liquid in the tumbler he still seemed to see her eyes staring at him shrewdly.

"Put your glass down a moment," she said. "On the floor—that will do. Now, just look here a moment." She was holding up her skinny forefinger. Past it he could see those two dark triangles. "That's right. Now—watch my finger—you are very tired, aren't you? You are going to lie down on the floor and go to sleep. You will sleep—very comfortably—for ten minutes. When you wake, you will walk over to that door and lock it. The key is in the lock. Then you will take out the key and push it under the door with one of the knitting needles that are lying on the small table by the door. Ahhh! You are so sleepy." She yawned, deeply. Matt was yawning too. His head flopped sideways on to the carpet and he lay motionless, deep asleep.

While he slept it was very quiet in the room. The house was too secluded in its own grounds among the builders' yards for any sound from the town to reach it; only faintly from far away came the throb of the motorway. Mrs. Jordan sat impassively listening to it. She did not sleep; she had done enough sleeping and soon would sleep even deeper. She sat listening, and thinking about her husband; sometimes the lopsided smile crooked down one corner of her mouth.

After ten minutes the sleeping boy woke up. Drowsily he staggered to his feet, walked over to the door, locked it, removed the key and, with a long wooden knitting needle, thrust it far underneath and out across the polished dining-room floor.

Returning to the old lady he stared at her in a vaguely bewildered manner, rubbing one hand up over his forehead.

"My head aches," he said in a grumbling tone.

"You need a drink. Open another bottle," she said. "Listen: the clock is going to strike the half-hour."

On the other side of the room the clock gave its silvery chuckle.

Graham Masterton

Bridal Suite

GRAHAM MASTERTON WAS BORN IN 1947, AND SENDS ME A *mysterious paragraph about himself. He and his wife and three children divide their time between Epsom Downs in England and Key West in Florida. He is a skilled underwater swimmer and a collector of rare umbrellas. Eh? Maybe living in Philip Marlowe territory does things to a man.*

His novels include The Manitou *(filmed by the late William Girdler),* The Sphinx, The Djinn, *and* Charnel House. *He specializes in visiting myths from the past on the present. If "Bridal Suite" is in some ways more traditional, nevertheless until recently it could hardly have been published.*

They arrived in Sherman, Connecticut, on a cold fall day when the leaves were crisp and whispery, and the whole world seemed to have crumbled into rust. They parked their rented Cordoba outside the front steps of the house, and climbed out. Peter opened the trunk and hefted out their cases, still new, with price tags from Macy's in White Plains, while Jenny stood in her sheepskin coat and smiled and shivered. It was a Saturday, mid-afternoon, and they had just been married.

The house stood amongst the shedding trees, white weather-boarded and silent. It was a huge old colonial, 1820 or thereabouts, with black-paint railings, an old coach lamp over the door, and a flagged stone porch. All around it stretched silent leafless woods and rocky outcroppings. There was an abandoned tennis court, with a sagging net and rusted posts. A decaying roller, overgrown with grass, stood where some gardener had left it, at some unremembered moment, years and years ago.

There was utter silence. Until you stand still in Sherman, Connecticut, on a crisp fall day, you don't know what silence is. Then suddenly a light wind, and a scurry of dead leaves.

They walked up to the front door, Peter carrying the suitcases. He looked around for a bell, but there was none.

Jenny said: "Knock?"

Peter grinned. "With that thing?"

On the black-painted door was a grotesque corroded brass knocker, made in the shape of some kind of howling creature, with horns and teeth and a feral snarl. Peter took hold of it tentatively and gave three hollow raps. They echoed inside the house, across unseen hallways and silent landings. Peter and Jenny waited, smiling at each other reassuringly. They had booked, after all. There was no question but they had booked.

There was no reply.

Jenny said: "Maybe you ought to knock louder. Let me try."

Peter banged louder. The echoes were flat, unanswered. They waited two, three minutes more. Peter, looking at Jenny, said: "I love you. Do you know that?"

Jenny stood on tippy-toes and kissed him. "I love you, too. I love you more than a barrelful of monkeys."

The leaves rustled around their feet and still nobody came to the door. Jenny walked across the front garden to the living-room window and peered in, shading her eyes with her hand. She was a small girl, only five-two, with long fair hair and a thin oval face. Peter thought she looked like one of Botticelli's muses, one of those divine creatures who floated two inches off the ground, wrapped in diaphanous drapery, plucking at a harp. She was, in fact, a *sweet* girl. Sweet-looking, sweet-natured, but with a slight sharpness about her that made all that sweetness palatable. He had

35

met her on an Eastern Airlines flight from Miami to La Guardia. He had been vacationing, she had been visiting her retired father. They had fallen in love, in three months of beautiful days that had been just like one of those movies, all out-of-focus swimming scenes and picnics in the grass and running in slow motion across General Motors Plaza while pigeons flurried around them and passing pedestrians turned and stared.

He was an editor for Manhattan Cable TV. Tall, spare, given to wearing hand-knitted tops with floppy sleeves. He smoked Parliament, liked Santana and lived in the village amidst a thousand LPs, with a grey cat that liked to rip up his rugs, plants and wind chimes. He loved Doonesbury and never knew how close it got to what he was himself.

Some friends had given them a polythene bag of grass and a pecan pie from the Yum-Yum Bakery for a wedding present. Her father, dear and white-haired, had given them three thousand dollars and a water-bed.

"This is crazy," said Peter. "Did we book a week at this place or did we book a week at this place?"

"It looks deserted," called Jenny, from the tennis court.

"It looks more than deserted," complained Peter. "It looks run down into the ground. *Cordon bleu* dining, they said in *Connecticut*. Comfortable beds and all facilities. It looks more like Frankenstein's castle."

Jenny, out of sight, suddenly called: "There's someone here. On the back terrace."

Peter left the cases and followed her around the side of the house. In the flaking trees, black-and-white wood warblers flurried and sang. He walked around by the tattered tennis-court nets, and there was Jenny, standing by a deck chair. In the chair, asleep, was a grey-haired woman, covered by a blanket of dark green plaid. On the grass beside her was a copy of the New Milford newspaper, stirred by the breeze.

Peter bent over the woman. She had a bony, well-defined face, and in her youth she must have been pretty. Her mouth was slightly parted as she slept, and Peter could see her eyeballs moving under her eyelids. She must have been dreaming of something.

He shook her slightly, and said: "Mrs. Gaylord?"

Jenny said: "Do you think she's all right?"

"Oh, she's fine," he told her. "She must have been reading and just dozed off. Mrs. Gaylord?"

The woman opened her eyes. She stared at Peter for a moment with an expression that he couldn't understand, an expression that looked curiously like suspicion, but then, abruptly, she sat up and washed her face with her hands, and said: "Oh, dear! My goodness! I think I must have dropped off for a while."

"It looks that way," said Peter.

She folded back her blanket, and stood up. She was taller than Jenny, but not very tall, and under a grey plain dress she was as thin as a clothes horse. Standing near her, Peter detected the scent of violets, but it was a strangely closeted smell, as if the violets had long since died.

"You must be Mr. and Mrs. Delgordo," she said.

"That's right. We just arrived. We knocked, but there was no reply. I hope you don't mind us waking you up like this."

"Not at all," said Mrs. Gaylord. "You must think that I'm awful . . . not being here to greet you. And you just married, too. Congratulations. You look very happy with each other."

"We are," smiled Jenny.

"Well, you'd better come along inside. Do you have many bags? My handyman is over at New Milford this afternoon, buying some glass fuses. I'm afraid we're a little chaotic at this time of year. We don't have many guests after Rosh Hashanah."

She led the way towards the house. Peter glanced at Jenny and shrugged, but Jenny could only pull a face. They followed Mrs. Gaylord's bony back across the untidy lawn and in through the door of a sun room, where a faded billiard table mouldered, and yellowed framed photographs of smiling young men hung next to yachting trophies and varsity pennants. They passed through a set of smeary french doors to the living room, dark and musty and vast, with two old screened fireplaces, and a galleried staircase. Everywhere around there was wood panelling, inlaid flooring and dusty drapes. It looked more like a neglected private house than a *"cordon bleu* weekend retreat for sophisticated couples."

"Is there . . . anybody else here?" asked Peter. "I mean, any other guests?"

"Oh, no," smiled Mrs. Gaylord. "You're quite alone. We are very lonely at this time of year."

"Could you show us our room? I can always carry the bags up myself. We've had a plenty hard day, what with one thing and another."

"Of course," Mrs. Gaylord told him. "I remember my own wedding day. I couldn't wait to come out here and have Frederick all to myself."

"You spent your wedding night here too?" asked Jenny.

"Oh, yes. In the same room where you will be spending yours. I call it the bridal suite."

Jenny said: "Is Frederick—I mean, is Mr. Gaylord—?"

"Passed over," said Mrs. Gaylord. Her eyes were bright with memory.

"I'm sorry to hear that," said Jenny. "But I guess you have your family now. Your sons."

"Yes," smiled Mrs. Gaylord. "They're all fine boys."

Peter took his luggage from the front doorstep and Mrs. Gaylord led them up the staircase to the second-floor landing. They passed gloomy bathrooms with iron claw-footed tubs and amber windows. They passed bedrooms with unslept-in beds and drawn blinds. They passed a sewing room, with a silent pedal sewing machine of black enamel and inlaid mother-of-pearl. The house was faintly chilly, and the floorboards creaked under their feet as they walked towards the bridal suite.

The room where they were going to stay was high-ceilinged and vast. It had a view of the front of the house, with its driveway and drifts of leaves, and also to the back, across the woods. There was a heavy carved-oak closet, and the bed itself was a high four-poster with twisting spiral posts and heavy brocade drapes. Jenny sat on it, and patted it, and said: "It's kind of hard, isn't it?"

Mrs. Gaylord looked away. She seemed to be thinking about something else. She said: "You'll find it's most comfortable when you're used to it."

Peter set down the cases. "What time do you serve dinner this evening?" he asked her.

Mrs. Gaylord didn't answer him directly, but spoke instead to Jenny. "What time would you like it?" she asked.

Jenny glanced at Peter. "Around eight would be fine," she said.

"Very well. I'll make it at eight," said Mrs. Gaylord. "Make yourself at home in the meanwhile. And if there's anything you want, don't hesitate to call me. I'm always around someplace, even if I am asleep at times."

She gave Jenny a wistful smile and then, without another word, she left the room, closing the door quietly behind her. Peter and Jenny waited for a moment in silence until they heard her footsteps retreating down the hall. Then Jenny flowed into Peter's arms, and they kissed. It was a kiss that meant a lot of things: like, I love you, and thank you, and no matter what everyone said, we did it, we got married at last, and I'm glad.

He unbuttoned her plain wool going-away dress. He slipped it from her shoulder and kissed her neck. She ruffled his hair with her fingers and whispered: "I always imagined it would be like this."

He said: "Mmh."

Her dress fell around her ankles. Underneath, she wore a pink gauzy bra through which the darkness of her nipples showed and small gauzy panties. He slipped his hand under the bra and rolled her nipples between his fingers until they knurled and stiffened. She opened his shirt, and reached around to caress his bare back.

The fall afternoon seemed to blur. They pulled back the covers of the old four-poster bed and then, naked, scrambled between the sheets. He kissed her forehead, her closed eyelids, her mouth, her breasts. She kissed his narrow muscular chest, his flat stomach.

From behind the darkness of her closed eyes, she heard his breathing, soft and urgent and wanting. She lay on her side, with her back to him, and she felt her thighs parted from behind. He was panting harder and harder, as if he was running a race, or fighting against something, and she murmured: "You're worked up. My God, but I love it."

She felt him thrust inside her. She wasn't ready, and by his unusual dryness, nor was he. But he was so big and demanding that the pain was a pleasure, too, and even as she winced she was shaking with pleasure. He thrust and thrust and thrust, and she cried out, and all the fantasies she'd ever dreamed of burst in front of her closed eyes—fantasies of rape by brutal Vikings with steel armour and naked thighs, fantasies of being forced to show herself to prurient emperors in bizarre harems, fantasies of being assaulted by a glossy black stallion.

He was so fierce and virile that he overwhelmed her, and she seemed to lose herself in a collision of love and ecstasy. It took her whole minutes to recover, minutes that were measured out by a painted pine wall clock that ticked and ticked, slow as dust falling in an airless room.

She whispered: "You were fantastic. I've never known you like that before. Marriage must definitely agree with you."

There was no answer. She said: "Peter?"

She turned, and he wasn't there. The bed was empty, apart from her. The sheet was rumpled, as if Peter had been lying there, but there was no sign of him.

She said, in a nervous voice: "Peter? Where are you?"

There was silence, punctuated only by the clock.

She sat up. Her eyes were wide. She said, so softly that nobody could have heard: "Peter? Are you there?"

She looked across the room, to the half-open door that led to the bathroom suite. Late sunlight fell across the floor. Outside, in the grounds, she could hear leaves shifting and the faint distant barking of a dog.

"Peter—if this is supposed to be some kind of a game—"

She got out of bed. She held her hand between her legs and her thighs were sticky with their lovemaking. She had never known him to fill her with such a copious flow of semen. It was so much that it slid down the inside of her leg on to the rug. She lifted her hand, palm upwards, and frowned at it in bewilderment.

Peter wasn't in the bathroom. He wasn't under the bed, or hiding under the covers. He wasn't behind the drapes. She searched for him with a pained, baffled doggedness, even though she knew that he wasn't there. After ten minutes of searching, however, she had to stop. He had gone. Somehow, mysteriously, gone. She sat on the end of the bed and didn't know whether to giggle with frustration or scream with anger. He must have gone someplace. She hadn't heard the door open and close, and she hadn't heard his footsteps. So where was he?

She dressed again, and went to look for him. She searched every room on the upper landing, including the bureaux and the closets.

She even pulled down the ladder from the attic and looked up there, but all Mrs. Gaylord had stored away was old pictures and a broken-down baby carriage. Up there, with her head through the attic door, she could hear the leaves rustling for miles around. She called: "Peter?" anxiously; but there was no reply, and so she climbed down the ladder again.

Eventually, she came to one of the sun rooms downstairs. Mrs. Gaylord was sitting in a basketwork chair reading a newspaper and smoking a cigarette. The smoke fiddled and twisted in the dying light of the day. On the table beside her was a cup of coffee with a wrinkled skin forming on top of it.

"Hallo," said Mrs. Gaylord, without looking around. "You're down early. I didn't expect you till later."

"Something's happened," said Jenny. She suddenly found that she was trying very hard not to cry.

Mrs. Gaylord turned around. "I don't understand, my dear. Have you had an argument?"

"I don't know. But Peter's gone. He's just disappeared. I've looked all around the house and I can't find him anywhere."

Mrs. Gaylord lowered her eyes. "I see. That's most unfortunate."

"Unfortunate? It's terrible! I'm so worried! I don't know whether I should call the police or not."

"The police? I hardly think that's necessary. He's probably gotten a case of cold feet, and he's gone out for a walk on his own. Men do feel like that sometimes, when they've just been wed. It's a common complaint."

"But I didn't even hear him leave. One second we were—well, one second we were resting on the bed together, and the next thing I knew he wasn't there."

Mrs. Gaylord bit at her lips as if she was thinking.

"Are you sure you were on the bed?" she asked.

Jenny stared at her hotly, and blushed. "We are married, you know. We were married today."

"I didn't mean that," said Mrs. Gaylord, abstractedly.

"Then I don't know what you *did* mean."

Mrs. Gaylord looked up, and her momentary reverie was

41

broken. She gave Jenny a reassuring smile, and reached out her hand.

"I'm sure it's nothing terrible," she said. "He must have decided to get himself a breath of fresh air, that's all. Nothing terrible at all."

Jenny snapped: "He didn't open the door, Mrs. Gaylord! He just vanished!"

Mrs. Gaylord frowned. "There's no need to bark at me, my dear. If you're having a few complications with your new husband, then it's most certainly not my fault!"

Jenny was about to shout back at her, but she put her hand over her mouth and turned away. It was no good getting hysterical. If Peter had simply walked out and left her, then she had to know why; and if he had mysteriously vanished, then the only sensible thing to do was search the house carefully until she found him. She felt panic deep inside her, and a feeling which she hadn't felt for a very long time—loneliness. But she stayed still with her hand against her mouth until the sensation had passed, and then she said quietly to Mrs. Gaylord, without turning around: "I'm sorry. I was frightened, that's all. I can't think where he could have gone."

"Do you want to look around the house?" asked Mrs. Gaylord. "You're very welcome."

"I think I'd like to. That's if you don't mind."

Mrs. Gaylord stood up. "I'll even help you, my dear. I'm sure you must be feeling most upset."

They spent the next hour walking from room to room, opening and closing doors. But as darkness gathered over the grounds and the surrounding woods, and as the cold evening wind began to rise, they had to admit that wherever Peter was, he wasn't concealed or hiding in the house.

"Do you want to call the police?" asked Mrs. Gaylord. They were standing in the gloomy living room now. The log fire in the antique hearth was nothing more than a heap of dusty white ashes. Outside, the wind whirled in the leaves, and rattled at the window frames.

"I think I'd better," said Jenny. She felt empty, shocked, and hardly capable of saying anything sensible. "I think I'd like to call some of my friends in New York, too, if that's okay."

"Go ahead. I'll start preparing dinner."

"I really don't want anything to eat. Not until I know about Peter."

Mrs. Gaylord, her face half-hidden in shadow, said softly: "If he's really gone, you're going to have to get used to it, my dear; and the best time to start is now."

Before Jenny could answer her, she had walked out of the living room door and along the corridor to the kitchen. Jenny saw an inlaid mahogany cigarette box on a side table, and for the first time in three years she took out a cigarette and lit it. It tasted flat and foul, but she took the smoke down, and held it, her eyes closed in anguish and isolation.

She called the police. They were courteous, helpful, and they promised to come out to see her in the morning if there was still no sign of Peter. They had to warn her, though, that he was an adult, and free to go where he chose, even if it meant leaving her on her wedding night.

She thought of calling her mother, but after dialling the number and listening to it ring, she set the phone down again. The humiliation of Peter having left her was too much to share with her family or her close friends right now. She knew that if she heard her mother's sympathetic voice, she would only burst into tears. She crushed out the cigarette and tried to think who else to call.

The wind blew an upstairs door shut, and she jumped in nervous shock.

Mrs. Gaylord came back after a while with a tray. Jenny was sitting in front of the dying fire, smoking her second cigarette and trying to keep back the tears.

"I've made some Philadelphia pepper soup, and grilled a couple of New York steaks," said Mrs. Gaylord. "Would you like to eat them in front of the hearth? I'll build it up for you."

Throughout their impromptu dinner, Jenny was silent. She managed a little soup, but the steak caught in her throat, and she couldn't begin to swallow it. She wept for a few minutes, and Mrs. Gaylord watched her carefully.

"I'm sorry," said Jenny, wiping her eyes.

"Don't be. I understand what you're going through only too well. I lost my own husband, remember."

43

Jenny nodded, dumbly.

"I think it would better if you moved to the small bedroom for tonight," suggested Mrs. Gaylord. "You'll feel more comfortable there. It's a cosy little room, right at the back."

"Thank you," Jenny whispered. "I think I'd prefer that."

They sat in front of the fire until the fresh logs were burned down, and the long-case clock in the hallway began to strike two in the morning. Then Mrs. Gaylord cleared away their plates, and they mounted the dark, creaking staircase to go to bed. They went into the bridal suite to collect Jenny's case, and for a moment she looked forlornly at Peter's case, and his clothes scattered where he had left them.

She suddenly said: *"His clothes."*

"What's that, my dear?"

She flustered: "I don't know why I didn't think about it before. If Peter's gone, then what's he wearing? His suitcase isn't open, and his clothes are lying right there where he left them. He was *naked*. He wouldn't go out on a cold night like this, naked. It's insane."

Mrs. Gaylord lowered her gaze. "I'm sorry, my dear. We just don't know what's happened. We've looked all over the house, haven't we? Maybe he took a robe with him. There were some robes on the back of the door."

"But Peter wouldn't—"

Mrs. Gaylord put her arm around her. "I'm afraid you can't say what Peter would or wouldn't do. He *has*. Whatever his motive, and wherever he's gone."

Jenny said quietly: "Yes. I suppose you're right."

"You'd better go get some sleep," said Mrs. Gaylord. "Tomorrow, you're going to need all the energy you can muster."

Jenny picked up her case, paused for a moment, and then went sadly along the landing to the small back bedroom. Mrs. Gaylord murmured: "Goodnight. I hope you sleep."

Jenny undressed, put on the frilly rose-patterned nightdress she had bought specially for the wedding night, and brushed her teeth at the small basin by the window. The bedroom was small, with a sloping ceiling, and there was a single bed with a colonial patchwork cover. On the pale flowery wallpaper was a framed sampler, reading, "God Is With Us."

She climbed into bed and lay there for a while, staring up at the cracked plaster. She didn't know what to think about Peter any more. She listened to the old house creaking in the darkness. Then she switched off her bedside lamp and tried to sleep.

Soon after she heard the long-case clock strike four, she thought she detected the sound of someone crying. She sat up in bed and listened again, holding her breath. Outside her bedroom window the night was still utterly dark, and the leaves rattled like rain. She heard the crying noise again.

Carefully, she climbed out of bed and went to the door. She opened it a little way, and it groaned on its hinges. She paused, her ears straining for the crying sound, and it came again. It was like a cat yowling, or a child in pain. She stepped out of her room and tippy-toed halfway along the landing, until she reached the head of the stairs.

The old house was like a ship out at sea. The wind shook the doors and sighed between the shingles. The weathervane turned and grated on its mounting, with a sound like a knife being scraped on a plate. At every window, drapes stirred as if they were being touched by unseen hands.

Jenny stepped quietly along to the end of the landing. She heard the sound once more—a repressed mewling. There was no doubt in her mind now that it was coming from the bridal suite. She found she was biting at her tongue in nervous anxiety, and that her pulse rate was impossibly quick. She paused for just a moment to calm herself down, but she had to admit that she was afraid. The noise came again, clearer and louder this time.

She pressed her ear against the door of the bridal suite. She thought she could hear rustling sounds, but that may have been the wind and the leaves. She knelt down and peered through the keyhole, although the draught made her eyes water. It was so dark in the bridal suite that she couldn't see anything at all.

She stood up. Her mouth was parched. If there was someone in there—who was it? There was so much rustling and stirring that it sounded as if there were two people there. Maybe some unexpected guests had called by while she was asleep; although she was pretty sure that she hadn't slept at all. Maybe it was Mrs. Gaylord. But if it was her, then what was she doing, making all those terrifying noises?

Jenny knew that she had to open the door. She had to do it for her own sake and for Peter's sake. It might be nothing at all. It might be a stray cat playing around in there, or an odd downdraught from the chimney. It might even be latecoming guests and, if it was, then she would wind up embarrassed. But being embarrassed had to be better than not knowing. There was no way she could go back to her small bedroom and sleep soundly without finding out what those noises were.

She put her hand on the brass doorknob. She closed her eyes tight, and took a breath. Then she turned the knob and jerkily opened the door.

The noise in the room was horrifying. It was like the howl of the wind, only there was no wind. It was like standing on the edge of a clifftop at night, with a yawning chasm below, invisible and bottomless. It was like a nightmare come true. The whole bridal suite seemed to be possessed by some moaning, ancient sound; some cold magnetic gale. It was the sound and the feel of fear.

Jenny, shaking, turned her eyes towards the bed. At first, behind the twisted pillars and drapes, she couldn't make out what was happening. There was a figure there, a naked woman's figure, and she was writhing and whimpering and letting out sighs of strained delight. Jenny peered harder through the darkness, and she saw that it was Mrs. Gaylord, as thin and nude as a dancer. She was lying on her back, her claw-like hands digging into the sheets, her eyes closed in ecstasy.

Jenny stepped into the bridal suite, and the wind gently blew the door shut behind her. She crossed the rug to the end of the bed, her mind chilled with fright, and stood there, looking down at Mrs. Gaylord with a fixed and mesmerized stare. All around her, the room whispered and moaned and murmured, an asylum of spectres and apparitions.

With complete horror, Jenny saw why Mrs. Gaylord was crying out in such pleasure. *The bed itself, the very sheets and underblankets and mattress, had taken on the shape of a man's body, in white linen relief, and up between Mrs. Gaylord's narrow thighs*

46

thrust an erection of living fabric. The whole bed rippled and shook with hideous spasms, and the man's shape seemed to shift and alter as Mrs. Gaylord twisted around it.

Jenny screamed. She didn't even realize that she'd done it until Mrs. Gaylord opened her eyes and stared at her with wild malevolence. The bed's heaving suddenly subsided and faded, and Mrs. Gaylord sat up, making no attempt to cover her scrawny breasts.

"You!" said Mrs. Gaylord, hoarsely. "What are you doing here?"

Jenny opened her mouth but she couldn't speak.

"You came in here to spy, to pry on my private life, is that it?"

"I—I heard—"

Mrs. Gaylord climbed off the bed, stooped, and picked up a green silk wrap, which she loosely tied around herself. Her face was white and rigid with dislike.

"I suppose you think you're a clever girl," she said. "I suppose you think you've discovered something momentous."

"I don't even know what—"

Mrs. Gaylord tossed her hair back impatiently. She didn't seem to be able to keep still, but kept on pacing around the bridal suite, loaded with tension. Jenny, after all, had interrupted her lovemaking, however weird it had been, and she was still frustrated. She gave a sound like a snarl, and paced back around the room again.

"I want to know what's happened to Peter," said Jenny. Her voice was shaky but for the first time since Peter's disappearance, her intention was firm.

"What do you think?" said Mrs. Gaylord, in a caustic voice.

"I don't know what to think. That bed—"

"This bed has been here since this house was built. This bed is the whole reason this house was built. This bed is both a servant and a master. But more of a master."

"I don't understand it," said Jenny. "Is it some kind of mechanism? Some kind of trick?"

Mrs. Gaylord gave a sharp, mocking laugh. "A trick?" she asked, fidgeting and pacing. "You think what you saw just now was a trick?"

"I just don't see how—"

Mrs. Gaylord's face was sour with contempt. "I'll tell you how, you witless girl. This bed was owned by Dorman Pierce, who lived here in Sherman in the 1820s. He was an arrogant, dark, savage man, with tastes that were too strange for most people. He took a bride, an innocent girl called Faith Martin, and after they were married he led her up to his bridal suite and *this* bed.''

Jenny heard the wind moaning again. The cold, old wind that stirred no drapes nor aroused any dust.

''What Dorman Pierce did to his new bride on this bed that first night—well, God only knows. But he used her cruelly and broke her will, and made her a shell of the girl she once was. Unfortunately for Dorman, though, the girl's godmother got to hear of what had happened, and it was said that she had connections with one of the most ancient of Connecticut magic circles. She may even have been a member herself. She paid for a curse to be put upon Dorman Pierce, and it was the curse of complete submission. In future, *he* would have to serve women, instead of women serving *him.* ''

Mrs. Gaylord turned towards the bed, and touched it. Its sheets seemed to shift and wrinkle by themselves.

''He lay in this bed one night and the bed absorbed him. His spirit is in the bed even now. His spirit, or his lust, or his virility, or whatever it is.''

Jenny frowned. ''The bed did what? *Absorbed* him?''

''He sank into it like a man sinking into quicksand. He was never seen again. Faith Martin stayed in this house until she was old, and every night, or whenever she wished it, the bed had to serve her.''

Mrs. Gaylord pulled her wrap tighter. The bridal suite was growing very cold. ''What nobody knew, though, was that the enchantment remained on the bed, even after Faith's death. The next young couple who moved here slept on this bed on their wedding night, and the bed again claimed the husband. And so it went on, whenever a man slept on it. Each time, that man was absorbed. My own husband, Frederick was— Well, he's in there, too.''

Jenny could hardly stand to hear what Mrs. Gaylord was going to say next.

She said: ''And *Peter?*''

Mrs. Gaylord touched her own face, as if to reassure herself that

48

she was real. She said, ignoring Jenny's question: "The women who decided to stay in this house and sleep on this bed all made the same discovery. For each man who was absorbed, the bed's strength and virility grew that much greater. That's why I said that it's more of a master than a servant. Right now, with all the men that it has claimed, it is sexually powerful to an enormous degree."

She stroked the bed again, and it shuddered. "The more men it takes," she whispered, "the more demanding it becomes."

Jenny whispered: "Peter?"

Mrs. Gaylord smiled vaguely, and nodded, her fingers still caressing the sheets.

Jenny said: "You knew what was going to happen, and you actually let it? You actually *let* my Peter—"

She was too shocked to go on. She said: "Oh, God. Oh, my God."

Mrs. Gaylord turned to her. "You don't have to *lose* Peter, you know," she said, cajolingly. "We could both share this bed if you stayed here. We could share all of the men who have been taken by it. Dorman Pierce, Peter, Frederick, and all the dozens of others. Have you any idea what it's like to be taken by twenty men at once?"

Jenny, feeling nauseous, said: "Yesterday afternoon, when we—"

Mrs. Gaylord bent forward and kissed the sheets. They were snaking and folding with feverish activity, and to Jenny's horror, they were beginning to rise again into the form of a huge, powerful man. It was like watching a mummified being rise from the dead; a body lifting itself out of a starched white shroud. The sheets became legs, arms and a broad chest, and the pillow rose into the form of a heavy-jawed masculine face. It wasn't Peter, it wasn't any man; it was the sum of *all* the men who had been caught by the curse of the bridal suite, and dragged into the dark heart of the bed.

Mrs. Gaylord pulled open her wrap, and let it slither to the floor. She looked at Jenny with glittering eyes, and said: "He's here, your Peter. Peter and all his soulmates. Come and join him. Come and give yourself to him . . ."

Skinny and naked, Mrs. Gaylord mounted the bed, and began to run her fingers over the white shape of the sheets. Jenny, with rising panic, crossed the room and tried the door handle, but the door seemed to be wedged firmly shut. The windless wind rose again, and an agonized moaning filled the room. Now Jenny knew what that moaning was. It was the cries of those men trapped for ever within the musty substance of the bridal bed, buried in its horsehair and its springs and its sheets, suffocatingly confined for the pleasure of a vengeful woman.

Mrs. Gaylord seized the bed's rising member, and clutched it in her fist. "See this?" she shrieked. "See how strong it is? How proud it is? We could share it, you and I! Come share it!"

Jenny tugged and rattled at the door, but it still refused to open. In desperation she crossed the room again and tried to pull Mrs. Gaylord off the bed.

"Get away!" screeched Mrs. Gaylord. "Get away, you sow!"

There was a tumultuous heaving on the bed, and Jenny found herself struck by something as heavy and powerful as a man's arm. She caught her foot on the bed's trailing sheets, and fell. The room was filled with ear-splitting howls and bays of fury, and the whole house was shuddering and shaking. She tried to climb to her feet, but she was struck again, and she knocked her head against the floor.

Now Mrs. Gaylord had mounted the hideous white figure on the bed, and was riding it furiously, screaming at the top of her voice. Jenny managed to pull herself up against a pine bureau, and seize an old glass kerosene lamp which was standing on top of it.

"Peter!" she shouted, and flung the lamp at Mrs. Gaylord's naked back.

She never knew how the kerosene ignited. The whole of the bridal suite seemed to be charged with strange electricity, and maybe it was a spark or a discharge of supernatural power. Whatever it was, the lamp struck Mrs. Gaylord on the side of the head and burst apart in a shower of fragments, and then there was a soft *woofff* sound, and both Mrs. Gaylord and the white figure on the bed were smothered instantly in flames.

Mrs. Gaylord screamed. She turned to Jenny with staring eyes and her hair was alight, frizzing into brownish fragments. Flames danced from her face and her shoulders and her breasts, shrivelling her skin like a burning magazine.

But it was the bed itself that was most horrifying. The blazing sheets struggled and twisted and churned, and out of the depths of the bed came an echoing agonized roar that was like a choir of demons. The roar was the voice of every man buried alive in the bed, as the fire consumed the material that had made their spirits into flesh. It was hideous, chaotic, unbearable and, most terrible of all, Jenny could distinguish Peter's voice, howling and groaning in pain.

The house burned throughout the rest of the night, and into the pale cold dawn. By mid-morning it was pretty much under control, and the local firemen trod through the charred timbers and wreckage, hosing down the smouldering furniture and collapsed staircases. Twenty or thirty people came to stare, and a CBS news crew made a short recording for television. One old Sherman citizen, with white hair and baggy pants, told the newsmen that he'd always believed the place was haunted, and it was better off burned down.

It wasn't until they moved the fallen ceiling of the main bedroom that they discovered the charred remains of seventeen men and one woman, all curled up as small as monkeys by the intense heat.

There had been another woman there, but at that moment she was sitting in the back of a taxi on the way to the railroad station, wrapped tightly in an overcoat, her salvaged suitcase resting on the seat beside her. Her eyes, as she watched the brown-and-yellow trees go past, were as dull as stones.

Christopher Priest

The Miraculous Cairn

CHRISTOPHER PRIEST IS A LANKY FIGURE MUCH IN EVI-
*dence at science fiction conventions, discussing the mystique of
creativity and cursing publishers for putting rocket ships on his
psychological novels. He was born in 1943 and was educated at
Manchester Warehousemen, Clerks' Orphan School, three false
clues in one name. For six years he was articled to a firm of char-
tered accountants, then he worked for a greetings-card manufacturer and a mail-order publisher. No wonder he became a full-time
writer in 1968, encouraged by a commission to expand two of his
short stories into his first novel,* Indoctrinaire. *His other novels include* Fugue for a Darkening Island, Inverted World *(winner of the
British Science Fiction Association Award),* The Space Machine
(which won the Ditmar Award) and A Dream of Wessex.*

Chris is another of the science fiction writers I wanted to coax
into this anthology, and both of us were pleased when I succeeded:
he'd been suffering a writer's block (virtually the worst thing that
can befall a writer, an absolute inability to write) and brooding
over the Situations Vacant columns. I hoped to present some
stories which could hardly be published elsewhere. This is one of
them.*

I

The island of Seevl lies like a dark shadow over my memories of childhood. It was always physically there, sprawling across the horizon opposite Jethra Harbour, blurring sometimes into the low clouds of storms, standing out at other times as a black, rugged outline against the southern sky. Its landscape was not unlike that of the mountains around Jethra, but there was a saying amongst us that the rocks and soil our ancestors had no use for had been thrown out to sea to make Seevl.

The closeness of Seevl to Jethra had created an inevitable bond—family ties, trading agreements, old alliances—but although to the Jethrans it was just an off-shore island, politically it was a part of the Dream Archipelago. Journeys between mainland and island were forbidden, except with official permission from the Seigniory, but a ferry still ran every day in defiance of the ban, openly and commercially. Officialdom turned a blind eye, because trade was important to Jethra, and crucial to Seevl. I myself travelled to Seevl many times, three or four times a year, for several years of my childhood.

II

It was twenty years since I had visited Seevl, and sixteen years since leaving Jethra. The last time I saw the city was when I left to go to university in Old Haydl, and I had never returned. Twenty years of mixed fortune, with most of the success on the surface, misleadingly. I had a passable education, an interesting career. I had avoided war-service so far, and was now probably too old to be caught up in it, except incidentally. Many friends of my own age (I was thirty-four) had volunteered, but it was not for me. As a teacher I was officially exempted, and if I searched my conscience I knew that the work I was doing was more useful than any war-work might have been. I had done well in teaching, or well enough to have self-esteem and the respect of my colleagues.

Internally, though, those twenty years had been less successful, and it was returning to Jethra, with Seevl looming on the horizon, that brought it to mind.

Jethra was the old capital of our country, but because of the war and the need for decentralized government, there had been an exodus to the newer, less exposed cities inland. There was still a token government presence in Jethra, but the Seignior's Palace was unoccupied, and the Senate House had been bombed at the outbreak of war. Now there was just the fishing, and a certain amount of light industry, and Jethra had become a large, desolate ghost of a city.

A return to the place of childhood is a gathering of reminders. For me, Jethra was life with my parents, schooling, old friends with whom I had lost contact . . . and Seevl. Not an uncommon grouping of memories, perhaps, but between them they had the effect of reminding me of what I had become. This became clear as I sat on the train going to Jethra, thinking of the past. I had not actually chosen to make this journey, because there was family business I had to resolve, but neither did I make it unwillingly. I was curious to see Jethra again, and nervous of travelling to Seevl, but I felt it was time, after twenty years, to confront the past.

III

When I was a child, the closeness of Seevl had a foreboding quality for everyone, and certainly for the other children at school. "Send you to Seevl," was the ultimate childish threat, with unstated connotations of eternal damnation and terror. In our alternate world of invented myth, Seevl was populated by bogeymen and creeping horrors, and the actual landscape of the island was thought to be a nightmare terrain of crevasses and volcanic pools, steaming craters and shifting rocks. This vision was as true for me, in an imaginative sense, as it was for all Jethra children, but with a child's unconscious ability to see the world from a number of different viewpoints, I also knew Seevl for what it really was.

It was no less horrifying to me in reality, but its horrors were acutely personal.

I was an only child. My parents, both Jethrans, had had another child before me, but she died a year before I was born. I came into a world where my life was guarded for reasons I could not begin to understand until I had almost grown up. In some ways I can now sympathize with the protective way my parents brought me up, but it meant that when I was more than just a child—in my early and middle teens—I was still being treated as some precious object that had to be guarded against all the possible dangers and threats of life. While youngsters of my own age were hanging around in gangs, and getting into scrapes, and learning about sex, I was expected to be at home and sharing my parents' friends and interests. These were numerous, and although some were not uninteresting, they were hardly the normal activities of a teenager. Other filial duties, though, I entered into with a sense of duty and numb acceptance, suppressing the urge to evade them. The most unwelcome of these was to go with my parents on their regular visits to see my father's brother on Seevl.

My Uncle Torm was a few years younger than my father, but had married at about the same time: there was a photograph in our living room of the two young men with their brides, and although I recognized the youthful versions of my father, mother and uncle easily enough, it took me years to realize that the pretty young woman holding Torm's arm in the photograph was my Aunt Alvie.

In the picture she was smiling, and I had never seen Alvie smile. She was wearing a gay, flowery dress, and I had never seen Aunt Alvie in anything except an old nightgown and a patched cardigan. Her hair was short and wavy, cut attractively about her face, and Aunt Alvie's hair was long and greasy and grey. And the girl in the picture was standing beside her new husband, raising one leg to show her knee coquettishly to the camera, and my Aunt Alvie was a bedridden cripple.

Torm and Alvie had moved to Seevl soon after their marriage, just before the war started. He had taken a clerical job at a catholic seminary in the remotest part of the Seevl mountains; his reasons for this I do not understand to this day, but I do know that it caused a bitter, if short-lived, row between him and my father.

They were there with their new baby on Seevl when war broke out, and were unable to return to Jethra. By the time the war had settled into its interminable routine of attritional skirmishes, under which circumstances a certain amount of movement between Seevl and Jethra was possible, Aunt Alvie had been taken ill and was not to be moved.

It was in this climate that my parents made their occasional weekend visits to Seevl, to see Torm and Alvie, and to take me with them. For me they were weekends of unrelieved dreariness and depression: a voyage to a bleak, windswept island, to a cramped and dark house on the edge of a moor, and a house at that where a sickbed was the centre of attention, and where the conversations at best were about other adult relatives and at worst about sickness and pain and false hopes of a miraculous recovery. The only distraction from all this, and the ostensible reason for my being there, was Torm and Alvie's daughter, my cousin Seri. She was a few months older than me, and plump and rather stupid, and we were the worst kind of companions to each other. The prospect of her company did nothing to relieve those long days of dread before a visit, and afterwards the memory of it did nothing to help me recover from the profound moods of depression that always followed.

IV

As I left the station, a young woman in Seigniorial uniform opened a car door and walked across to me.

"Are you Lenden Cros?" she said to me.

"Yes."

"I am Serjeant Reeth. I am your escort."

We went to the car, and I placed my bag on the back seat. She held the door open for me, like a chauffeuse, but before I was properly seated she walked around to her own side. She started the engine.

"Where are we going?" I said.

"The ferry does not sail until the morning. We will stay overnight at the Grand Shore Hotel."

She drove out of the station square, and turned into a main road leading towards the centre. I watched the buildings of the city through the window. We had lived in the suburbs, and I knew the centre only superficially. I recognized buildings, names of streets, and some had vague but poignant associations for me. As a child, I had known Jethra's centre as the place where my father worked, where my mother sometimes went shopping, and the street names were landmarks from their territory. The city now looked disused and unloved: there were office blocks, shops, civic buildings, but many of them were boarded up and litter blew across the steps. There was not much traffic in the streets: several cars in various stages of decay, a few trucks, a surprising number of horse-drawn vehicles.

We were held up for a few seconds at a large intersection.

I said: "Are you from Jethra?"

"No."

"You seem to know where you are going."

"I arrived this morning. I've had time to explore."

The traffic moved on, and the conversation ended.

I had never stayed at the Grand Shore Hotel, had never even been through its doors. It was the largest, most expensive hotel in town. In my childhood it had been the scene of society weddings, business conferences and many glittering civic occasions. We drew up in the car park outside the main entrance, with its imposing and solid façade of smoke-dirtied red brick.

Serjeant Reeth stood back as I registered for my room. The clerk pushed across two pieces of white card for my signature. One was for a room in my own name, the other, an adjacent number, was for Serjeant Reeth.

A porter took my bag, and led us up the wide, curving staircase to the next floor. There were mirrors and chandeliers, a plush carpet on the stairs, gold paint on the plaster ceiling-mouldings . . . but the mirrors were unpolished, the carpet was worn and the paint was peeling. The hotel's grandeur was inherited from the days before the war. The muted sounds of our climbing seemed like memories of those famous parties of the past.

The porter opened the door to my room, and went in ahead of me. Serjeant Reeth went to her own door and inserted the key. For a moment she glanced back at me, and something in her expression took me by surprise: I detected a curiosity, a quick interest?

I tipped the porter, and he left. He had placed my bag on a low table by the door, so I took out my clothes and hung them in the

57

wardrobe. I went to the basin, washed off the grime from the train journey, and put on clean clothes. Then I sat on the edge of the bed and looked around at the dingy room.

It was an unexpected position from which to contemplate my past; I had imagined that we would have gone straight across to Seevl, and had not realized that we were, of course, dependent on the ferry. How were we to spend the evening? I supposed the policewoman would have arranged that too.

I recalled the look that Serjeant Reeth had given me, as we went into our rooms. She reminded me of someone I had once known, a girl of about the same age, with similar build and colouring. She was one of many lovers I had had at one time, when a succession of young women had passed through my life. Perhaps if I had met Serjeant Reeth then, she would have been one of them, but I was older now. I knew that such affaires almost always ended in emotional disaster; I had made no casual pick-ups for years, preferring the less intense discontents of sexlessness.

Serjeant Reeth was the same sort of reminder of the past as Jethra itself had become, and she induced in me much the same quality of depression.

I was thirsty, so I left my room and went towards the staircase, thinking I would visit the bar. When I reached the head of the stairs I thought I should, out of politeness, see if the policewoman would join me.

She answered my knock on her door after only a moment's delay, as if she had been standing by the door, waiting for me.

"I'm going downstairs for a drink," I said. "Will you join me?"

"That would be nice. Thank you."

We went downstairs and found the bar. It was locked, and there were no lights on inside. We went into the lounge, rang a bell, and in a moment an elderly waiter came to serve us.

When he had taken our order and left the lounge, I said, making conversation: "Have you worked as an escort before, Serjeant Reeth?"

"No . . . this is the first time."

"Does the work come up very often?"

"I'm not sure. I have only been in the Seigniory for a year."

Just then the waiter returned with our drinks.

"Will you be dining in this evening?" he said to me.

"Yes."

When he had gone I looked around the lounge; we were the only people there. I liked the airy, gracious feeling in the room, with the big windows and long velvet drapes, the high Consortship light-shades, and the broadbacked wicker chairs grouped about the low tables. There were dozens of potted plants, great spreading ferns and tall parlour-palms, lending a feeling of sedate livingness to an otherwise decaying hotel. All the plants were green and alive, so someone must still be looking after them, dusting them and watering them.

We sat in silence for several minutes, and I had plenty of opportunity to try to assess my companion of the next day or two. I placed her age at about twenty-four or five. She was no longer wearing her cap, but the uniform—stiff, sexless and unflattering—effectively neutered her. She wore no make-up, and her hair was drawn back into a bun. She seemed shy and uncommunicative, and unaware of my regard.

At last, it was she who broke the silence.

"Have you been across to Seevl before?"

"I was taken there several times as a child," I said. "What about you?"

"No."

"Do you know what it's like there?"

"I'm told it's bleak. Is that how you remember it?"

"More or less. It's twenty years since I was there. It won't have changed much." I tried my drink, swallowing much of it, hoping it would ease the conversation. "I used to hate going across there. I always dreaded it."

"Why?"

"Oh . . . the mood of the place, the scenery," I said vaguely, avoiding specific memories. The seminary, Alvie, the open moors and the dead towers. "I can't describe it. You feel it as soon as you land."

"You sound like my brother. He says he can always tell if a house is haunted."

"I didn't say the place was haunted," I said, quick to the defence. "It's a question of the landscape. And the wind . . . you can always hear the wind."

Jethra itself was built in the shadow of the Murinan Hills, but beyond these, to the west, was a wide, straight valley that led northwards into the foothills of the northern range. For all but a few short weeks at the height of summer, a polar wind came down the valley and escaped out to sea, whining across Seevl's treeless fells and moors. Only on the eastern side of the island, nearest to Jethra, were there villages of any size, and the only port, Seevl Town, was there. One of my clearest childhood memories of Seevl was seeing it in the springtime. I could look out to the south from my bedroom window, and see the blossoms shining pink and white and bright red on the trees along the boulevards in Jethra, and beyond, out in the blue Midway Sea, there would be Seevl, still with its wintertime crust of snow.

Serjeant Reeth's mention of a brother had given me, for the first time, a little information about her background. I asked her about him. He was also in the Seigniory, she told me, serving with the Border Police. He was hoping for promotion, because his unit was soon to be shipped across to the southern continent. The war was still confused and confusing: neither side would admit to being the first to send an expeditionary force to the south—claims and counter-claims came from both sides—but almost every week there was news of more troops being sent out. That very morning, before setting out from home to catch the train, I had heard news of government claims that the enemy was building a transit-camp on one of the islands in the Dream Archipelago. If this was true it marked a new stage in the war, because the political status of the islands was controlled by a Covenant of Neutrality.

It was the precarious state of the neutrality that had involved me with the Seigniory: the request from the Father Confessor that I should visit my uncle's house to sort out his belongings had been channelled through the Seigniorial Visa Department. If it had come direct to me, if the priests at the seminary had had my address, I could have slipped across unofficially. But that was not to be. Thus my need to be escorted, thus Serjeant Reeth.

I was telling her the reason for my trip—the need to sign papers, to permit furniture to be burnt or given away—when the waiter returned. He was carrying two menu-folders, so discreetly implying that the dining-room staff were ready for us. While we perused the menu the waiter drew the curtains, then led us down the corridor to the dining room.

V

My last visit to Seevl. I was fourteen.

There were examinations at school and I was trying to concentrate on them, but I knew that at the end of the week we were going to see my uncle and aunt and cousin. It was summer, and Jethra was dusty and windless. Sitting by my bedroom window, distracted from my revision, I looked frequently out to sea. Seevl was green then, a dark, tough green; a coloured lie, a deceit of lushness. Day followed day, and I thought about feigning illness: a migraine attack, a sudden bout of gastroenteritis, but at last the day arrived and there was no avoiding it. We were out of the house soon after dawn—in the cool, lovely light of summer, when no one else is about—and hurried down to the tram-stop to catch the first of the day.

What were these visits for? Unless my parents spoke in some adult code I have never been able to decipher, they went out of a combination of habit, guilt and family obligation. I never heard anything of interest discussed, in the way I now know educated adults can discuss matters (and both my parents were educated, and so was my uncle, although I cannot be sure about Alvie); there was news to impart, but it was stale news, trivial events in the family, not even interesting when fresh. Everything that passed between the four adults was familial or familiar: an aunt or cousin who had moved house or changed jobs, a nephew who married, a great-uncle who had died. Sometimes, photographs were passed around Alvie's sickbed: Cousin Jayn's new house (hasn't he done well?), or this is us on holiday, or isn't she a lovely baby? Family banality it was; it seemed so when I was a child and it seems so now. It was as if they had no ideas they could externalize, no sense of the abstract, or if they had it was deemed dangerous, not to be spoken of.

News of the family and old conversations revisited were a levelling device: it was almost as if they were instilling a sense of mediocrity into Alvie, to bring her to their level, to make her, that is, no longer ill. Mediocrity as medicine.

And where were their recollections? Did they have no past together, that they could reminisce about? My only hint of this forgotten past was the photograph taken before I was born, the one that sat in our living room. I was genuinely fascinated by it. When was it taken, and where? What were they doing that day? Who took the photograph? Was it a happy day, as seemed from the picture, or did something occur later to mar it? Why did none of them ever mention it?

It was probably Alvie's sickness. It suffused everything in past and present: her pain, her discomfort, her doctor and her pills. Death surrounded Alvie's sickbed, and occupied it. The disease was creeping through her. Every time we visited her she was a little worse. First her legs lost all sensation; then she became incontinent; then she could not take solid food. But if her decline was steady, it was also slow. News of further deterioration came by letters, so that whenever I saw her I did so with the prospect of seeing her arms withering, or her face decaying away, or her teeth falling out; the ghoulish imagination of childhood was never satisfied, disappointed even, once I had resigned myself to having to visit her again. There was always an inverse surprise: how well she looked! Only later, as the depressing news was exchanged, would we hear of new horrors, new agonies. Yet the years dragged by and Alvie was still there in her bed, propped up by eight or nine pillows, her hair in a lank skein over one shoulder. She grew fatter, and paler, more grotesque, but these would come to anyone who never got exercise, who never went outside. Her spirit was unfailing: her voice was always pitched on one note, sounding sad and dull and dreary, but the things she said were self-consciously normal. She reported her pain and setbacks, she did not complain about them. She knew the disease was killing her, but she talked of the future, even if it was a future of the narrowest vision (what would I like for my next birthday, what was I going to do when I left school?). She was an example to us all.

Whenever we made our visits, one of the priests would come in to see Alvie. I always suspected that no one ever came from the seminary unless there was someone there from the outside world to witness it. Alvie had "courage"; she had "fortitude"; she "bore her cross." I hated the priests in their black clothes, waving their white hands sanctimoniously over the bed, blessing not only Alvie but my family too. I sometimes thought it was the priests who were killing her; they were praying not for a cure but a lingering death, and they were doing it to make a theological point to their students. My uncle was godless, his job was just a job. There was Hope in religion, and to prove it to him the priests were killing Alvie: no one works in the service of the Lord as one toils in the vineyards. We shall save.

The last visit:

The boat was late; the man in the harbour office told us the engine was being repaired, and for a joyous moment I thought the trip would have to be cancelled . . . but then the ferry appeared in the harbour, coming slowly to the quay to collect us, and the handful of other passengers who stood with us.

It seemed, as soon as the boat was outside the harbour, that we were almost upon Seevl: the grey, limestone cliffs were dead ahead . . . but it was an hour's voyage to Seevl Town, the boat swinging far out to sea to avoid the shoals beneath Stromb Head, then turning in again to take the sheltered passage beneath the cliffs. I stood apart from my parents, staring up at the cliffs, watching for the occasional glimpses of the high fells beyond, and feeling the onset of the real, stomach-turning dread I always felt as we arrived. It was cold at sea, and though the sun was rising quickly the wind came curling down on to the passage from the cliffs above. My parents were in the bar with the other passengers, and I shared the deck with crates of livestock, packing-cases, newspapers, cases of drink, two tractors.

The houses of Seevl Town, built up in terraces on the hills around the harbour, were constructed from the grey rock of the island, the roofs whitened around the chimney-stacks with bird droppings. An orange lichen clung to the walls and roofs, souring the houses, making them seem not warm, but crumbling. On the highest hill, dominating the town, stood the derelict remains of a rock-built tower. I never looked directly at this, fearing it.

As the boat glided in on the still water my parents came out of the saloon and stood beside me, one to each side, like an escort, preventing flight.

There was a car to be hired in Seevl Town; an expensive luxury in Jethra, but a necessity for the wild interior of the island. My father had booked it a week before, but it was not ready and we had to wait an hour or more in a cold office overlooking the harbour. My parents were silent, trying to ignore me as I fidgeted and made fitful attempts to read the book I had brought.

Around Seevl Town were the few farms on the island, rearing their scrawny animals and growing their hybrid cereals on the barren soil of the eastern side. The road climbed up through these smallholdings, following the perimeters of the fields, and turning through sharp angles and steep climbing corners. The surface had been metalled once but now it was decaying, and the car lurched uncomfortably in the potholes and the wheels often spun on the gravelly sides. My father, driving, stayed silent, trying to master not only the dangerous road but also the controls of the unfamiliar vehicle; my mother sat beside him with the map, ready to direct him, but we always got lost on Seevl. I sat in the back, ignored by them both, except when my mother would turn to see what I was doing; I always did nothing, staring out of my window in mute suspension of thought.

It took nearly an hour to reach the first summit of the fells, by which time the last farm, the last hedge, the last tree, were miles behind us. There was a last glimpse of Seevl Town as the road went over the crest, and a wide view of the gun-metal sea, flecked with islets, and the indistinct shape of the mainland coast.

On the moors the road rose and fell with the whim of the country, winding through the scrub-covered land. Sometimes, the car would come out from a high pass, where on each side great crags of limestone loomed over the scree-slopes, and the blast of wind from the north would kick the car to the side. My father drove slowly, trying to avoid the potholes; the map lay unconsulted on my mother's knee, because Father knew the way. Yet he always made mistakes, took the wrong turn or followed the wrong fork, and then Mother would sit quietly at his side until he realized. The map would be taken from her, the car would be reversed, and we would go back the way we had come to the place where we went wrong.

I left all this to them, although, like Mother, I usually knew when we went wrong. My interest was not with the road, but the landscape it passed through. I never failed to be appalled by the gigantic emptiness of Seevl, and Father's wrong turnings had for me the double advantage of not only delaying our eventual arrival at the seminary, but also of opening up more of the island to my eyes. The road often passed the dead towers of Seevl. I knew the islanders never went near these, but I did not know why; whenever the car passed one I could scarcely look towards it for fear, but my parents never even noticed. If we passed slowly, I would cower in my seat in anticipation of some ghoul of legend making a rush for the car.

Later in the journey the road itself deteriorated into a rough track, consisting of two gravel paths divided by a strip of long, coarse grass that scraped against the floor of the car.

Another hour passed, and then the road went down into a shallow valley where four of the dead towers stood like sentinels along the ridge. The valley was treeless, but there were many sprawling thorn-bushes, and in the lowest part, beside a wide stream, was a tiny hamlet with a view of the sea and the mainland. A part of Jethra could be seen: a black spread against the side of the Murinan Hills, and it seemed so close and foreign. Outside the village we climbed the high fells again, and I looked forward to one of the scenic surprises of the journey: the island was narrow for a distance, and crossing the moors the road touched on the southern side. For a few minutes we had a view of the Midway Sea beyond Seevl, with island after island spreading across it as far as the horizon. I never really considered Seevl to be a part of the Dream Archipelago. That was a different place: a lush, tropical maze of islands, hot and tranquil, forested or barren . . . but always dozing in the equatorial sun, and peopled by a strange race with customs and language as bizarre as their food, clothes and homes. But this fleeting glimpse, from the window of a car lurching along an unmade road on a cold grey island, was as close as I would ever be. The rest was dream.

Another valley; another hamlet. I knew we were approaching the seminary, and in spite of myself I was staring ahead, looking for the first sight of it.

VI

After dinner, Serjeant Reeth and I returned to our rooms, she because she said she wanted a bath and to wash her hair, and I because I could think of nowhere else to go. I sat for a while on the edge of my bed, staring at the carpet, then went to my suitcase and found the letter from the Father Confessor at the seminary. It was strange to read his ponderous, circumlocutory sentences, full of a stiff intent not only to engage my sympathies but also to intimidate me, and try to reconcile this with my adolescent bitterness about him and his priests. I remembered one occasion of many: I had been walking on a lawn at the seminary, innocently close to one of the flowerbeds, and a priest had appeared and reprimanded me severely. They could never leave it at that, because they had insights into the universe and I did not, and so I was warned of hell and my imminent and inevitable destiny. That priest was possibly now this reverend father, and the same implied threat was there: you must attend to your uncle's affairs, or we will fix the fates for you.

I lay back on the bed, thinking about Seevl, and wondering what it would be like to return. Would it depress me, as Jethra had done in the afternoon? Or would it scare me, as it had done in childhood? The priests and their heavenly machinations held no terror for me; Alvie was dead, and now so was Torm, both joining my parents, and a generation was gone. The island itself—as scenery, as a place—interested me, because I had only ever seen it with child's eyes, but I did not look forward to its emptiness. The dead towers . . . they were another matter, one I put aside. I had never come to terms with those, could only shun them as the islanders did. The difference, though, the factor that wrenched me into adult perspective, was the presence of Serjeant Reeth.

Her name was Bella; this she told me during dinner, and I, with wine inside me, had been unable to stop myself smiling. I had not known that policewomen had names like Bella, but there it was. She had an innocent quality to her, a certain wide-eyed ingenuousness; I liked it, but it made me feel my age. It seemed during the meal that our roles were reversing, that I, being older, was becoming her guardian for the journey. It had been too easy to forget that she was a member of the Seigniory, that if I spoke too freely or took her into my confidence, what I said might go into her report, might find its way on to a file.

Now I was alone again, it became a matter of personal reassurance. However much I might rationalize my fears, I did feel considerable trepidation about visiting Seevl again. If my Seigniory escort had been someone else—a man, perhaps, or someone older than myself—I might have sought psychological dependence on their presence . . . but because Bella was who she was, I felt differently. It would be I who took her to Seevl, not the other way around.

It was still too early to go to bed, so I found a book in my case, and lay on the bed to read it. Some time later, I was subconsciously aware that Bella must have returned to her room, because I heard her moving around.

Then, making me start a little, there was a tap on my door.

"Yes?" I called.

"Are you asleep, Lenden?"

"No . . . come in."

The door opened, and she put her head around. She had a towel wrapped about her hair.

"I'm sorry to be a nuisance, but I'm trying to dry my hair. The plug on my drier is the wrong one. You haven't got an adaptor, have you, or a screwdriver so I can change the plug?"

She came into the room, closing the door behind her. I stared at her in surprise. She had changed out of her uniform, and was wearing a loose, silken wrap. Her face was pink, and where her robe was open at the neck I could see her skin had that glowing cleanliness that follows a hot bath. The wrap was thin and white, and I could not help but see that she was full-breasted, dark-nippled. Damp ringlets of hair fell from under the towel.

"I've got a penknife," I said, trying not to reveal my reaction. "We can take a plug off something in here."

She stood by the door, holding her electric drier as I looked around for some appliance I could plunder. There was an electric radiator by the wall, but it had no independent plug. Then I saw the bedside lamp.

"Turn on the central light," I said. "I'll use this."

"I know it sounds stupid," she said, and gave me a little embarrassed smile. "I have to dry my hair like this, otherwise it goes frizzy."

I found my penknife, and started to unscrew the plug. She made me feel capable.

"Sit down, Bella. It'll only take a couple of minutes."

She sat on the edge of the bed, folding one knee over the other, while I kneeled on the floor, picking at the screws of the plug with the knife-blade. I did not look up at her; I was suddenly too conscious of her presence, her young body, her casually revealing wrap.

At last I got the plug off.

"Give me the drier," I said, looking up at her. The towel had loosened, and more hair was falling free. I wanted to reach up and stroke it. She put a hand to the towel, rubbed it gently against her head with an up-and-down motion.

She said: "Do you think we're the only people staying in the hotel?"

"It's very quiet. I haven't seen any other guests."

The closed bar, the silent lounge. We had been alone at dinner, with the lights on around our table, but the rest of the room had been darkened. The attentive waiters, standing by the serving-door, responsive to every move we made, every request. Yet the menu had been a full one; the food had been freshly cooked, and was attractively served.

"I looked in the register this morning," Bella said. "No one else has booked in for more than a week."

I looked up at her, but quickly bent my head over the plug. She was still towelling her hair; as she raised her arm she stretched the thin fabric of the robe across her body. The garment was working loose.

"It's the quiet season," I said.

"I tried room-service just now, to see about the plug. No one answered."

I screwed the back on the plug, and passed the drier up to her.

"That's fixed it," I said.

68

"Do you mind if I dry my hair here? It won't take long, and I'd like company."

I sat opposite her, in the one easy-chair in the room. She leaned down to connect the drier, then unwound the towel and played the warm stream of air over her. She swung her head, loosening the hair, then combed it through, playing the heat across it.

She was awakening things in me that had been dormant too long; I wished she had not come, yet I could not resist the feelings in me. With her hair loose she looked so young! As she dried her hair she was looking directly at me, with her head cocked on one side. She combed out several strands, holding them away from her head in the hot current, and as the hair dried it fell in a light cascade about her shoulders.

"Why don't you have your hair like that during the day? It's much more attractive."

"Regulations. The collar must be seen."

"Isn't it a strange job for a girl to have?"

"Why?" she said. "The pay's good, and it's a secure job. I get a lot of travel, and meet people."

"It just seems unfeminine."

She was fingering the vee of her wrap, where the fabric crossed loosely above her breasts. "Do I seem unfeminine?"

I shook my head, knowing that I had not meant it that way.

Her hair was dry. She bent down to unplug the drier, and for an instant, as her wrap fell forward, I caught a glimpse of her breast.

"Would you like me to stay?" She was sitting erect on the bed, looking at me.

I turned away, not knowing what to say. She got up from the bed, gathering the robe around her, and walked across to me. She gripped my arm lightly, just above the elbow. Her face was close to mine, and she was breathing quickly. I wanted to stroke her breasts, wanted to kiss her.

Still not meeting her gaze, I said: "I'd like you to, but—"

I willed her to interrupt me before I had to invent an excuse, but she stayed silent.

"Do you find me attractive?" she said.

"Of course I do."

She released my arm and picked up the drier, coiling the flex around it. She walked slowly towards the door.

"Please don't go!" I said.

"I thought you wanted me to."

"Not yet . . . I want to explain. It's not your fault, and please don't be hurt."

"I made a mistake," said Bella.

"No . . . I'm not ready, that's all. I can't say why."

She paused, with her head down, then turned and came back to me. For a moment her fingers twined themselves around my arm, and she kissed me quickly on the cheek. Before I could put my arm around her she stepped back.

"Goodnight, Lenden."

She went quickly from the room, closing the door quietly behind her. I stood where I was, my eyes closed, deeply ashamed of myself. I could hear Bella in her room: a drawer opening and closing, water running, then silence. At last, when I could bear to, I went to the mirror and stood looking at myself for a long time, stretching the skin around my eyes, smoothing the tiredness.

I undressed and went to bed. I woke at periods through the night, straining to hear some sound of Bella, urging her mentally to come back to my room . . . for that, at least, would have resolved an uncertainty. Through it all, the nearness of her, the little glimpses of her young body, I had been attracted to her as I had not been attracted for a long time. Even so, deep down, I was terrified she would return. This struggle between attraction and repulsion had dogged my life. Ever since Seevl.

VII

The ticking clock by Alvie's bed, and the gusting wind rattling the window in its loose frame; these were the only sounds in the pauses between conversation. I sat by the draughty window, looking down into the gardens outside and watching a black-robed priest tending one of the flowerbeds with a rake. The lawns and beds of the seminary's grounds were brightly incongruous on Seevl, an island within an island, constantly watered and fertilized and prodded.

When we went in the winter months only the lawns survived, but today there were clusters of tough-looking flowers, gripping the paltry earth with shallow roots. If I craned my neck I could see the huge vegetable garden where the students were made to work, and on the other side of the grounds, invisible from Alvie's room, was a small livestock farm. The seminary tried to keep itself, but I knew that food was brought in from outside, because that was part of my uncle's job to organize. Why had the priests lied about this, when I was shown around the seminary once? They must have known my uncle ordered food and fuel-oil from Seevl Town, so what was the point of maintaining the fiction that they were entirely independent of the world?

The priest at the flowerbed had glanced up when I first sat by the window, but since then he had ignored me. How long before he, or one of the others, came to see Alvie?

I looked across to the rising ground beyond the seminary walls. The skyline was a long, straight crag, with sloping scree beneath it, and below that the rank wild grass of the moors. There was one of the dead towers out there, a short way from the seminary, but it was one of the less conspicuous ones on Seevl, standing not against the sky, but against the duller background of the crag.

My parents had started to discuss me: Lenden was taking examinations, Lenden had not been studying properly, Lenden was not doing well. I sometimes wished I had the sort of parents who boasted about their child, but their method, at least with relatives, was to try to embarrass me into making greater efforts. I loathed them for it: the embarrassment I felt was the sort that made me resentful, even less willing to apply myself. I looked over at Seri, who was sitting by herself at a table in the corner of the room, apparently reading a book. She was listening, of course, while pretending not to, and when she saw me turn in her direction she looked back with a blank stare. No support there.

"Come here, Lenden," said Aunt Alvie; it was the sort of moment I always dreaded.

"Go to your aunt, Lenden," said my father.

Reluctantly I left my seat by the window, and went to stand beside the head of the bed. She stretched out a palsied hand, and took mine.

"You must work harder," she said. "For the sake of your future. For me. You want me to get well, don't you?"

"Yes," I said, although I did not see the connection. I was acutely aware of my parents watching me, of Seri's feigned indifference, and the embarrassment intensified.

"When I was your age," Aunt Alvie said, "I won every prize at school. It wasn't as much fun as being lazy, but in the end I was glad. You do understand, don't you?" She wanted my future to be like her present; she wanted to inflict her illness on me. I shrank away from her, as if her disease were contagious, but the pressure on my hand increased. "Now kiss me."

I was always having to kiss Alvie: when we arrived, before and after every meal, as we departed. It was part of the dread. I leaned forward, presenting my cheek to her cyanotic lips, but my reluctance held me back and she pulled my hand towards her. As her lips touched coldly against my skin I felt her pressing my hand against her breast; her coarse cardigan, the thin nightdress, the flaccid flesh. In turn, I kissed her cold white cheek, then tried to move away, but my hand was still clasped against her chest.

"Promise me you'll try harder from now on," Alvie said.

"I promise."

I tugged my hand away, and, so released, I stumbled back from the bed and returned to my chair. My face was hot with the indignity of the interview, and I saw a satisfied look on my father's face. We had endless rows at home about the marks I got at school, and now he had recruited an ally. Sitting by the window, staring sightlessly out across the lawns, I waited for them to find another topic to discuss. But they would not leave me.

"Why don't you go out for a walk, Lenden?"

I said nothing.

"Seri, take Lenden to see your den."

"I'm reading," Seri said, in a voice that tried to convey preoccupation.

"Seri!" said Uncle Torm. "Take your cousin for a walk. You'd like to see Seri's den, wouldn't you, Lenden?"

"Yes," I said. We were being dispatched; something adult and perhaps interesting was going to be discussed. Medical treatment, no doubt, details of bedpans and suppositories. I should not have minded hearing about those.

Seri and I looked at each other with mutual resignation, and she closed her book. She led me out of the room, down the gloomy and must-smelling corridor and out of the house. We crossed the garden, and came out through a gate in a brick wall into the main grounds of the seminary. Here Seri hesitated.

"What do you want to do?"

"Have you got a den?"

"That's what *they* call it. It's my hide-out."

"Can I see it?" I sometimes climbed a tree in the garden at home, to be by myself, but I had never had a proper hide-out. "Is it secret?"

"Not really. But I don't let anyone in I don't want there."

"Will you let me in?"

"I suppose so."

We walked along a gravel drive edging one of the lawns. From one of the open windows there came the sound of voices chanting a psalm. I walked with my feet scuffing up the gravel, to drown the sound, because it reminded me of school.

We came at last to one of the long wings of the seminary building. Seri led me towards some railings beside the base of the main wall, beyond which were some narrow stone steps leading down to a basement. A priest, hoeing a flowerbed, paused in his work to watch us.

Seri ignored him, and went down the steps. At the bottom she got down on her hands and knees and crawled through a low, dark hatchway. When she was inside she turned around and stuck out her head to look at me. I was still waiting at the top of the steps.

"Come on, Lenden. I'll show you something."

The priest was working again, but glancing back over his shoulder to look at me. I went quickly down the steps, and crawled in through the hatchway.

Seri's hide-out had once been some kind of store or cellar, because there were no windows, and the hatch was the only way in or out. The ceiling was high enough for us to stand erect. It was dark and cool, and Seri was lighting three or four candles placed high on a shelf. The tiny cell smelled of match phosphor and candlewax, and soot. There were two up-ended boxes to sit on, and from some-where Seri had found an old mat for the floor.

"What do you do in here?" I said enviously, thinking at once of all the fantasies I could live out if it were my own.

"That's what I'm going to show you."

The candles cast a weak yellow light, although now my eyes had adjusted from the bright daylight it seemed perfectly adequate. I sat down on a box.

I had been expecting Seri to sit on the other box, but she came and stood in front of me.

She said: "Do you want to know a secret, Lenden?"

"What sort of secret?"

"The special sort."

"All right," I said, without much interest, still very much under the cloud of Aunt Alvie and the others, and so assuming it was going to be something to do with that.

"How old are you, Lenden?"

"Fourteen."

"I'm fifteen. Have you got any hair yet?"

"Hair?" Of course I had hair; it was constantly falling in my eyes, and I was always being told to cut it.

"This is a dead secret. Just between you and me."

Before I realized what she was talking about, Seri quickly raised the front of her skirt, and with her other hand pulled down the front of her pants. I saw a tangly black bush of hair, at the junction of her legs.

I was so surprised that I almost fell off the box. Seri let go, and the elastic in her pants snapped them back into place, but she did not release the skirt. She held this high against her chest, looking down at herself. Her pants were dark-coloured and woollen, and the elastic bit into the plump flesh of her stomach.

I was acutely embarrassed—my own pubic hair had started growing some months before, and it was a matter of mystery, as-tonishment and shame, all mixed up together—but I was also com-pulsively interested.

"Let me see again," I said.

74

She stepped back, almost as if she was uncertain, but then came forward again.

"You pull it down," she said, thrusting her abdomen towards me.

Nervously, I reached forward, took the top of her pants in my fingers, and pulled the cloth down until I could just see the first growth of hair.

"Further!" she said, knocking my hand out of the way. She pulled the pants down, front and back, so that they clung around her thighs. Her triangle of hair, curling and black, stood unambiguously before me. I could not stop staring at her, feeling hot and prickly, and with a sudden and quite unmistakable stirring of arousal. I said nothing.

"Do you want a feel?" Seri said.

"No . . ."

"Touch me. I want you to feel."

"I'm not sure I should."

"Then let me have a look at you."

That, by presenting an awful alternative, resolved my doubts. I was too shy to let anyone see me. I reached out and put my fingers on her hair. It was coarse and wiry, and I recoiled in surprise, mentally but not physically. Seri moved her body against my fingertips.

"Lower down, Lenden. Feel lower down."

I turned my hand, so that it was palm up, and reached for the junction of her legs. It felt different there: less hair, a fold of skin. I snatched my hand away.

"What's the matter?"

"I don't know," I said, looking away. But I looked back, and Seri had moved much closer.

"Touch me again. Go right inside."

"I . . . can't."

"Then I'll touch you."

"No!" The thought of anyone, anyone at all, exploring my body; it was unimaginable. I was still growing, there was too much unexplained. I was ashamed of my body, of growing up.

"You can put your finger right inside, if you want to," Seri said. "I don't mind."

She seized my wrist and brought my hand up against her. Her body was warm, and the hairs curled against my palm. She pressed herself on my hand, encouraging my fingers to explore the cleft beyond. I felt the soft damp flaps of skin, and my fingertip played on the warm recess behind. I was in a heat of excitement, eager to do anything. I wanted to slip into her, sink my fingers, my hand into her. But then, just as I was going in to her, she stepped back and let the skirt fall.

"Seri—"

"Ssh!" She crouched by the square of daylight that was the hatch, and listened. Then she straightened, and hoisted up her pants with a sinuous movement of her hips.

"What are you doing?" I was distressed by her sudden withdrawal.

"Keep quiet," she said, softly. "I think there's someone outside."

"You're just teasing me, making an excuse!"

"No . . . really. I heard something fall. Did you hear a clattering noise?"

"No. Let me touch you again."

"Not now. I'm frightened."

"Then when?"

"In a minute. We'll have to go somewhere else. Do you still want to?"

"Of course I do! Let's go now!" I was excited beyond anything in my previous experience. And this was Seri! My stupid cousin!

"I know somewhere safe. Outside the seminary . . . a short walk."

"And then I can . . . ?"

"Anything you like, Lenden."

She made me crawl first through the hatch, and she blew out the candles as I did so. I stood up at the bottom of the steps, then jumped with surprise. The priest we had seen earlier was standing at the top of the steps, leaning down with one hand on the railings, as if listening. He backed away as I looked up. I went up the steps, and saw him hurry across to where he had dropped his hoe on the path. By the time Seri had joined me at the top he was back at work, hoeing the soil with quick, sharp movements.

He did not look up as Seri and I walked hurriedly along the gravel path, but as we passed through the gate I looked back. He was standing with the hoe in his hand, staring towards us.

"Seri, that priest was watching us."

She said nothing, but took my hand and led me running through the long wild grass outside the seminary grounds.

VIII

A hired car was waiting for us in Seevl Town, with a Seigniory pass attached to the windscreen. I sat in the front seat beside Serjeant Reeth as she drove slowly up the narrow streets towards the hills.

I was in a complex state of emotions, and this revealed itself by a forced exterior calm and an unwillingness to talk. She needed me to direct her, so I sat, as once my mother had sat, with the map on my knee, wondering if we would need it.

Last night had not been mentioned. Bella had appeared at breakfast, crisp in her uniform, once more the policewoman. Her straightforward proposition, my embarrassed refusal; I could hardly bear to think of them, yet how I wanted to speak of them! I did not want Bella to think she had made a mistake, but still I was incapable of explaining. I wanted some formula by which we could bring the incident forward into today, in an acceptable form, but by her silence and mine we were simply pretending nothing had happened.

She had, however, awakened my awareness of her sexuality, and that could not be pretended away, either by silence or by her starchy uniform. Waiting on Jethra dockside for the ferry, sitting together in the saloon of the boat, walking through Seevl Town to collect the car; I could not ignore her physical presence, could not forget that young body in the loose silk wrap.

Now we drove, and sometimes, as she shifted gear in the antiquated car, her hand or her sleeve would brush lightly against my knee; to see if it was as accidental as it seemed I moved my leg away, unobtrusively, and it did not happen again. Later, I let my leg move back, for the touch excited me.

Once, at a junction on the higher slopes of the moors, we went to the map for guidance. Her head bent down beside mine: another moment of physical nearness, but it ended as soon as we found the correct turning.

Watching the sombre green of Seevl's fells, my thoughts moved imperceptibly away from that intrigue to the other, the larger: the island and the seminary. My recollection of the road was unreliable, but the mood induced by the scenery was a familiar companion, twenty years absent. To someone seeing it for the first time, as Bella was seeing it, Seevl would seem wild, barren, grossly empty. There was the roundness of line that betrayed the millennia of harsh winters and unrelenting gales; where the rock was exposed, no plantlife clung to it except in the most sheltered corners, and then was only the hardiest of mosses, or the lowliest of lichens. There was a violent splendour to it, a scenic ruggedness unknown in our country. Yet to me, who had been along this route before, actual and mental, the scenery was merely the context. We passed through it as a hand reaching through luxuriant grass passes into a snake's nest. The moors were neutral, but contained a menace, and for me they were always coloured by it.

As Bella drove unsteadily along the narrow road I was already imagining ahead, seeing that valley at the other end of the island, with the cluster of grim buildings, the lawns and the incongruous flowerbeds.

Seevl was an island made for night. Although on this day the sky was clouded, the sun broke through from time to time, casting for brief periods a bright, unnatural radiance on the barren, grossly empty. There was the roundness of line that a damp stillness, chill and sad, filming the windscreen of the car. We had the windows closed and the heater on, yet the cold reached us. I shivered every now and then, shaking my shoulders, pretending to be more cold than I really was, because it was the island chilling me and I did not want Bella to know.

She drove slowly, steering more cautiously over the rutted track than ever my father had done. The car was in low gear for much of the time, the engine's note changing continually, making me irrationally irritable. Still we said nothing to each other, beyond intermittent consultations of the map. I watched for familiar landmarks—a cluster of standing stones, a fall of water, the dead towers—and sometimes I could direct her without referring to the map. My memory of the landscape was partial: there were long sections of the road that seemed new to me, and I was sure we had lost our way, then something I remembered would appear, surprising me.

We stopped for lunch at a house in one of the little hamlets, and here some preparation was revealed: we were expected, a meal was ready. I saw Bella sign a document, a form that would recompense the woman for her service.

When we reached the narrow part of the island, and travelled along the road above the southern cliffs, Bella pulled the car on to the side and stopped the engine. We were shielded from the wind by a high, rocky bank, and the sun warmed us.

We stood outside the car, looking across the glistering seascape, the view that as a child I had only been able to glimpse from my parents' moving car.

"Do you know any of the islands' names?" I said.

Bella had removed her cap, left it on the driver's seat in the car, and wisps of hair blew lightly around her face.

"A few. Torquin is the biggest; we have a base there now. My brother will probably pass through Torquin. And one of them must be Derril, where the Covenant was made. I'm not sure which one that is, though."

"Have you ever been in the Archipelago?"

"Only here."

Only Seevl, the offshore island.

The islands we could see were different shades of green, some dark, some light. It was said that of the ten thousand inhabited islands not one was like any other, that a true islander, if planted blind in a foreign island, would know its name by smell and sound alone. All I, a mainlander, knew was that the islands we could see from here were a part of the Dream Archipelago known as the Torqui Group, that they were primarily dependent on dairy-farming and fishing, and that the people spoke the same language as my own. This was school-knowledge, half-remembered, all but useless.

"Did you ever want to run away to the islands?" Bella said.

"When I was a kid. Did you?"

"I still do, sometimes."

"At least you have come to Seevl."

"At least."

Talking about something outside ourselves had eased the tension between us; it was as if we had slipped unconsciously into another language. It came naturally to speak in the same tongue, so I said: "Bella, about last night—"

"Lenden, I'm sorry about that."

"That's what *I* was going to say."

"But it is I who should say it. I shouldn't have gone to your room. I made a stupid mistake."

I found her hand, and squeezed it quickly. "No, not a mistake. I wanted you . . . but I just wasn't ready."

"Can we forget it?"

"That's what I want."

Yes, to forget the misunderstanding, and the shame that followed . . . but not to forget what still might be. I thought about that for a while, as we leaned together against the side of the car, watching the sea.

I said: "We'll have to stay at the seminary tonight. You know we can't get back to Seevl Town?"

"Yes, I know."

"They'll probably give us rooms in the college."

"That's all right. I went to a convent."

She went around to the driver's door, and opened it. We drove on. I knew it would take at least another hour from there, and the afternoon was drawing on. Bella said nothing, concentrating on the difficult drive, and I surrendered to my memories and the oppressive mood of the island.

IX

Seri held my hand, and we leaped and ran across the rough ground, the coarse grasses whipping against our legs. It was the first time I had ever left the seminary grounds, and never until then had I recognized how the stout walls became a symbolic defence against the rest of the island. Out here the wind seemed stiffer and colder, and we were more exposed.

"Where are we going?" I said, gasping because I was out of breath.

"Somewhere I know." She released my hand, and went on ahead.

"Let's do it here." Some of the tension that had built up inside her hide-out had been dissipated by our sudden escape, and I wanted to go on before she changed her mind.

"Out in the open?" she said, rounding on me. "I told you this was a secret!"

"There's long grass," I said lamely.

"Do you still want to do it?"

"Yes!" I said, sure of that if nothing else.

"Then come on."

She set off again, leaping down a shallow slope towards a stream. I held back for a moment, staring guiltily towards the seminary. There was someone there, outside the walls, walking in our direction. I knew at once that it was the priest with the hoe, although he was too far away for me to be sure.

I ran after Seri, and jumped across the narrow stream to join her.

"There's someone following us. That priest."

"He won't find us!"

It was now quite obvious where Seri was taking me. The ground sloped up steeply from the stream, rising towards the high crag in the distance. A short way from us, built with the limestone rock of the island, was the dead tower.

I looked back, and saw we were out of sight of the priest if he was still following us. Seri marched on, a long way ahead of me, scrambling up the hillside through the windswept grass.

The tower was not noticeably different from any other of its sort I had seen on Seevl: it was about as tall as a four-storey house, with window-frames higher up which once had contained glass, but which now were broken. There was a door in the base, hanging open on its hinges, and all around in the grass were pieces of broken brick and tile. The tower was not wide: perhaps fifteen feet in diameter, and hexagonal. There had once been a roof, built in candle-snuffer shape, but now it was all fallen, and only two or three beams stood out to reveal its former design.

Seri was waiting for me by the open door.

"Hurry, Lenden!"

"I'm coming," I said, stepping over a heap of masonry, and looking up at the tower as it loomed over me. "We're not going inside, are we?"

"Why not? It's been here for years . . . it's quite safe."

All I knew about the towers of Seevl was that no one went near them; yet Seri stood by the door as if it were just another hide-out. I was torn between my dread of the tower, and what Seri would offer me inside.

"I thought these towers were . . . dangerous," I said.

"It's just an old ruin. Something to do with the college, when it was a monastery. Years ago."

"But they're all over the island!"

Seri shrugged dismissively, and went through the door. I hesitated a few seconds longer, then followed her. She closed the door behind us.

Daylight came in through two windows set high under the ceiling, which was a bare skeleton: dusty joists and broken planking. A fallen beam lay at an angle across the room, propped up against the wall. The floor was littered with glass, plaster and pieces of rock.

"See . . . there's nothing to worry about." Seri kicked a few pieces of rock out of the way, to clear a space on the wooden floor. "It's just an old dump."

"Are you still going to let me touch you?" I said.

"If you want to."

"I do . . . but that priest was following us. You said it was secret."

Seri started to say something, but changed her mind and turned away. She opened the door, and peered out; I stood behind her, looking over her shoulder. We both saw the priest. He had reached the stream and was walking along the bank, trying to find somewhere to cross.

Seri closed the door again. "He won't come here. Not to the tower."

"But he's coming!" It was obvious that he was following us.

"Lenden, none of the priests will come here. They say the tower is evil. They're terrified of the place . . . that's why it's safe for us.''

I glanced around nervously. ''What's evil about it?''

''Nothing . . . it's just their superstition. They say something wicked happened. A long time ago.''

''But he's still coming,'' I said.

''You wait and see what he does.''

I went to the door and opened it a fraction of an inch. I peered through the slit, looking down the hill for the priest. He was some way away, standing still, looking up towards me. I closed the door, and told Seri this.

''You see?'' she said.

''But he'll wait until we come out. What then?''

''It's none of his business,'' she said. ''He won't know what we're doing. I know him . . . it's Father Grewe. He's always poking around, wondering what I'm up to. I'm used to it. Shall we start?''

''If you want to.'' The mood had left me.

''Get undressed then.''

''Me? I thought you—''

''We both undress.''

''I don't want to.'' I looked at the rubble-strewn floor, shyly. ''Not yet, anyway. You do it first.''

''All right. I don't mind.''

She reached up under her skirt, and pulled her pants down her legs. She tossed them on the floor.

''Now you take something off,'' she said. I hesitated, then complied by taking off my pullover.

Seri undid two buttons on the side of her skirt, and it slid down her legs. She turned away from me to drape the garment over the beam, and for a moment I saw the pinkness of her buttocks, slightly dimpled. ''Now you.''

''Let me feel you first. I've never done . . .''

Some compassion softened her determination to make me undress at the same rate as her. She smiled, quickly, then sat down on the floor, keeping her knees together and reaching forward to clasp her ankles. I could see none of her secrets, just the pale curve of her thighs, rounding towards her buttocks. Her sweater finished at her waist.

"All right. But be very gentle. You were jabbing me before."

She sat back, resting her elbows on the floor behind her, and then she parted her legs. I saw the black thatch of hair, the whorl of pink skin, revealed but mysterious. Staring at her I moved forward, crouching down. I was suddenly as excited as I had been before; it switched on like a motor, compelling me towards her almost against my will. I felt a tightness in my throat, a sweatiness in my palms. That passive, lipped organ, lying between her thighs like an upright mouth, waited for my touch. I reached forward, ran fingertips across the lips, felt the warmth of them, the moistness behind. Seri sucked in her breath, tensing herself.

Something small and hard whacked against the door, startling us both. Seri swung away from me, turning to one side; my hand brushed against the top of her thigh, then she was away from me.

"What was that!" I said.

"Don't move." She went to the door, eased it open and peered out.

I heard, distantly: "Seri, come out of that place. You know it is forbidden."

She closed the door. "He's still out there."

She sounded surprised, as if she had forgotten him. I had not, and I looked around for my pullover. "Is he coming in?"

"I told you . . . he won't come near us. I'll have to go and talk to him." She picked up her skirt and stepped into it, buttoning it again at the waist. "Wait here, and don't let him see you."

"But he knows I'm here. I'll come with you. We ought to be going back to the house anyway."

"No!" she said, and I saw the quickness of her temper. "There's more to do, more than just touching. That's only the beginning." Her hand was on the door. "Stay here . . . keep out of sight, and I'll be back in a few moments."

The door slammed behind her. I peeped through the crack, saw her running down through the long grass to where the priest waited. He seemed angry, but she was uncowed, standing near to him and kicking idly at the grasses while he spoke.

84

There was a faint, musky fragrance on my fingertips, where I had touched her. I drew back from the door, and looked around at the filthy interior of the tower. Without Seri I felt ill at ease in the old ruin. The ceiling was sagging; what if it fell on me? The constant wind of Seevl blustered around the tower, and a piece of broken wood, hanging by the window-frame, knocked to and fro.

Minutes passed, and as the aroused excitement faded for the second time, I began to wonder guiltily about the possible consequences of being caught here. Suppose the priest told Torm and Alvie that we had been up to something, or that we were gone long enough for them to guess anyway? If they knew the truth, or even a part of it, there would be a terrible scene.

I heard the voice of the priest, in a freak silence of the wind; he was saying something sharply, but Seri's response was laughter. I returned to the door, put my eye to the crack and looked out at them. The priest was holding Seri by the hand, tugging her, but she was pulling back from him. To my surprise, I realized that I was not witnessing a conflict, but what seemed to be a game. Their hands slipped apart . . . but it was an accident, because they joined again immediately and the playful pulling went on.

I stepped back, very puzzled.

X

We were in a part of the seminary I had never seen before: an office just behind the main entrance. We had been greeted by a Father Henner, thin, bespectacled, and younger than I had expected; condolences on the death of my uncle, a tragic loss, a servant of God. He handed over the key to the house, and we went for a meal in the refectory. Father Henner did not eat with us; Bella and I ate alone at a table in one corner of the room. Night was falling beyond the stained-glass windows.

I could hear the wind, made louder, it seemed, by the airy space above us, the high, buttressed roof.

"What are you thinking, Lenden?" Bella said, over the sounds of the students clattering their dishes at the other end of the hall.

"I'm wishing we didn't have to stay. I don't like this place."

Afterwards, Father Henner took us across to the house, leading the way through the grounds with a battery flashlight; our feet crunched on the gravel pathway, the trees moved blackly against the night sky and the vague shape of the moors beyond. I unlocked the door and Father Henner turned on a light in the corridor. A dim, low-wattage bulb shed yellow light on the shabby floor and wallpaper. I smelt damp rot and mould.

"You'll find that much of the furniture has already been removed," said Father Henner. "Your uncle bequeathed the more valuable pieces to the college, and some of the effects belonged to us already. As you know, we have been unable to trace the daughter, so with your permission the rest may be destroyed."

The daughter . . . ah, Seri. Where are you now, Seri? She left the island soon after Alvie died, but no one knew where she went. My parents would never mention her, and I never asked. Today she would be somewhere in the Archipelago.

"What about my uncle's papers?" I said.

"They're still here. We can arrange for them to be incinerated, if you will separate the valuable ones."

I opened a door into a room off the corridor. It had been my uncle's office, but now it was empty, with pale squares on the walls where pictures had been; a dark patch of damp spread up from the stone floor.

"Most of the rooms have been cleared. There's just your dear aunt's room. And the kitchen. There are utensils there."

Bella was standing by the door to my aunt's room. Father Henner nodded to her, and she turned the handle. I experienced a sudden compulsion to back away, fearing that Alvie would still be there, waiting for me.

Father Henner went back to the main door. "Well, I'll leave you to your work. If there's anything you need, I shall be in my office during the day."

I said: "We need somewhere to stay."

Father Henner opened the door, and his black habit blew in the sudden wind from outside. "You may use the house, of course."

"We were expecting you to give us rooms," Bella said.

"In the college?" he said to her. "I'm afraid that would not be possible. We have no facilities for women."

Bella looked at me questioningly; I, stricken with a dread of spending a night in the house, shook my head.

"Are there proper beds here?" Bella said, pushing open the door and peering into the room, but my aunt's folding screen was there, making its temporary corridor into the room and blocking the view of the rest.

Father Henner was outside. "You'll have to make do. It's only for one night, after all. God be with you."

He went, and the door slammed behind him. Quietness fell; the thick walls effectively muted the wind, at least here in the centre of the house, away from the windows.

"What are we going to do, Lenden? Sleep on the floor?"

"Let's see what's in there."

Aunt Alvie's room; my dear aunt.

Pretending to Bella that it was just an ordinary room, pretending to myself, I went past her and walked in. The central light was beyond the folding screen, so the way was shadowed. At the end, facing us, someone from the seminary had stacked two huge piles of old documents; tomorrow I should have to go through them. Dust lay in a gritty film on the top sheets. Bella was behind me; I looked beyond the screen to see the rest of the room. The double bed, Alvie's bed, was still there, dominating everything. Tea-chests had been brought in to the room, two extra chairs were crammed against the wall, books lay in uneven piles on the table beneath the window, picture-frames rested on the mantelpiece . . . but the bed, piled high with pillows, was the focus of the room, as ever. By its head was the bedside table: dusty old pill-bottles, a notebook, a folded lace handkerchief, a telephone, lavender water. These I remembered.

Alvie still lay in the bed. Only her body was missing.

I could smell her, see her, hear her. Above the bed, on the wall behind the top rail of the brass-fitting, were two dark marks on the wallpaper. I remembered then: Alvie had had a characteristic gesture, reaching up behind her to grip the rail with both hands, perhaps to brace herself against pain. Her hands, years of her hands gripping like that, had left the stains.

The windows were black squares of night; Bella drew the curtains, and dust cascaded down. I could hear the wind again, and thought: Alvie must have known this wind, every night, every day.

"Are you all right, Lenden?"

"Of course."

"Well, there's a bed, at least."

"You have it," I said. "I'll sleep on the floor."

"There'll be another bed somewhere. In one of the other rooms."

"Father Henner said they had been cleared."

"Then . . . will you share? Or I could go on the floor."

We stood there in awful indecision, each for our own reasons. At last we came to silent agreement, changing the subject, pretending to look for enough space on the floor for me to lie down, but it was inevitable we would share. We were both tired, and chilled by the cold house. I let Bella take charge, and she tidied the bed, shaking out the old sheets to air them a little, turning them over. Spare pillows went on the floor, extra covers were found. I busied myself, trying to help, distracting myself from the thought: Alvie's bed, Alvie's bed.

At last the bed was ready, and Bella and I took it in turn to use the bathroom upstairs. I went first, and when Bella went after me I sat on the edge of Alvie's bed, listening to the sounds of her footsteps on the bare boards above. Here, in this room, my fears were conjoined: the shadow of my past and how it barred me from Bella, the memories of Alvie, and the winds and darknesses of Seevl that surrounded the house. I heard Bella above me, walking across the room, and she started down the wooden staircase. I made a sudden decision, stripping off my outer clothes and sliding in between the sheets.

Bella switched off the central light as she came in. She saw that I was in the bed, but her expression remained neutral. I watched, and did not watch, as she undressed in the glow from the table-lamp. The blouse and skirt of her uniform; suspender-belt and stockings; black pants and a sensible bra. She stood naked, looking away from me, finding a tissue to blow her nose on.

As she lay down beside me I felt her skin cold against mine, and realized she was shaking.

"I'm freezing," she said, and turned off the light. "Will you hold me?"

My arm went easily around her; she was slim and her body shaped itself naturally against mine. I could feel the plump weight of her breast on my arm, the prickle of her hair against my thigh. I was getting excited, but did not move, hoping to conceal it.

She ran a hand lightly over my stomach, then up to my breasts. "You've still got clothes on."

"I thought—"

"Don't be frightened, Lenden."

She slipped her hand inside my bra, caressed my nipple, kissed me on the neck. Pressing herself to me she unhooked the bra and slid it down my arms. Her head ducked down, and with her hand cupping me she took a nipple in her mouth, sucking and pulling on it. Her hand crept down, went beneath the fabric of my pants and her fingers slipped expertly between my legs. I stiffened, excited and terrified.

Later, Bella sat astride me, her hair falling loose and touching my face. I caressed her beautiful breasts, playing with the small firm nipples, licking and kissing them. She guided my hand to her sex, but as soon as my fingers felt the bristle of hair, I snatched away. Again I was guided there, again I pulled back.

"Touch me, Lenden, oh, touch me . . . ."

Bella was kissing my face, my neck, my shoulders, but I could not touch her. I shrank from her as once before I had shrunk from Seri, but Bella took my wrist in her hand, thrust my clenched fingers between her legs, clamped down on me, thrusting herself against my knuckles in repeated spasms. Afterwards, she sprawled across me, her sweat dripping down from her temples and into my open mouth.

I left her in the bed and stood, shivering, by the window. I leaned against the wall by the frame, staring out into the gusty night. The dark was impenetrable. There were no lights, not even the subdued glow of a cloudy night, and I could not see the bulk of the moors.

Bella turned on the table light, and after she had lit a cigarette I turned to look back at her. She was lying with the cigarette between her lips, her hands gripping the brass rail of the bed above her head. Her hair fell down across her shoulder, partially covering one breast.

"You do prefer men, don't you?" she said.

I simply shook my head, and waited by the window until she had finished her cigarette and turned out the light. In the darkness I returned to the bed. Bella did not stir, and I curled up against her, resting my head on her shoulder. I started to drift towards sleep, and I laid my hand gently on her breast. The bed smelled of bodies.

XI

While Seri was outside the dead tower with the priest something happened to me, and I cannot explain it. There was no warning of it, and I had no premonition of fear.

My main preoccupations were intense sexual frustration, and curiosity about what Seri was doing with the priest. She had suddenly and unexpectedly illuminated an area of my life I had always kept in the shade. I wanted the knowledge of her that she was offering, and I wanted the consequent knowledge of myself.

But she had told me to wait, to stay out of sight . . . and I was prepared to do both, but not for long. I had expected her to get rid of the priest somehow, but instead she was out there apparently playing with him.

So preoccupied, I barely noticed a low, snuffling sound that came to me over the noise of the wind. I was picking up my pullover, retrieving Seri's pants. I was going out to join Seri, because I wanted to know what she was doing.

I was stuffing her pants into the pocket of my skirt when I heard the noise again. It surprised me: because I had heard it the first time without really thinking about it I had subconsciously ignored it, but when it came again it was both strange and half-familiar. It was like nothing I had ever heard before. It was animalistic, but there was a human quality to it too, as if some beast had managed to form half a word before reverting to its usual grunt. Still I felt no fear, but a sense of curiosity. I suspected that Seri had returned, and was playing a joke on me. I called her name, but there was no answer.

Something about the animal quality of the noise had made me hesitate. I stood in the centre of the crumbling tower, looking around, thinking for the first time that perhaps some predatory beast was in the vicinity. I listened, trying to filter out the persistent noise of the wind, trying to distinguish the sound again. But there was no more of it.

A beam of Seevl's bright cool sunlight was striking in through one of the high windows and illuminating the wall beside the door. This, like the rest of the tower, was decaying away, and a short distance from the doorpost the plaster and brickwork had fallen away, leaving a jagged hole about the size of a man's head. Beyond, the cavity of the wall was revealed, with the great, grey bricks of the main structure dimly visible behind. It was one of several holes in the wall, but it caught my attention because some instinct told me that this was the source of the noise. I stepped towards it, still suspecting Seri of some complicity; perhaps having got rid of the priest she had returned quietly to the tower, and was fooling around outside the door.

Something moved inside the cavity, and although I was staring straight at the place I saw only a dark, quick movement. The sun went in, as one of the low clouds covered it, and it seemed suddenly much colder. Moments later the sun came out again, but the chill remained; I knew then that it was in me.

I placed my hand on the brickwork, leaning slightly towards the hole, trying to see down into it. I did not want to go too close, yet I was convinced someone, or something, was in there, and I wanted to know what it was. There were no more movements, no more noise, but an almost tangible sense of presence remained.

I was no longer alone in the tower.

"Is that you, Seri?" I said, and the sound of my voice seemed too loud and too feeble, simultaneously. I cleared my throat, noisily, giving Seri a chance to declare herself . . . but there was no response.

I moved my hand further into the hole, until I touched the bricks on the far side of the cavity. There was something warm in there, because I could feel a gentle heat, as of a living body. I reached down, into the dark.

There was a violent noise, a movement that I felt without seeing, and something grabbed my hand.

It pulled, dragging my arm down into the hole until my shoulder scraped painfully against the bricks. I screamed in surprise, gasping in terror. I tried to pull back, but whatever it was that had taken hold had sharp claws or teeth and they were biting into my skin. My face was jammed sideways against the wall, the skin of my bare upper arm was grazing against the rough bricks.

"Let go!" I shouted, helplessly, trying to tug my arm away.

As the thing had grabbed me I had instinctively balled my hand into a fist, and I could feel it contained in something wet and very warm, hard on one side, soft on the other. I pulled again, and the grip of the teeth tightened. Whatever it was in there was no longer dragging me down, but was holding me. Whenever I pulled back, the sharp teeth tightened around me. They were backwards-pointing, so that to pull against them was only to drag my flesh against their edge.

I unballed my fingers slowly, painfully aware that to loosen them was to expose them. The tips pressed against something soft, and I clenched my fist reflexively again. I shuddered, wanting to scream again, yet lacking the breath.

It was a mouth that had seized me. I knew that from the moment it had taken hold, yet it was too horrible to believe. Some animal, crouching in the wall, some huge, rank animal had taken my arm in its mouth, and was holding me. My knuckles were jammed against the hard roof of the mouth, my tightly balled fingers were against the coarse surface of the tongue. The teeth, the fangs, had closed about my arm, just above the wrist.

I tried turning my arm, attempting to twist it free, but the instant I moved the teeth closed more tightly on me. I shouted in pain, knowing that the flesh must have been torn in many places, and that I was surely bleeding into the animal's mouth.

I shifted my feet, trying to balance, thinking that if I could stand firmly I could pull harder, but as the animal had dragged me down it had pulled me over. Most of my weight was on the shoulder jammed against the bricks. I moved a foot, shifted some of my weight on to it. The fangs tightened on me again, as if the animal sensed what I was doing.

The pain was indescribable. The strength that held my fingers closed was draining away, and I could feel my fist loosening. Again my fingertips touched the hot, quivering surface of the tongue, and drooped down towards the throat. Miraculously, I still had the sensation of touch, and I could feel the hard gums, the slick sides to the tongue. It was the most disgusting thing I had ever felt in my life: wild, feral, bestial.

The animal, having firm hold of me, was trembling with some kind of incomprehensible excitement. I could feel the head shivering, and the breath rasped in and out over my arm, cold against the wounds as it inhaled, wet and hot as it exhaled. I could smell its stench now: sweet with the saliva of gross animalism, rancid and fetid with the smell of carrion.

I tugged once more, in desperate, disgusted terror, but the agony of the biting teeth redoubled. It felt as if it had almost bitten through me; I had a ghastly, flashing image of withdrawing my arm at last, and seeing it severed through, the sinews dangling from the stump, the blood pumping away. I closed my eyes, gasping again with horror and revulsion.

The tongue started moving, working around my wrist, stroking my palm. I felt as if I were going to faint. Only the pain, the intense, searing agony of torn muscle and crushed bone, kept me conscious to suffer longer.

Through the veils of pain I remembered Seri was outside. I shouted for help, but I was weakened and my voice came out as a hoarse whisper. The door was only a few inches from me. I reached over with my free hand and pushed at it. It swung outwards, and I could see down the slope, across the long grass. The brilliant cold sky, the dark rising moors . . . but no sign of Seri. I was alone.

Staring through tear-filled eyes, unable to focus, I stayed helpless, leaning against the rough brickwork as the monster in the wall slowly ate my arm. Outside, the wind made light-coloured patterns on the thick, waving grass.

The animal began to make a noise, a reprise of the first sound it had made. It growled deep inside its throat, and beneath my helpless fingers the tongue was quivering. It sucked in breath and the head tensed, and then there came a second growl. Somehow, the sound made my fevered imagining of the animal more detailed: I saw a wolf's head, a long snout, flecks of foam. The pain intensified, and I sensed the animal's increased excitement. The throat-noises were coming regularly now, in a fast rhythm, faster and faster as its hold on my arm tightened. The agony was so acute that I was sure it must almost have bitten through, and I tried once more to pull away, quite ready to lose my hand for the sake of release. The animal held on, chewing more viciously, snarling at me from its hidden den below. My head was swimming; unconsciousness could not have been far away.

The animal noises were now coming so quickly that they seemed to join into one continuous howl; the pain was intolerable. But then, unaccountably, the jaw sagged open and I was released.

I slumped weakly against the wall, my arm still dangling inside the cavity. The pain, which surged with every heartbeat, began to diminish. I was crying with relief and agony, and with terror of the animal which was still there below. I dared not move my arm, thinking that one twitch of a muscle would provoke another attack, yet I knew my chance had come to snatch away what was left of my arm.

My tears stopped, because I was afraid. I listened carefully: was the animal breathing, was it still there? I did not know if my arm had lost all sensation, but I could not feel the animal's foul breath moving across me. The pain was almost indiscernible; my arm must be numb. I imagined, rather than felt, the fingers hanging uselessly from the mangled wrist, blood pulsing down into the animal's open snout below.

A deep revulsion stirred me at last, and, not caring if the animal should attack me again, I stood away from the wall, withdrawing my shattered arm from the cavity. I staggered away, and rested my good hand against the low-lying beam. I looked at the damage done to me.

The arm was whole, the hand was undamaged.

I held it before me, disbelieving what I saw. The sleeve of my blouse had been torn as I was dragged through the brickwork, but there were no marks on the skin, no lacerations, no teeth-marks, no blood. I flexed my fingers, bracing myself against the anticipated pain, but they moved normally. I turned my hand over, looking at it from all sides. Not a mark, not even a trace of the saliva I had felt running across me.

The palm was moist, but I was sweating all over. I touched the arm gingerly, feeling for the wounds, but as I pressed down on the sore areas the only sensation I could feel was of fingertips squeezing against good flesh. There was not even a ghost of the pain I had suffered.

There was a faint, unpleasant odour on my hand, but as I sniffed at the backs of my fingers, at my palm, it faded away.

The door was open. I snatched at my pullover, which lay on the floor, and lurched outside. I was holding my wounded, undamaged arm across my chest, as if I was in pain, but it was just a subconscious reflex.

The long grass swept around me in the wind, and I remembered Seri. I needed her then: to explain, to soothe, to calm me. I wanted another human being to see me, and give me the reassurance I could not give myself. But Seri had vanished, and I was alone.

At the bottom of the slope, near the stream, a good distance from the tower: a figure in black stood up. His habit was caught in the band at his waist, and as he turned he was pulling at it, making it hang normally. I ran towards him, rushing through the grass.

He turned his back on me as soon as he saw me, and strode quickly away. As I dashed towards him he reached the brook, leaped over it and hurried up the slope beyond.

"Wait, Father!" I shouted. "Please wait!"

I came to a place where the grass was flattened, and in its centre lay Seri. She was on her back, with her skirt rolled up above her waist. Her sweater had been pushed up to her neck, revealing plump little breasts, pink-tipped. Her eyes were closed, and her arms lay on the ground above her head. Her knees were raised, and her legs were wide open.

"Seri!"

She opened her eyes and saw me.

"Do you still want to touch me, Lenden?" she said, and giggled.

I looked at the place; a pale, creamy fluid trickled from the reddened lips.

A wave of nausea came over me, and I backed away from her, unable to look at her. She was still laughing, and as she saw my reaction her laughter became shrill and hysterical. She rolled around in the flattened grass, writhing as she must have writhed before.

I kept a distance between us, waiting for her to sober. I remembered that I had her pants in the pocket of my skirt, and I found them and threw them at her. They landed on her naked belly.

"You're . . ." I tried to find a word forceful enough to convey the revulsion in me, but failed. "You're *filthy!*"

Her crazy laughing stopped, and she lay on her side to look at me. Then, deliberately, she opened her legs in tacit invitation.

I turned from her and ran away, towards the seminary, towards the house. I sobbed as I ran, and the torn sleeve of my blouse flapped around my arm. I stumbled as I crossed the stream, drenching my clothes; I tripped many times, cutting my knee, tearing the hem of my skirt. Bloodied, hysterical, bruised and soaked through, I ran into the house and burst into my aunt's sickroom.

My uncle and my father were supporting Alvie above a chamber-pot. Her white, withered legs dangled like bleached ropes; drops of orange liquid trickled from her. Her eyes were closed, and her head lolled.

I heard my uncle shouting. My mother appeared, and a hand was slapped over my eyes. I was dragged, screaming, into the corridor.

All I could say, again and again, was Seri's name. Everyone seemed to be shouting at me.

Later, Uncle Torm went out on the moors to find Seri, but before they returned we had got back into our car and were driving, through the evening and night, towards Seevl Town.

It was the last time I went to Seevl. I was fourteen. I never saw Seri again.

XII

We burned my uncle's papers in the yard behind the house: black charred ashes floated up, then were whisked away by the wind. There were also some clothes, and some chairs and a table the priests did not want. They burned slowly, and I stood by the fire, watching the flames reflectively.

Bella, standing by the doorway, said: "Why do you keep staring at the moors?"

"I didn't know that I was."

"There's something out there. What is it?"

"I was watching the blaze," I said.

"Have you ever been out on the moors?"

"No." I kicked a chair leg that had rolled from the fire, and sparks flew. Something in the fire spat, and a cinder shot across the yard.

Bella came towards me, took my arm tenderly.

"It doesn't matter, about last night."

I said nothing because I knew she was right, but also that it did matter.

"Was that your first time?" she said.

"Of course not."

"I meant, with someone like me?"

"No."

What was she like, that was so different? She meant perhaps: was she my first female lover? I smiled sadly, thinking of the men I had loved, the women too. More women than men, over the years, because I only went to men in desperation. I, always the passive lover: excited and slightly appalled by their relish in caressing my body, envying them their lack of inhibition, and determined with each new partner that *this* one would be different, *this* one would find me active. No, in that sense, Bella was no different. I had not changed. I had thought a few years' abstention, a gaining in maturity, would cure me of the irrational fear. I should not have put it to the test; I had been weak, thinking that the return to Seevl would, in itself, be some kind of exorcism. I had fallen for Bella's youth, her hesitancy, her pretty body; these had drawn me, once again, to failure. I had not known that I had dried up, become a husk.

"I'm only trying to understand," Bella said.

"So am I."

"We're alone." Bella, speaking softly. "Be frank with me."

"I am, I think."

"Will we see each other again? After this?"

"Yes," I said, postponing.

"I can travel freely. Let me visit your home."

"All right. If you'd like to."

It seemed to satisfy her, but she stood with her hand on my arm as we watched the fire.

I wondered what it was she saw in me; surely she had other friends? I was several years older than her, and she made me feel it, with her economical body, her youthful mannerisms. I had my first grey hairs, my breasts had started to sag, my waist was full, my thighs were thick. I was the older woman, more mature and presumably more experienced, yet it was she who pursued. I found it very affecting and flattering.

If it had been anywhere else: not Seevl, not Alvie's room and Alvie's bed. Would it have been any different?

The inevitable failure . . . but also the inevitable seeking for an excuse.

The real excuse, if there was any at all, lay out there under the crag of Seevl's moors.

That morning I had risen before Bella, and climbed from Alvie's bed to go to the window. From there I had been sure I would be able to see the tower where it all had happened, but I looked and I had not been able to see. The seminary gardens were just as I re-called them—although less well tended than I had thought—and so was the view across to the high, limestone crag. But there was no sign of the tower.

Bella was right: all that morning, as I worked through my un-cle's papers, I had looked frequently towards the moors, wonder-ing where the tower had gone.

There must have been a rational explanation: it had become unsafe, it had been demolished.

Or the other sort of rational explanation: that it was not there, that it had never been there. I shied away from that, unable to face the consequences.

Bella was still holding my arm, resting her cheek lightly against my shoulder.

She said: "I've a confession, Lenden."

I was lost in my own thoughts, and barely heard her.

"Is it important?" I said.

"I don't know. It might be. There's a file on you, in the Seign-iory. Does that surprise you?"

"No, not really." There were files on everybody, we were at war.

"I read your file. I know a lot about you."

"What sort of thing?" A tremor of concern.

"Nothing political."

No surprise; my isolation was almost total. "What then?"

"About your private life. I suppose that's worse really." I had drawn away from her, to face her. "The file told me the sort of person you are . . . the fact that you have had women lovers. There was a picture of you."

"When did you see this?"

"When the assignment was posted. I volunteered for this, I wanted to meet you. I thought . . . it's hard to say. I've been very lonely."

"And it's hard to meet the right people," I said. "I've been through all that too."

"You don't mind?"

"I object to it being on file. But I don't mind what you did."

The fire was almost out. There was an old broom in the yard, and I used it to sweep the charred wood and ashes into a small neat pile. A few flames flickered, but they would not burn much longer.

There was nothing left for us to do at the house, and we had a long drive to catch the evening ferry. I took the key back to Father Henner's office, while Bella carried our stuff to the car. Walking back through the grounds, alone, I knew that this was my last chance to find the tower. I left the path and walked through the gardens until I came to the wall. I found a gate, went through, and stood looking across the rough ground.

I could not see the tower, could not even see where it might have been. I was standing there looking for it, when Bella found me.

She slipped her hand into mine.

"Something happened here once, didn't it?"

I nodded, and held her hand tightly.

"A long time ago?"

"Twenty years ago. I'm not sure what it was. I think I must have imagined it. It all seems different now."

"I was just a child, twenty years ago," Bella said.

"So was I."

But thinking, as we drove back through the fells, it seemed different again. I was sure the tower was there, that it was simply that I had not seen it.

Bella talked, in the car, on the ferry, and we made our plans for future meetings . . . but we parted on the quay in Jethra, and I have not heard from her since.

Robert Bloch

The Rubber Room

ROBERT BLOCH WAS BORN IN 1917, AND FOR MUCH OF THE time is the most charming and pleasant man you could imagine. Some say it is his Mr. Hyde who writes his horror stories, but it seems to me that the opposite is true: when he feels compassion for his audience he writes his horror stories, when he's feeling evil he makes some of the most atrocious puns imaginable. Luckily he's kept busy writing short stories (collected in Cold Chills, Yours Truly Jack the Ripper, Dragons and Nightmares, Pleasant Dreams *and nearly a dozen more books), novels (including* The Scarf, Firebug, *the Lovecraftian* Strange Eons, *and* Psycho, *which was filmed by someone or other), and film and television scripts. His short story "That Hellbound Train" won a Hugo, and at the first World Fantasy Convention he was given a Life Achievement Award. Psychological horror is his particular skill, and it has never been darker inside one of his characters than here.*

Emery kept telling them he wasn't crazy, but they put him in the rubber room anyway.

Sorry, fella, they said. Only temporary, we got a space problem here, overcrowded, move you to another cell in a couple hours, they said. It's better than being in the tank with all them drunks, they said. Okay, so you had your call to the lawyer but just take it easy until he gets here, they said.

And the door went clang.

So there he was, stuck way down at the end of the cell-block in this little room all by himself. They'd taken his watch and his wallet, his keys and his belt, even his shoelaces, so there was no way he could harm himself unless he bit his own wrists. But that would be crazy, and Emery wasn't crazy.

Now all he could do was wait. There wasn't anything else, no choice, no options, no way, once you were here in the rubber room.

To begin with, it was small—six paces long and six paces wide. A reasonably active man could cover the distance between the walls in one jump but he'd need a running start. Not that there was any point in trying, because he'd just bounce harmlessly off the thick padding.

The windowless walls were padded everywhere from floor to ceiling and so was the door. The padding was seamless so it couldn't be torn or pried away. Even the floor was padded, except for a ten-inch square at the left far corner which was supposed to serve as a toilet facility.

Above him a tiny light bulb burned dimly behind its meshed enclosure, safely beyond reach from the floor below. The ceiling around it was padded too, probably to deaden sound.

Restraint room, that's what they said it was, but it used to be called a padded cell. Rubber room was just popular slang. And maybe the slang wouldn't be so popular if more people were exposed to the reality.

Before he knew what he was doing, Emery found himself pacing back and forth. Six paces forward, six paces back, over and over again, like an animal in a cage.

That's what this was, actually—not a room, just a cage. And if you stayed in a cage long enough you turned into an animal. Ripping and clawing and smashing your head against the walls, howling for release.

If you weren't crazy when you came in you'd go crazy before you got out. The trick, of course, was not to stay here too long.

But how long was too long? How long would it be before the lawyer arrived?

Six paces forward, six paces back. Grey spongy padding muffled his footsteps on the floor and absorbed the light from above, leaving the walls in shadow. Shadows could drive you crazy too. So could the silence, and being alone. Alone in shadows and silence, like he'd been when they found him there in the room—the other room, the one in the house.

It was like a bad dream. Maybe that's the way it feels when you're crazy, and if so he must have been crazy when it happened.

But Emery wasn't crazy now. He was perfectly sane, completely under control. And there was nothing here that could harm him. Silence can't harm you. What was the old saying? Violence is golden. No, not *violence.* Where had that come from? Freudian slip. To hell with Freud, what did he know? Nobody knew. And if he kept silent nobody ever would. Even though they'd found him they couldn't prove anything. Not if he kept silent, let his lawyer do the talking. Silence was his friend. And the shadows were his friends too. Shadows hid everything. There had been shadows in the other room and no one could have seen clearly when they found him. You just *thought* you saw it, he'd tell them.

No, he'd forgotten—he mustn't tell them, just let the lawyer talk. What was the matter with him, *was* he going crazy here after all?

Six paces forward, six paces back. Keep walking, keep silent. Keep away from those shadows in the corners. They were getting darker now. Darker and thicker. Something seemed to be moving there in the far corner to the right.

Emery felt the muscles tightening in his throat and he couldn't control them; he knew that in a moment he was going to scream.

Then the door opened behind him and in the light from the corridor the shadow disappeared.

It was a good thing he hadn't screamed. They would have been sure he was crazy then, and that would spoil everything.

But now that the shadow was gone Emery relaxed. By the time they took him down the hall and into the visitor's room he was quite calm again.

His lawyer waited for him there, sitting on the other side of the grille barrier, and nobody was listening.

That's what the lawyer said. Nobody's listening, you can tell me all about it.

Emery shook his head and smiled because he knew better. Violence is golden and even the walls have ears. He wanted to warn his lawyer that they were spying on him but that would sound crazy. The sane thing to do was not to mention it, just be careful and say the right things instead.

He told the lawyer what everybody knew about himself. He was a decent man, he had a steady job, paid his bills, didn't smoke or drink or get out of line. Hardworking, dependable, neat, clean, no police record, not a troublemaker. Mother was always proud of her boy and she'd be proud of him today if she were still alive. He'd always looked after her and when she died he still looked after the house, kept it up, kept himself up, just the way she'd taught him to. So what was all this fuss about?

Suppose you tell me, the lawyer said.

That was the hard part, making him understand, but Emery knew everything depended on it. So he talked very slowly, choosing his words carefully, sticking to the facts.

World War II had happened before he'd been born, but that was a fact.

Emery knew a lot of facts about World War II because he used to read library books when Mother was alive. Improve your mind, she said. Reading is better than watching all that violence on the television, she said.

So at night when he couldn't sleep he read for hours sitting up in bed in his room. People he worked with down at the shop called him a bookworm but he didn't care. There was no such thing as a bookworm, he knew that. There were worms that ate microorganisms in the soil and birds that ate worms and animals that ate birds and people who ate animals and microorganisms that ate people— like the ones that ate Mother until they killed her.

Everything—germs, plants, animals, people—kills other things to stay alive. This is a fact, a cruel fact. He could still remember the way Mother screamed.

After she died he read more. That's when he really got into history. The Greeks killed the Persians and the Romans killed the Greeks and the barbarians killed the Romans and the Christians killed the barbarians and the Moslems killed the Christians and the Hindus killed the Moslems. Blacks killed whites, whites killed Indians, Indians killed other Indians, orientals killed other orientals, Protestants killed Catholics, Catholics killed Jews, Jews killed Our Saviour on the Cross.

Love one another, Jesus said, and they killed him for it. If Our Saviour had lived, the gospel would have spread around the world and there'd be no violence. But the Jews killed Our Lord.

That's what Emery told the lawyer, but it didn't go down. Get to the point, the lawyer said.

Emery was used to that kind of reaction. He'd heard it before when he tried to explain things to girls he met after Mother died. Mother hadn't approved of him going with girls and he used to resent it. After she was gone the fellows at work told him it would do him good. Get out of your shell, they said. So he let them set up some double-dates and that's when he found out that Mother was right. The girls just laughed at him when he talked facts.

It was better to stay in his shell, like a snail. Snails know how to protect themselves in a world where everyone kills to live, and the Jews killed Our Saviour.

Facts, the lawyer said. Give me some facts.

So Emery told him about World War II. That's when the real killing began. Jewish international bankers financed the Napoleonic wars and World War I, but these were nothing compared to World War II. Hitler knew what the Jews were planning and he tried to prevent it—that's why he invaded those other countries, to get rid of the Jews, just as he did in Germany. They were plotting a war to destroy the world, so they could take over. But no one understood and in the end the Jew-financed armies won the war. The Jews killed Hitler just like they killed Our Saviour. History repeats itself, and that's a fact too.

Emery explained all this very quietly, using nothing except facts, but from the way his lawyer looked at him he could see it was no use.

So Emery went back into his shell. But this time he took his lawyer with him.

He told him what it was like, living alone in his house, which was really a big shell that protected him. Too big at first, and too empty, until Emery began to fill it up with books. Books about World War II, because of the facts. Only the more he read the more he realized that most of them didn't contain facts. The victors write the histories and now that the Jews had won they wrote lies. They lied about Hitler, they lied about the Nazi Party and its ideals.

Emery was one of the few people who could read between the lies and see the truth. Reminders of the truth could be found outside of books, so now he turned to them and started to collect them. The trappings and the banners, the iron helmets and the iron medals. Iron crosses were reminders too—the Jews had destroyed Our Saviour on a cross and now they were trying to destroy the crosses themselves.

That's when he began to realize what was happening, when he went to the antique shops where such things were sold.

There would be other people in these shops and they stared at him. Nobody said a word but they were watching. Sometimes he thought he could hear them whispering behind his back and he knew for a fact that they were taking notes.

It wasn't just his imagination because pretty soon some of the people down at work started asking him questions about his collection—the pictures of the party leaders and the swastika emblems and badges and the photographs of the little girls presenting flowers to the Führer at rallies and parades. Hard to believe these little girls were now fifty-year-old women. Sometimes he thought if he met one of those women he could settle down with her and be happy; at least she'd understand because she knew the facts. Once he almost decided to run an ad in the classified section, trying to locate such a woman, but then he realized it might be dangerous. Suppose the Jews were out to get her? They'd get him too. That was a fact.

Emery's lawyer shook his head. His face, behind the grille, was taking on an expression which Emery didn't like. It was the expression people wear when they're at the zoo, peering through the bars or the wire screens at the animals.

That's when Emery decided he'd have to tell his lawyer the rest.

It was a risk, but if he wanted to be believed his lawyer must know all the facts.

So he told him about the conspiracy.

All these hijackings and kidnappings going on today were part of it. And these terrorists running around with ski-masks over their faces were part of the plan too.

In today's world, terror wears a ski-mask.

Sometimes they called themselves Arabs, but that was just to confuse people. They were the ones behind the bombings in Northern Ireland and the assassinations in South America. The international Jewish conspiracy was in back of it all and behind every ski-mask was a Jewish face.

They spread throughout the world, stirring up fear and confusion. And they were here too, plotting and scheming and spying on their enemies. Mother knew.

When he was just a little boy and did something naughty Mother used to tell him to behave. Behave yourself or the Jew-man will get you, Mother said. He used to think she was just trying to frighten him but now he realized Mother was telling the truth. Like the time she caught him playing with himself and locked him in the closet. The Jew-man will get you, she said. And he was all alone in the dark and he could see the Jew-man coming through the walls and he screamed and she let him out just in time. Otherwise the Jew-man *would* have taken him. He knew now that this was the way they got their recruits—they took other peoples' children and brainwashed them, brought them up to be political terrorists in countries all over the world—Italy, Ireland, Indonesia, the Middle East—so that no one would suspect the real facts. The real facts, that the Jews were responsible, getting ready for another war. And when the other nations had destroyed themselves, Israel would take over the world.

Emery was talking louder now but he didn't realize it until the lawyer told him to hold it down. What makes you think these terrorists are after you, he asked. Did you ever see one?

No, Emery told him, they're too clever for that. But they have their spies, their agents are everywhere.

The lawyer's face was getting red and Emery noticed it. He told him why it was getting so hot here in the visitor's room—their agents were at work again.

Those people who saw Emery buying the flags and swastikas and iron crosses had been planted in the stores to spy on him. And the ones down at work who teased him about his collection, they were spies too, and they knew he'd found out the truth.

The terrorists had been after him for months now, planning to kill him. They tried to run him down with their cars when he crossed the street but he got away. Two weeks ago when he turned on the television there was an explosion. It seemed like a short-circuit but he knew better; they wanted to electrocute him only it didn't work. He was too smart to call a repairman because that's what they wanted—they'd send one of their assassins instead. The only people who still make house-calls today are the murderers.

So for two weeks he'd managed without electricity. That's when they must have put the machines in the walls. The terrorists had machines to make things heat up and at night he could hear a humming sound in the dark. He'd searched around, tapping the walls, and he couldn't find anything, but he knew the machines were there. Sometimes it got so hot he was soaked with sweat, but he didn't try to turn down the furnace. He'd show them he could take it. And he wasn't about to go out of the house because he knew that's what they wanted. That was their plan, to force him out so they could get at him and kill him.

Emery was too smart for that. He had enough canned goods and stuff to get by and it was safer to stay put. When the phone rang he didn't answer; probably someone at the shop was calling to ask him why he didn't come to work. That's all he needed—come back to work so they could murder him on the way.

It was better to hole up right there in his bedroom with the iron crosses and the swastikas on the walls. The swastika is a very ancient symbol, a sacred symbol, and it protected him. So did the big picture of the Führer. Just knowing it was there was protection enough, even in the dark. Emery couldn't sleep any more because of the sounds in the walls—at first it had been humming, but gradually he could make out voices. He didn't understand Hebrew, and it was only gradually that he knew what they were saying. Come on out you dirty Aryan, come out and be killed.

Every night they came, like vampires, wearing ski-masks to hide their faces. They came and they whispered, *come out, come out, wherever you are.* But he didn't come out.

Some history books said Hitler was crazy, and maybe that part was true. If so, Emery knew why. It was because he must have heard the voices too and known they were after him. No wonder he kept talking about the answer to the Jewish question. They were polluting the human race and he had to stop them. But they burned him in a bunker instead. They killed Our Saviour. Can't you understand that?

The lawyer said he couldn't understand and maybe Emery should talk to a doctor instead. But Emery didn't want to talk to a doctor. Those Jew doctors were part of the conspiracy. What he had to say now was in the strictest confidence.

Then for Christ's sake tell me, the lawyer said.

And Emery said yes, he'd tell him. For Christ's sake, for the sake of Our Lord.

Two days ago he'd run out of canned goods. He was hungry, very hungry, and if he didn't eat he'd die. The terrorists wanted to starve him to death but he was too smart for that.

So he decided to go to the store.

He peeked through all the windows first but he couldn't see anyone in a ski-mask. That didn't mean it was safe, of course, because they used ordinary people too. The only thing he could do was take a chance. And before he left he put one of the iron crosses around his neck on a chain. That would help protect him.

Then, at twilight, he went to the supermarket down the street. No sense trying to drive, because the terrorists might have planted a bomb in his car, so he walked all the way.

It felt strange being outside again and though Emery saw nothing suspicious he was shaking all over by the time he got to the store.

The supermarket had those big fluorescent lights and there were no shadows. He didn't see any of their spies or agents around either, but of course they'd be too clever to show themselves. Emery just hoped he could get back home before they made their move.

The customers in the store looked like ordinary people; the thing is, you can never be sure nowadays. Emery picked out his canned goods as fast as possible and he was glad to get through the line at the checkout counter without any trouble. The clerk gave him a funny look but maybe it was just because he hadn't shaved or changed clothes for so long. Anyway he managed, even though his head was starting to hurt.

It was dark when he came out of the store with his bag of groceries, and there was nobody on the street. That's another thing the Jew terrorists have done—made us afraid to walk on the street alone. See what it's come to? Everyone's scared just being out at night!

That's what the little girl told him.

She was standing there on the corner of the block when he saw her—cute little thing, maybe five years old, with big brown eyes and curly hair. And she was crying, scared to death.

I'm lost, she said. I'm lost, I want my Mommy.

Emery could understand that. Everybody's lost nowadays, wants someone to protect them. Only there's no protection any more, not with those terrorists around waiting for their chance, lurking in the shadows.

And there were shadows on the street, shadows outside his house. He wanted to help but he couldn't risk standing out here talking.

So he just went on, up the porch steps, and it wasn't until he opened the front door that he realized she had followed him. Little girl crying, saying please Mister, take me to my Mommy.

He wanted to go in and shut the door but he knew he had to do something.

How did you get lost, he asked.

She said she was waiting in the car outside the market while Mommy shopped but when Mommy didn't come back she got out to look for her in the store and she was gone. Then she thought she saw her down the street and she ran after her only it turned out to be another lady. Now she didn't know where she was and would he please take her home?

Emery knew he couldn't do that, but she was crying again, crying loud. If they were anywhere around they'd hear her, so he told her to come in.

The house smelled funny from not being aired out and it was

very hot inside. Dark too with all the electricity turned off on account of the terrorists. He tried to explain but she only cried louder because the dark frightened her.

Don't be scared, Emery said. Tell me your Mommy's name and I'll phone her to come and get you.

So she told him the name—Mrs. Rubelsky, Sylvia Rubelsky—but she didn't know the address.

It was hard to hear because of the humming in the walls. He got hold of the flashlight he kept in the kitchen for emergencies and then he went into the hall to look up the name in the phone book.

There weren't any Rubelskys listed. He tried other spellings—Rubelski, Roubelsky, Rebelsky, Rabelsky—but there was nothing in the book. Are you sure, he asked.

Then she said they didn't have a phone.

That was funny; everybody has a phone. She said it didn't matter because if he just took her over to Sixth Street she could point out the house to him.

Emery wasn't about to go anywhere, let alone Sixth Street. That was a Jewish neighbourhood. Come to think of it, Rubelsky was a Jewish name.

Are you Jewish, he asked her.

She stopped crying and stared at him and those big brown eyes got wider and wider. The way she stared made his head hurt more.

What are you looking at, he said.

That thing around your neck, she told him. That iron cross. It's like Nazis wear.

What do you know about Nazis, he asked.

They killed my Grandpa, she said. They killed him at Belsen. Mommy told me. Nazis are bad.

All at once it came to Emery in a flash, a flash that made his whole head throb.

She was one of *them*. They'd planted her on the street, knowing he'd let her into the house here. What did they want?

Why do you wear bad things, she said. Take it off.

Now she was reaching out towards the chain around his neck, the chain with the iron cross.

It was like that old movie he saw once long ago, the movie about the Golem. This big stone monster got loose in the Jewish ghetto, wearing the Star of David on its chest. A little girl pulled the star off and the Golem fell down dead.

That's why they sent her here, to pull off the iron cross and kill him.

— No way, he said. And he slapped her, not hard, but she started to scream and he couldn't have that, so he put his hands around her neck just to stop the screaming and there was a kind of cracking sound and then—

What happened then, the lawyer asked.

I don't want to talk about it, Emery said.

But he couldn't stop, he *was* talking about it. At first, when he didn't find a pulse, he thought he'd killed her. But he hadn't squeezed that hard, so it must have happened when she touched the iron cross. That meant he'd guessed right, she was one of *them*.

But he couldn't tell anyone, he knew people would never believe that the terrorists had sent a little Jew-girl here to murder him. And he couldn't let her be found like this. What to do, that was the question. The Jewish question.

Then he remembered. Hitler had the answer. He knew what to do.

It was hot here and even hotter downstairs. That's where he carried her, downstairs, where the furnace was going. The gas furnace.

Oh my God, said the lawyer. Oh my God.

And then the lawyer stood up fast and went over to the door on the other side of the grille and called the guard.

Come back here, Emery said.

But he didn't listen, he kept whispering to the guard, and then other guards came up behind Emery on his side of the grille and grabbed his arms.

He yelled at them to let him go, not to listen to that Jew lawyer, didn't they understand he must be one of *them?*

Instead of paying attention they just marched him back down the hall to the rubber room and shoved him inside.

You promised you'd put me in another cell, Emery said. I don't want to stay here. I'm not crazy.

One of the guards said easy does it, the doctor is coming to give you something so you can sleep.

And the door went clang.

Emery was back in the rubber room, but this time he didn't pace and he didn't call out. It wouldn't do any good. Now he knew how Our Saviour had felt, betrayed and waiting for the crucifixion.

Emery had been betrayed too, betrayed by the Jew lawyer, and now all he could do was wait for the Jew doctor to come. Put him to sleep, the guard had said. That was how the conspiracy worked—they'd put him to sleep for ever. Only he wouldn't let them, he'd stay awake, demand a fair trial.

But that was impossible. The police would tell about hearing the little girl scream and breaking into the house and finding him. They'd say he was a child-molester and a murderer. And the judge would sentence him to death. He'd believe the Jews just like Pontius Pilate did, just like the Allies did when they killed Our Führer.

Emery wasn't dead yet but there was no way out. No way out of the trial, no way out of the rubber room.

Or was there?

The answer came to him just like that.

He'd plead insanity.

Emery knew he wasn't crazy but he could fool them into believing it. That was no disgrace—some people thought Jesus and the Führer were crazy too. All he had to do was pretend.

Yes, that was the answer. And just thinking about it made him feel better. Even if they shut him up in a rubber room like this he'd still be alive. He could walk and talk and eat and sleep and think. Think about how he'd tricked them, all those Jew terrorists who were out to get him.

Emery didn't have to be careful now. He didn't have to lie, the way he'd lied to the lawyer. He could admit the real truth.

Killing that little Jew-girl wasn't an accident, he knew what he was going to do the minute he got his hands around her throat. He squeezed just as hard as he could because that's what he'd always really wanted. To squeeze the necks of those girls who laughed at him, squeeze the guys at work who wouldn't listen when he told them about his collection and yes, say it, he wanted to squeeze Mother too because she'd always squeezed him, smothered him, strangled away his life. But most of all he squeezed the Jews, the dirty kike terrorists who were out to destroy him, destroy the world.

And that's what he had done. He hadn't cracked the little girl's neck, she wasn't dead when he carried her downstairs and opened the furnace door.

What he had really done was solve the Jewish question.

He'd solved it and they couldn't touch him. He was safe now, safe from all the terrorists and evil spirits out for revenge, safe forever here in the rubber room.

The only thing he didn't like was the shadows. He remembered how they'd been before, how the one in the far corner seemed to get darker and thicker.

And now it was happening again.

Don't look at it, he told himself. You're imagining things. Only crazy people see shadows moving. Moving and coiling like a cloud, a cloud of smoke from a gas furnace.

But he had to look because it was changing now, taking on a shape. Emery could see it standing in the corner, the figure of a man. A man in a black suit, with a black face.

And it was moving forward.

Emery backed away as the figure glided towards him softly and silently across the padded floor, and he opened his mouth to scream.

But the scream wouldn't come, nothing was coming except the figure looming up before Emery as he pressed against the wall of the rubber room. He could see the black face quite clearly now—only it wasn't a face.

It was a ski-mask.

The figure's arms rose and the hands splayed out and he saw little black droplets oozing from the smoky wrists as the fingers curled around his throat. Emery struck out at the eyes behind them. But there was nothing under the mask, nothing at all.

It was then that Emery really went mad.

* * *

114

When they opened the door of the rubber room the shadow was gone. All they found was Emery and he was dead.

Apoplexy, they said. Heart failure. Better write up a medical report fast and close the case. Close the rubber room too while they were at it.

Just a coincidence of course, but people might get funny ideas if they found out. Two deaths in the same cell—Emery, and that other nut last week who bit open his own wrists, the crazy terrorist guy in the ski-mask.

Giles Gordon

Drama in Five Acts

GILES GORDON SAYS IT ALL AS TERSELY AS I COULD, SO LET *him do so. "GG was born in Edinburgh in 1940 and lived there until 1962 when he came to London to work in publishing. He resigned from Victor Gollancz Ltd. in 1972 where for five years he'd been editorial director (before which he'd been an editor with Penguin Books) to be able to devote more time to his own writing. He now works as a literary agent with Anthony Shiel Associates where he represents, among other authors, Michael Moorcock, and writes his own books. He's published five novels* (The Umbrella Man, About a Marriage, Girl with Red Hair, 100 Scenes from Married Life *and* Enemies *and has just completed a novel,* Ambrose's Vision) *and three collections of short stories* (Pictures from an Exhibition, Farewell, Fond Dreams *and* The Illusionist). *He has edited a number of anthologies including* Prevailing Spirits: a book of Scottish Ghost Stories, A Book of Contemporary Nightmares *and (with Fred Urquhart)* Modern Scottish Short Stories. *He lives in London with his wife Margaret Gordon, the children's book illustrator, and their three children, Callum, Gareth and Harriet. He is a member of the Writers' Guild, Writers' Action Group and the Society of Authors." The one point he fails to make is that much of his career has been devoted to extending the boundaries of fic-*

tion and experimenting with its form, but this story makes the point for him.

On the beach.

A beach. By the shore. Sand, sea, sky. The combination. Tone and texture.

More sand on the beach than in the house though the house built partly of sand, sand in the stone and in the cement.

What stone? What cement?

And who in their right mind, their upright mind, would want to pour sand on to a white carpet, the carpet in the living room? White, or dyed red, the carpet. Or, for that matter, another matter, any carpet?

A white carpet. Or a red carpet.

The texture of the carpet.

A horizontal surface on which to stand, kneel, lie, sleep, cohabit, relate.

I will not dye my carpet red. If it is red to start with, when purchased and laid, why then it is red. If I have chosen it that colour, I and she who is to me, why then it is red, the colour of red, the colour of blood and wine, of bandages and the besmirched linen battle flag, why then it is red, that colour, and lies on my floor, underneath my feet. And I wear a white suit of fine material on a hot day and grey soft leather shoes with high heels and stand on the red carpet. And the sun is pinned high in the sky, blue sky, dazzling sun, and the sun doesn't move and the Earth doesn't move.

Listen.

On the beach, or through the window of my summer house, the walls of the window being glass (there is sand in glass, too), the walls entirely glass, a glass house, I stare at the horizon, hoping that the sight will transform my eyes, my vision, hoping that my eyes and insights will be transformed.

Stand, looking.

Stare is too strong, too positive a word. I stand, happen to be standing. Look, happen to be looking.

The horizon is painted on, a line, blue against blue. Backcloth. Act One.

* * *

On the beach, a man dressed in . . . different clothes, strange to me because not mine, clothes that are not mine, pours liquid from an immaculate glass on to the sand, into the sand. The sand accepts. It is not in the habit of rejecting such offerings.

If you listen you may hear it, if your ear is cocked, tilted. The glass is turned, angled. The liquid descends, plunges in a line, a column, like a thin silver waterfall, a cascade. A dark patch appears on the sand, spreads, grows, then ceases to seep outwards.

My glass house is on the beach, on the sand. The end away from the sea.

A dark patch appears on my carpet.

You cannot *hear* the liquid falling. It is not sound that causes it to fall, persuades it to fall. It is the hand that tilts the glass. The stain spreads and I remember it in my dreams, will remember it spreading, day and night, from generation to generation, really. What the mind can encompass compared to the body!

What colour was the liquid in the glass?

Ah . . .

You smile at the question.

You did not think to ask about the texture, did not ask about the texture.

I look through the window. There is no glass there, between me and what I see. I see: the beach, the sea, the horizon, the sky. There are no holidaymakers on the beach with boiled bodies and bathing suits, no summer families playing ball games or lazing or feeling the water. It is not that kind of beach. A cluster of dark birds circle, circle the sky, their colour or tone (dark against light) not changing against sand, sea or sky. The sky rolls back, a domed head, extravagant, preposterous halo. What a physique. What a capacity. Cubic capacity, the world's skull.

On the beach, a man has been hacked at by another. Act Two. A man? A person.

Cruelly, though cruelty didn't enter into it. There hasn't been a war for years, decades, not on this shore, this coastline. Wars take place in the newspapers, or on television, in black and white or in colour.

A torso, live, wriggling, the body descending to the sea through a smudge of movement, life out of focus. It shunts, shuffles towards the water, the salt in the sea, to bathe what it imagines to be its wounds, but doesn't reach it, whether because of the slowness of its movement or because the tide retreats and retreats I cannot tell.

It is severed below the shoulders, a clean, ivory cut. Or was born that way. The blood has dripped. *Has* dripped. Years ago, years ago. Generations before. You cannot imagine, remember the cut. You turn away, in your memory, not daring to witness it.

You concentrate on the sword slashing. Shake your head, slowly, shake your head, shake your head, faster. You cannot imagine. No!

Your head doesn't move.

(My head doesn't move.)

Your body is static. Do you reject the choice of movement or is it that you cannot move your head from side to side?

On the beach, there is sand. Take away the sand and are you left with the beach? The beach is sand. The beach slopes towards the sea, touches the sea, the sea touches the sand.

The sand holds secrets, without telling, without speculating. The sand is, it goes without saying, so it does, inarticulate, silent. If it snores or snarls, cries or laughs, purrs or sings, the sound is not for your ears to hear, the conch of night. It churns over and over, over and over. And you are standing there, watching or not, standing there.

In your house.

Looking down the beach. And you stand on a marble floor, your feet encased in grey soft leather shoes, Italian with high heels, no more defined, no more precise than that, the heels high, too high for your age and the year of grace. And the house has gone, the glass has gone. Act Three. Or the house is being built. Built around you. Rebuilt. And there is no glass (who can see through glass?), you peer inside from outside, see nothing, you see through nothing, no house, landscape, seascape, the world, look.

What?

Look. And the inside of your head, your mind has moved. The body in your eye, your brain. Your flesh and blood.

On the beach, a red figure moving and squirming like a seething

119

tin of worms or snakes, living shrimps in melting butter but red, carved from solid gore but gleaming none the less, bleeding but no blood spilling, staining the sand. And another person makes for the foreshore but the tide pushes up, surges, a sudden swell of water, no creeping prettily a few inches hour by hour as the Moon pushes or pulls, devious menstrual whore.

I stand looking.

Isolated.

In my own body.

It is possible, more usual than not, to be isolated in the body of another?

I nod to myself. Yes.

What, am I weary?

In the isolation of another body, the body of another, we forget our own. I try to forget my own, the loaned, lent body, the hair I've sprouted which assists at disguising the truth.

The what?

The figure steals away, she gives thanks for the morrow, shivers at the arm, born that way. And I do not know, cannot tell. There are explanations behind these events though my life is clear enough to me.

She is not mine, nor I hers. So the glimpse, the glance, suggested to me.

The form sinks to the ground.

I stand there. I tell you, I'm steadfast.

I am out of myself, the mind—mine or another's—is around the ceiling, above my body, watching, listening, involved too, taking a responsible part in the proceedings, God yes. And there is no roof on the house. No walls or roof but a marble floor. Black marble. (There is sand in marble, too.) No one needs to polish it, either on their knees or upright with a mop.

And I stand there in underpants and singlet and socks, no suspenders necessary. And my bellow, my roar grows and grows and I am disgusted, verily. That is: I am frightened, afraid. My world trembles.

Down the beach, the thing, the action. Act Four.

And I will not, and I cannot, and I will not.

It is wondrous to behold. It is, too. A human wonder become more than humanity or human imagination can accommodate. It splits, one comes out of the other and there is breathing, living. No destruction, only growth. One comes out of the other and each is whole. And I see the legs, and the froth and foam between the legs, the spread angle of one, and it doesn't necessarily come from there but I think it does. And there are two, wondrous to behold, from one, the shadow and the shadow woman, and the sunlight blinds the eyes from the marble, and it is all red.

You close your eyes.

Your eyes scream.

It is all red.

Or whatever colour you think it is.

Expect it to be.

On the beach.

In the house, serenity, security. The white of the sheets, no more blood than is traditional, normal. The walls keep the wolves at bay as the cats are fed their bones and milk and they throb in their throats with pleasure.

The wolves watch, the walls are glass. The animals are outside. Their paws, when they try to enter, skid on the marble, they can get no nearer. Their feet are trapped in the sand.

There are no walls. There is no glass.

I stand on the beach.

Or the desert.

Not the desert, no, there is sea. And no palm trees, no camels or horses charging towards me.

I stand in the depths of the ocean. Touch down deep enough and there is sand. One step, and another: I can walk again. What joy!

I walk through the waters, I blur towards her, towards. No breasts.

Face to

face

but I don't see her, cannot, cannot cannot understand the features, their meaning, the nostrils in the kneecap, the hair in the eye, the stomach in the back, the mouth in the armpit, the chest in the foot, the arm in the thigh, the eyes in the arse, the ears in the navel. Orifices galore. The body is confused. Confusing.

Sand. Water. Sun.

Then suddenly, darkness.

I walked through the water. There was red, and glass, and a knife, the sand and the ivory, ebony cut.

Oh I saw so well, such things, and my mind blew, and my mind . . .

You stand, in a white suit, on the beach.

Act Five.

And there is me and only me and I saw them split, separate, the one come from the other, two where there had been one, and why and how and why and how.

And on the beach, solemnly, silently, no nonsense,

no scream, no illness, certainly no illness, no great yob of vomit streaking, trailing down into a basin

and in the morning.

In the morning.

In the morning.

Jack Sullivan

The Initiation

JACK SULLIVAN LIVES IN NEW YORK, WHERE HE TEACHES
English and humanities at New York and Columbia Universities.
More to the point, he lectures on the ghost story at (among other
places) the New School in Greenwich Village and Briarcliffe Col-
lege in Westchester County. He wrote the Monarch study notes on
Dracula, *and the monograph* Elegant Nightmares, *which develops*
Robert Aickman's insight that the ghost story is akin to poetry. He
plays Debussy on the piano and gives the Rebel yell after Pierre
Boulez concerts, and I based Diana's apartment in my novel To
Wake the Dead *on his. I suspect he would say that New York is*
sometimes even more dismaying than it appears in his story.

As the IRT lurched forwards, he felt an instant distance from
the other passengers. He had heard New Yorkers were like this,
inattentive out of long habit to the ugliness around them, especially the subway. But he hadn't expected people to be quite
this oblivious, not only to him, but to the train. He felt a kinship
with the train, as if they were both being ignored. No one
seemed to care that he had been in New York only a few weeks,
that this was all new to him: he was in the city for what had

123

turned out to be a successful job interview, and he was still struggling over whether to accept.

People stared at newspapers, floors, blank faces. Conversation hung in the thick air and tried to synchronize with moving lips, only to be cut off by the roar of the train. How could people hear each other, or not care if they couldn't?

To his left, two young women clutched and jabbed, mime-like, as they talked, their gestures cancelling each other out. Across from him, a middle-aged man muttered back at his *Daily News*. To his right, a drunk sprawled serenely beside his shopping bag, the noise lulling him further into sleep.

None of these paid the slightest attention to the old woman with the tin cup, the accordion, and the empty eye sockets, who staggered past. He wondered whether they even heard the accordion vibrato quivering through the greater noise. Suddenly he realized that after only a few weeks he too was unmoved, in danger of becoming like the others. Like them, he had given the woman no money. Why hadn't he? Guilt made a quick stab at him, retreated at the next grate of the train, and flooded back as resentment. If the others could ignore her, why couldn't he? At least he had noticed her, more than he could say for them. He had seen her fall momentarily against the man across, who had only sunk further into his *Daily News*, burying his head beneath a typically tasteless *News* headline about the "flap" over recent missing persons reported in Manhattan. The man didn't direct his mutterings at the old woman; he didn't seem angry, even annoyed. He didn't seem anything really. Why should he? The woman was gone now. And so was the guilt.

An awareness of the train began to fill in the space. The distance he felt from the others had returned, granting him the freedom to look, even stare about. Though an express, the train moved in a manic pattern of hesitancy and speed. It seemed unsure of itself, as if it might jump the rail. His head was a chamber of white noise, shrieking upward when the train grated on curves. The floor surged under his feet. Graffiti danced in front of his eyes. Miss Subway, the Salem girl, and Smokey the Bear grinned down from above. Speeding through a tunnel of its own, his mind decided to leave what it saw behind for a while.

That is probably why he was able to visualize this new thing,

124

something very particular, for some time before he knew what it was. In looking up at the ads, his left eye had been teased to the side by a flickering outside the window where nothing had existed a moment before but blackness streaked with lights. He turned full around to take it in better. In the darkness another train had materialized, its windows parallel to his own so he could look into them. It was a local his express had overtaken and would soon pass by. Several feet away, its windows as greasy as those he was looking through, it didn't reveal much. The dimness gave him time to realize that the train had not caught his eye so much as something inside it, as if the train had been an excuse to turn around. What he actually saw, now that he could no longer put it off, were backs of heads in windows, like a moving string of beads. All except one window, where the head was turned around. Was that what he was so anxious about facing directly? It was only a passenger on the other train, doing the same thing he was doing, peering through a dirty window. Maybe it was because the man was looking directly at him. And there was something disturbing about the face, even though he couldn't see much of it, perhaps because he couldn't. Also because something was picking at his mind: he'd seen the face before—and in the subway. Hadn't he?

No way really to know because through the distance and dinginess only the eyes, the mouth and the outline of a crumpled hat were visible. It was hard to see the nose and cheeks because the man had flattened his face, almost painfully it seemed, against the window, as if the face were trying to smash through the glass to reveal more of itself. The window mashed the mouth into what might have been an attempted smile, but the eyes had the usual dazed look of the subway rider.

It was not until after the face had passed back out of sight that he began to wonder why it had been staring at him. Even now he had no time, for a new sight captured him. A strange station was rushing by, one that shouldn't be there. The last local station he'd seen go by was 86th Street. He remembered going over the labyrinthian subway map, determined not to get lost. He was sure the next stop was listed as 96th Street. Where was he then? Dim lights glowed between unnumbered supports mazed with graffiti. No people on the platform, only graffiti swarming over the supports and walls.

As the deserted station vanished, he turned back around to sort out what he'd seen, only to feel his impressions pitched sideways with his body as the train ground abruptly to a stop. People pushing their way out of the train collided with people pushing their way in. Some cursed or frowned on the rebound, but only a few seemed to mean it.

He thought of robots and was struggling for a more damning image when he remembered he had to change trains himself. Feeling benign and superior, he stood up and waited by the door for the passengers on the platform to get in. Only when all the others were in did he make his move to get out. He was directly between the doors when they slammed on him, reverberating from his shoulders, jolting him out on the platform where he dumbly watched the express pulling away.

A local jerked to a stop on the other side, vomiting out a stream of passengers, sucking others in. This time he pushed, elbowed and muttered with the best of them. He was finally getting into the spirit of things. Somehow an old lady managed to muscle her way in front of him. The surprisingly intense satisfaction of jabbing her in the kidney was ruined by something he saw flooding out of the local.

He quickly calculated that this was the same local he'd seen in the tunnel. The man who had peered at him was getting out with the others, looking back as he moved. He was stung by resentment: he hated to be stared at, and there was no question that the man was staring at him, singling him out. A fucking drunk—but why should a drunk stare at him that way, twice in a row? And where had he seen him before?

It must have been on the subway. On the street he'd seen winos weaving and pleading for money; on the upper West Side he'd seen crazy people jerking and gibbering like chickens. They'd stared at him, sometimes lunged at him. But their eyes were full of pain, not menace. At least not calculated menace. The subway was different from the street. This man had no pain or pleading in his bloodshot eyes—only a kind of leering familiarity.

Hurrying towards the exit, the other passengers were reduced to backs of heads, as they had been on the train. Only the staring man with the greasy hat faced him, exactly as he had from the window.

The only newly visible detail was the sootiness of the face, which made it impossible to tell his race or whether he was as old as his bulging eyes suggested. The rest of the figure was blotted out by other moving bodies, but the logistics were still puzzling: either the man's head was turned completely around on his shoulders or the weird bastard was walking backwards. He started to laugh at the grotesqueness of it all, just to release his silly, uncalled-for tension. The man's expression, just shy of a grin, almost encouraged him to, but he felt paralysed, strangely humiliated.

As the old lady returned his punch in the kidney with an elbow in the stomach, the clear flash of pain was almost a relief. He decided to resolve things with a well-aimed blow to the back of the head, but the lady had already moved briskly on to the train, well ahead now, shoving aside a man armed with a briefcase.

He was on the train too before it occurred to him to look out the window for the moving figure, but it had disappeared. Funny how much anxiety he was feeling from seeing a strange leering old man. He wondered for the first time how women must feel, how they could stand living in the city at all.

In front of him a pale, balding man choked and gasped on smoke and obscenities blown and shouted triumphantly in his face by a black teenager who refused to put out his cigarette. With a quick movement that probably surprised himself, the victim slapped the cigarette from the sneering teenager's mouth and fled the train. The teenager, wielding a bottle as club, bolted out after him. Of course no one took the slightest interest in any of this. It undoubtedly happened all the time, with much worse things going unnoticed, just as the movies and news stories said it did. No one seemed to see the strange figure outside either, no one but him. It only seemed strange to him after all.

He made a determination that if he stayed in the city he would resist the subway. He wouldn't become like the others, those blank lobotomized clichés from B movies who called themselves New Yorkers.

As the doors closed, he noticed the old lady standing next to one of them, looking dazed, and realized that he hadn't been in the spirit of things when he slugged her at all. He'd done it out of outrage, but she'd punched at him out of a purely mechanical reflex:

no emotion behind it at all. She reminded him of the staring figure's expression, if anything one of deadening indifference. The spirit of the subway. But something else too, that he was at a loss to figure out.

He might have had a chance to had he not got drunk that night, visiting acquaintances uptown who had recently moved to New York for reasons he found increasingly hard to fathom, even though he would probably do it too.

"How can you stand it?" he asked, but the encircling beer cans, doubling as ashtrays, smoked and mocked his question. "The same way I stand suburbia, I suppose," he admitted, popping open another can.

He described the face on the train, but no one was impressed.

"Just another drunk."

"Yeah, the same greasy hat, the same spacey eyes, the same smirk. Just a bum like a hundred other bums."

"He's right. The horrible thing about New York is that there's nothing really weird about it. No mystery. You'll get used to it."

"You'll just have to adjust whether you like it or not if you're going to live here. And it's getting worse. People seem a little stranger in the subway than they used to—a little more out of it, a little less civilized. But you'll get used to it."

"But I don't want to get used to it," he said. "That's the point."

"What point?"

The floor boomed beneath them as a train rumbled under the street. Outside a tyre screeched, several horns blared. The conversation floated, suddenly disconnected from the talkers. Disco music leaped into the open window, pummelled their ears, and slunk away up the street.

"You're lucky your apparition doesn't have a goddamn portable radio."

At three a.m., waiting for the downtown train, he was more sleepy than drunk, but still fighting his mind. Focusing on the 168th Street station as a diversion, he stared up the stone arc and the elevated platform leading down from both ends into the dungeon-like space where he sat. A tremor shook his bench, and he walked to the edge of the platform to watch the train come in. Staring into the tunnel, past the other heads bobbing over the edge, he saw blackness, then a yellow glare which snarled as it came closer. He committed suicide by leaping on to the track, watching the train grow larger, waiting for a spectacular doom. He forgot the fantasy as the train pulled in as an oversized centipede with fat yellow appendages. Between its joints were cylinders held high by shadowy organisms. More cylinders were loaded on by other figures who had suddenly materialized on the platform, and the insect crawled back into darkness. Some kind of garbage train, he theorized, no longer sure how drunk he was. Down here, being high on drugs or booze was superfluous. This thought persisted as he saw the uptown train pull in ahead, tattooed all over with graffiti. "Death" was inscribed on one of the cars in massive purple letters with black borders. As it moved away, he felt himself coming down from his high. He collapsed on the bench, wishing it were a bed.

Or at least a train taking him to a bed. Closing his eyes, he heard the rumble of "death," still moving away, still audible, and thrust his mind ahead to meet it. Lumps of consciousness remained on the bench, too heavy to move, but the rest soared through the darkness, terrified of falling on the moving train. He glided briefly alongside one of the cars and swept through a window on to a seat. Much of the graffiti had blurred or vanished. From his corner seat on the train, he saw the "death" letters in a reverse purple image. Others like himself seeped into windows: alert, casually dressed, but civilized people who talked amiably and helped each other find seats. Suddenly one of them, a young man, got up and walked into the next car. A long scream came from the car, a scream that modulated from outrage to horror to pain. Interspersed with it was a hissing or panting sound, and a banging and scuffling on the floor. The man processed back in stiffly, corpse-like. Signs of a struggle were evident in his trousers, which were torn, exposing his buttocks, but the most noticeable change was in his downcast eyes, which looked defeated, hardened, and somehow older. The moment the man sat back down, staring mutely while the others continued to talk, a woman got up, walked into the next car, and screamed and fought as the man had. When she wandered back to her seat, apathetically, another got up. He watched this in mounting panic, realizing his turn would come. Whenever anyone sat back down, graffitied dates separated by a dash seemed to materialize above heads on the wall. The second date was the current year. He stood up, shaking and beginning to weep, trying to decide which way to run as a formerly thin woman came back from the other car, pregnant. Before she could sit down, something black and oily plopped to the floor and scurried out from under her long skirt. It looked like a filthy baby, but it crawled into someone's shopping bag before he could be sure. From the window on the door to the other car, he saw the face from the deserted station peering in at him, sliding his pants down with its eyes, gnashing its yellow teeth in impatience, beckoning that it was his turn.

He screamed and woke up, banging his head against the stone wall.

Now he was looking at another train from his bench at 168th Street. The doors were open, waiting. Still shaking off his nightmare, he hurried in before the doors shut. It wasn't easy to banish. He had dreamed of death before, but the dreams had rarely attacked with such a peculiar combination of recent memories and images that seemed to come from nowhere. And all that sordid sexual stuff. God, if he moved to New York he'd soon be needing a shrink, just like everybody else here.

He grasped the nearest handrail, determined not to sit down and fall asleep again. The dream died briefly, then was called to life again by the gathering noise and velocity of the train. He fought it back down by taking a walk, passing from car to car through blasting passages of darkness. He reached the front car without seeing another passenger distinctly, although he glimpsed them from the corners of his eyes. He wanted to keep moving, to stay ahead of the dream, but he found himself stalled at the front of the train, pressing against metal and glass. Once again he found himself looking through a murky window. Out of the blackness, lights and columns rushed at his face, like comets in 3D movies he'd seen as a kid, as a station appeared and vanished. Just before he realized it shouldn't be, another station rushed by. Jesus, he must have been dozing again. He turned around to the other passengers, hoping to see signs of surprise or confusion. They *should* be pissed: it was going to be inconvenient for all of them. Approaching a man in a fading tweed jacket, he shouted loud enough so that several people could hear.

"Excuse me, isn't this a local? Why doesn't the train stop? Why is it going through these stations?"

He knew the bastard wouldn't answer; he was getting to where he could tell. Something about people's expressions, a listlessness mixed with hostility. He was getting to know who could most likely be approached for directions in the subway and there weren't any of them on this car. No one looked up at him. As another station went by, he felt powerless, then angry, as he turned on a young woman to his left and shouted the question in her ear. No acknowledgement. Trembling a little, he put the question differently:

"Are you deaf? Stupid? What the hell is the matter with you?"

He grabbed for images to cripple his anxiety. One was of men working on the tracks, the most probable explanation, but it faded ominously as he realized that someone should have made an announcement. Another was of some stations somehow closing down for the night, but the absurdity of that theory only made him aware of his desperation. Another station went by.

Turning on the passenger to his right, he felt an unexpected exhilaration. He wasn't alone. One of the doors separating his car from the next was open. Through the window of the other, he could barely see a woman near the door, her arms and mouth flapping at other passengers in a gesture that must be panic.

He was so intent on reaching her and hearing another normal, nervous human voice that his body, twisting to the right, failed to pick up the creaking signals of the train. As the train stopped dead, violently, it flung him to the floor.

The doors banged open. He felt little pain, only numbness, spaciness, as he listened to the train wheeze and hiss at the darkness outside. Pulling himself back to his senses, he saw that it was very dark, almost black. A feeble glow, like a fading gas light, illuminated the graffiti-blackened posts that he saw through the open doors as he fell into the seat behind him. He was almost overpowered with the urge to flee through those doors, but he knew there was nothing out there but filth and empty benches. He thought he saw something shadowy rise from one of the benches with a crackling noise, like crumpled paper, but when he focused his eyes, it had gone. Must have been static from the train. The station was not really so mysterious. He had been through it before.

He was struggling to understand why the doors were opening at the empty stop when, like an admission of error, they suddenly closed and the train started again. No one had got out. Of course they hadn't. The train had only stopped to test its doors—maybe fix them. It had stopped so fast that there must have been something wrong with the brakes too. That's why it hadn't stopped at the other stations.

Then 86th Street went by and his fear returned.

As he struggled to smother it by telling himself he was on an express after all, he remembered the woman and decided to look for her in the next car. It felt good to move again, and passing the other passengers he felt more relief at realizing how many of them were asleep, or near it. No wonder they didn't care whether the doors opened—or care about anything: these were the people he'd heard about, the ones who lived on the subway. A fat woman in a dingy flannel shirt, barely awake, stared at his feet as he hurried by. A humped-over man in a wrinkled business suit, his tie lolling like a noose, did the same. A distorted picture of the man settled uneasily in his mind while he pushed open the doors to the next car. The woman fit. She was destitute, pathetic, obviously poor. But why would a business man not care where the train stopped, and why did he look so much like the woman, as if he'd been down here a long time?

The puzzle scattered as he opened the door into a near-empty car. The woman was gone.

Most of the other passengers were gone too. They couldn't have got off. They must have moved down to the next car. He was about to move to it himself when he saw a derelict sprawled directly in front of the door. His head was partially buried in a large shopping bag, his right hand groping for something inside. Probably food, for the derelict was surrounded by scattered chicken bones. He would have either to step on the man or ask him to move, but he didn't like the thought of either option. Besides the few strands of hair on the pinkish forehead and the usual oily clothes, there was a repulsive eagerness, and also a strange redundancy, about the way the man was rooting around in the shopping bag, stuffing fist-sized hunks of meat into an invisible mouth.

He was at the centre of the car, trying to decide what to do, when a sliding of metal and rush of air made him turn around. The fat woman, the man with the loose tie, and three others came through the door, walking stiffly. They stood by the door, shaking with the train, staring at the floor. They looked ravaged.

A thought pierced his brain from behind as a woman's scream of pain seemed to arc over the white noise from somewhere near the back of the train. He had just begun to understand that the doors of the train had opened not to let anyone out but to let someone on. The scream changed that. Not someone. At least two of them.

He didn't need to turn back around. The nausea seeping into his stomach told him that the man crouching by the other door had sprung up. Even above the blast of the train he thought he heard the man kick aside the shopping bag and begin advancing towards him. His panic spun him around anyway, to meet the dead staring eyes he had met before. Beneath the soot on its face and grease on its hands, wrinkles sprouted, bones protruded. But if he creaked and staggered a little, he also moved forward, steadily. He had, after all, just eaten. His body was now impelled forward by a different kind of hunger.

Suddenly the derelict halted a moment to look at something on the floor. A few bones, a partially eaten sausage, a wine bottle in a crumpled hat, a small jar that had rolled out of the shopping bag, its open mouth revealing a clear jelly-like substance. The derelict's eyes hesitated at the jar, trying to reach a decision. Then as he showed his yellow teeth to his victim, advancing again with new excitement, taking in the lower body before moving back to the eyes, he did something he had never quite managed before. He smiled.

John Burke

Lucille Would Have Known

JOHN BURKE WAS BORN IN 1922 AND BROUGHT UP IN Liverpool (a good start for a macabre writer, believe me: other Merseysiders who have written in the genre include Rosalie Muspratt, May Sinclair, G. G. Pendarves of Weird Tales *fame and Lady Eleanor Smith). He has written over a hundred books, including* Swift Summer *(his first novel, which won an Atlantic Award in Literature), several novels based on Hammer and Amicus horror films, and a trilogy about a nineteenth-century psychic investigator* (The Devil's Footsteps, The Black Charade, *and* Ladygrove). *He also wrote the original screenplay for Michael Reeves' film* The Sorcerers, *which gave Boris Karloff and Catherine Lacey the chance for unforgettable performances.*

In the context of this book his tale may seem a reassuringly traditional ghost story—but there is one detail which may look reassuring but which, in retrospect, grows worse and worse.

There was one vacant seat in the mini-bus. It was the nearside rear seat which Lucille had always chosen to occupy so that she could address a running commentary at the backs of the others' heads and, as she laughed on each occasion they went out, "Keep an eye on the lot of you, make sure you don't pick your noses or drop off to sleep." This time perhaps they could have found somebody else to make up the numbers; but it wouldn't have seemed right, not yet, not so soon. It would take time to get used to the idea of Lucille not being with them any more and organizing everything for them.

Mrs. Armstrong had suggested that this trip ought to be cancelled. But Madge Wright had insisted they must go ahead. It was not just a matter of their having paid in advance, though that in itself had been quite an expense: Lucille had never believed in cutting costs by amalgamating with other groups, in a larger coach on a vulgar package tour. Eleven was enough. Eleven, plus a driver, was manageable.

Now there were ten.

"Lucille," declared Madge, "would have wanted us to make the trip."

Two women and one of the men—Madge's own husband, actually—remained dubious. But Madge had always been so close to Lucille, had been with her just before she died, and was so obviously Lucille's natural successor, that they allowed themselves to be persuaded. And so on this Friday afternoon, ten days after the funeral, they were setting out on their annual Getaway Weekend Study Tour.

Over the last few years they had, between a Friday lunchtime and a Monday evening, taken in Country Houses of Derbyshire, Gardens of Lincolnshire, and Yorkshire's Victorian Heritage. This year Lucille had opted for Romantic Castles of the North-East. "The military history will appeal to the men," she had said. Lucille had always made a point of appealing to the men.

"Well." Madge took charge. "Let's sort ourselves out, shall we?" She would sit where she had always sat, beside the driver. Only this time it would not be merely to relay Lucille's instructions. This time things would be different. And there were other things to be altered. As she stood by the door, letting the other four women and five men squeeze past, she saw her husband on his way to the back. "Harold, come up here and sit behind me. Or behind the driver."

He settled himself on the offside back seat, across the aisle from Lucille's empty place.

"I'll sit where I've always sat."

"Harold, we don't have to make a religious rite of it."

"I'm used to it here."

Yes, thought the driver. Although they had all from time to time been shifted about to suit the last Mrs. Bellamy's whims, this last few years Mr. Wright had always sat level with her. Right at the back. He remembered them joking together and leaning towards each other, laughing, and sometimes tossing crazy remarks forward along the aisle.

She had been a right merry widow, had Mrs. Lucille Bellamy.

It had been one of her ideas to space husbands and wives out of phase up the two sides of the bus. With Madge seated beside the driver, and Madge's husband on the opposite side at the back, other husbands were placed opposite women other than their wives.

"You can sit next to your own spouse any day of the week." Fred, the driver, remembered Lucille shrilling that the very first time he had been hired to drive them. "Come on, now—much more interesting conversation if we're all mixed up. Lean across the aisle and make up to somebody new. Keep you awake!"

And each time she would reshuffle the order. Save for having Madge's husband always at her own side.

Her voice would ring down the aisle. "Madge, tell the driver to turn left at the next junction. I'm sure it's a more interesting route." Or: "Madge, do tell the driver to go more slowly, this is beautiful countryside, it's a shame to race through it. We're not doing a safari rally, or whatever they call it."

It had been suggested that Lucille herself should sit beside the driver, but she wouldn't have that. "No, got to keep an eye on you all. Can't be craning over my shoulder the whole time to see what you're up to."

They would laugh with her and at her. Sometimes ruefully. But nobody could take over the reins from Lucille. For one thing, the rest of them just didn't have that much spare time. Since her husband died, Lucille had had money and time to spend. If she didn't arrange things for the group, they might never get arranged.

Now somebody else would have to take over.

Fred changed down and began a long climb out of the valley, up above the town and on towards the shadowy ridges of Northumbria. Behind him there was not the usual babble of conversation. A glum lot. It would take them time to recover, he supposed. They were all conscious of that unoccupied seat.

"Sad about Mrs. Bellamy," he ventured quietly.

"Yes." Madge looked steadily at the road ahead.

That was another thing he remembered. All the others, however often they might see one another at whatever fêtes and functions or bridge parties they shared, were Mrs. This and Mr. That and Mrs. So-and-so. But the woman beside him and the one who used to sit far back were always Madge and Lucille, not only to each other but to everyone else in the party. Equals, almost; though not quite. Rivals, sort of, he supposed.

He said: "What exactly was it she died of?"

"Most unusual." Madge spoke in a clipped voice, apparently anxious to keep it all as brief and unemotional as possible and be done with it. "A rare form of osmotic oedema which didn't respond to the usual drugs."

He had forgotten that she was something in the medical world. "I'm afraid I haven't got much idea about—"

"Accumulation of surplus fluid in the body tissues. A variety of what used to be called dropsy."

"Oh. Yes, I see."

It sounded nasty and damp and sagging. Fred was squeamish about such things, and sorry he had raised the question.

"Poor Lucille didn't respond to the diuretics we used to draw out the salt, and the water along with it. We had to fall back on the old-fashioned method of drawing fluid off by tubes. As with poor old George the Fourth, you know."

"Er . . . yes."

"With *him,* the doctors tapped the fluid from his feet. Excruciatingly painful," said Madge with a strangely mellow smile. "With Lucille, something went wrong with the timing. The rate of extraction must have been wrong. Terrible shock to the system. I found her dead."

"*You* found her?"

"I was on duty that night. But I'd had to attend to another patient, and when I got back to Lucille it was too late. In effect," explained Madge with brisk finality, "you might say she drowned in her own body fluids."

They drove on towards their first stop at Raby castle.

Mrs. Armstrong, striding out at the head of the party, came to a halt by the notice board. "But it says here it's not open on a Friday."

Flustered, Madge consulted the brochure she had bought from the Tourist Board. "No. Oh, dear. Saturday and Sunday would be all right. But Friday . . . no, I don't know how I came to . . ."

There was one barely subdued comment. "Lucille would have known."

They climbed back aboard, disgruntled.

As he closed the door, Fred had a fleeting sensation of someone else edging past him at the last minute. He slewed round to count his passengers. Ten, just as before. Five married couples, as ever; and an empty seat where there had once been the domineering, know-it-all widow.

He drove on again.

Dark cloud shadows rolled in a sombre muddy tide down the slopes ahead, thickening into the pool of a dark plantation. On the crest he saw the road begin to curve and guessed that on the other side there would be a tight swing to the left. He slowed, and glanced in his mirror.

There was somebody in Lucille's old seat.

The slant of his mirror was such that it showed the road behind and a few heads in the coach, but cut out several on the nearside. Including the rear seat. Yet somehow he was sure somebody had moved into it—perhaps slid across from one of the other seats. When he had negotiated the awkward bend and was tilting downhill again, he cautiously twisted the mirror to get a glimpse of that corner.

Of course there was nobody there.

It was simply that on previous excursions he had been so conscious of her, calling out her instructions or jokes every five minutes. You were never allowed to forget she was there, in charge.

138

And the rest of them felt the same, he could tell it: not chattering, hardly exchanging even the most casual remark on the scenery.

Madge said: "Can't we go any faster? We'll never get there in time for dinner at this rate."

Her irritable tone jarred in a way Lucille's long-drawn-out sigh had never done—the sigh when there was some minor hitch or people had failed to respond as she wanted them to, as if she were on the verge of washing her hands of all of them and then loftily relenting.

"Fancies herself in Lucille's shoes already." The whisper drifted along the bus.

On their right was a heavy drystone sheepfold, but there were no sheep in sight. To their left the gaunt obelisk of an old lead-mine chimney stuck up against the tumultuous sky: a mine long since abandoned. The landscape grew bleaker, as flushed and mottled and dark and unpredictable as the sky: flushed but cold, growing colder.

Lucille would surely have known better than to specify this unrewarding route.

Their stop for the night was at a hotel above a gentle loop of the river Wear. When they booked in, the plump girl at the desk looked at the voucher Madge handed over and reached behind her for a set of keys.

"That's right. Four doubles and two singles."

"No," said Madge. "Five doubles. And of course a single for our driver."

"That's not what you confirmed, madam. It was going to be five doubles and one single when you first booked, but then you cancelled the single—"

"One of our members," said Madge, "has unfortunately passed on."

"I'm right sorry to hear that."

"But in any case it ought to have been five doubles and two singles. And then I wrote to cancel just one."

"That's not the way I've got it down here." The girl was patient but unyielding. "Now let's see how we can help."

It finished with Madge and her husband agreeing to take a single room each, since there were no other doubles available. The driver

139

was allocated a hot little room at the back of the building, uncomfortably close to the kitchen extractor.

There was further confusion when Madge admitted she had not in her letter confirmed a dinner booking for the party, assuming that this would be taken for granted. "But you see," said the girl, her voice hardening, "we've got a big formal party in tonight, and we have to fit everyone else round them. If you'd let us know in time . . ."

Fred was glad to retreat to the comfort of the public bar and have chicken in the basket and three pints of bitter for his supper.

The side window of the bar commanded a view along the terraced gardens of the hotel. One isolated lamp, an electric bulb in a converted old gas lamp standard, cast a faint glow like an illuminated float bobbing up and down in the rippling water below.

Between the lamp and the spray of light from the dining room, a woman walked slowly along a flagged path towards the wrought iron gate which led to the car park. She paused once and looked at the windows as if seeking some friend at one of the tables inside. Yet although the light fell full upon her face, there was no definition to her features. They were a badly blurred snapshot of someone Fred felt vaguely he ought to know. He put down his pint glass and rubbed the palm of his right hand across the pane to wipe away condensation. But there was no condensation. The garden was nice and bright, the terraces sharp-edged. Only the sauntering woman appeared hazy as she resumed her progress towards the curlicued gate.

It was only after she had walked through and vanished round a corner of the car park that Fred realized—was sure, in spite of the third pint of bitter—that she had not even paused to open the gate.

Next morning there was a groundswell of complaint as the five couples trudged out to the bus. The meal last night had been indifferently served and half cold. Breakfast this morning had been greasy. Madge had not made nearly as much fuss as Lucille would have done in such circumstances. And Mr. Brearley had stumbled off an ill-lit step in a grubby corridor and now was limping badly. Fred hurried to relieve him of his overnight case and brought up the rear, behind Mrs. Brearley and Mrs. Catchpole.

"But of course," Mrs. Brearley was insinuating, "Lucille and the Wrights were always in one another's pockets. I did sometimes wonder . . ."

"About Lucille and Madge's husband?"

"Oh, I've never said anything to a soul."

"I mean," said Mrs. Catchpole, "with Madge often away on duty all night at the hospital, and them so close . . ."

"I've never been one to hint at any such thing," said Mrs. Brearley.

There was no laughter in it. Not like the sly laughter the time they were visiting country houses, and there had been these jokes about Lucille and Madge's husband in that maze for so long. And all that chucking under the chin and the rest of it at the medieval banquet.

They climbed aboard and travelled on.

First to Durham, and then to Hylton castle ruins, where Madge read out the story about the Stars-and-Stripes emblem in the family crest, and they all muttered indifferently, "Yes, you can see it, can't you?" and then on to Newcastle and Tynemouth and, late in the afternoon, to the massive peel tower of Langley. Madge recited from memory all she had learnt about peel towers; and got most of it wrong.

That night they stayed at a hotel almost on Hadrian's Wall. In the morning Madge appeared in blustery, decisive mood.

"Well, now. Let's have a bit of a shake-up, shall we? Change places. Let's see if we get more talk if the husbands and wives sit side by side, eh?"

"But we've never done it that way."

"High time to try it."

But they glared at her and got into the bus and settled themselves in the same order as the day before.

Fred headed for the river Coquet and Warkworth castle.

They had gone less than two miles when Mrs. Brearley, sitting immediately behind Madge, announced that she wanted to be sick. Fred pulled into the side. Mrs. Brearley scrambled out, with Madge leaning well away to allow her plenty of room. She stooped over a gap in the ragged brown stone wall, and vomited into brown and mauve scrub on the other side.

"I thought the bacon was even greasier than yesterday's," commented Mrs. Armstrong.

But when Mrs. Brearley returned she said: "It's sitting over that wheel that did it. Makes me feel funny."

"Then we must change some places." Madge was pleased by the thought of getting her own way after all.

The others looked at her with growing disapproval.

Mrs. Brearley palely said: "No, I wouldn't want anyone else to suffer." Then she nodded, as if someone had prompted her with a brilliant suggestion. "Yes, that'll do nicely."

She made her way to the back of the bus and to the seat which had always been Lucille's.

There was silence save for the faint whine of the breeze along the shallow hillside. A shocked, tremulous silence; until Fred revved his engine more noisily than was necessary, and began to grind uphill fiercely in low gear. At the top of the hill he glanced automatically in his mirror.

It did not quite cover the seat which Mrs. Brearley had vacated. But it showed enough to convince him that someone—one of the women, he was sure—had moved forward into the place behind Madge.

Madge put up one hand to dab at the side of her neck, as if a fly or strand of hair were tickling it; or someone were whispering in her ear.

They visited Warkworth, and then Alnwick.

"And this was one of the Percy castles," announced Madge.

"Surely," said Mrs. Armstrong, "it belonged to the Nevilles."

"I'm sure I read somewhere . . ."

Madge flipped through the pages of her brochure.

It did not need to be spoken aloud: *Lucille would have known.*

On the way to Dunstanburgh no word was exchanged in the bus. Glimpsing his passengers' expressions from time to time in his mirror, Fred had a disturbing sensation that they were all retreating from him. There wasn't really anyone at all in the bus. They were thinning, growing weaker, incapable of talking or of doing anything for themselves. Even Madge had ceased to dab at her neck and was staring hypnotically ahead, waiting for some unuttered command.

In the seat behind her, the someone or something was growing stronger.

Fred twisted his mirror abruptly.

This time there was no doubt. Growing in substance every second, Lucille sat smiling at the back of Madge's head.

The bus veered, its wheels slithering along the narrow grassy verge and narrowly escaping a scrape against the stone wall. Fred gulped; straightened up, slowed; and concentrated on the road ahead.

The others couldn't have seen her, or they'd have said something. He wasn't going to mention it. He didn't want them reporting him back to the company for being drunk and putting the wind up them. Really, they were the ones who had put the notion of her into his head, because that was all they could think about today. Should never have come.

At Dunstanburgh he stayed well back when they began to clamber silently over the castle ruins. He had no head for heights. Even looking up as Madge appeared in a gaping embrasure made him dizzy.

She was saying something. They seemed to be crowding in on her and forcing her back. One more step and she would be out and down. He wanted to shout a warning but dared not risk it.

There was another figure in the shelter of a turret, watching. Waiting—in no hurry.

When Madge came down she was in tears. The others were remote, as if dismissing her and waiting for more competent guidance.

"I'm doing my best," she cried.

They stared in blank accusation.

Only her husband blinked and shook himself in an effort to wake up. But all he could manage was: "Madge, could you have saved Lucille?"

"No one could have saved her."

"You didn't actually *help* her?"

"I did all I was supposed to do."

"I mean, you didn't help her on her way?"

"Charles, you can't mean . . . you're not accusing me . . ."

"I thought you might have got the wrong idea. About that one

143

time, you know, when Lucille was at our place and you came back early off night duty."

"Just that one time?" she said with sudden cold fury. "And was it such a wrong idea?"

"Then you did know. I mean, suspect. Madge . . ."

She walked on. Fred was sure nobody else had heard. Not that Harold Wright had lowered his voice: just that none of them was capable of registering anything at all. So there was a right turn-up. If Madge *had* done it because her husband was up to fun and games with Lucille . . .

The truth of it was something none of them would ever know now.

Lucille would have known.

They were on the road towards Bamburgh when Madge, jerking as if prompted by someone close to her, said: "Let's have a look at Hawkby on the way."

"Don't think I know that one, Mrs. Wright."

"The next turning but three to the right. Not as impressive as Bamburgh, but we ought to take it in while we're in the neighbourhood."

Sure enough there was a faded little signpost pointing towards Hawkby. The road ran gently downhill and ended in a small village overshadowed by castle ruins like the teeth of some stranded monster tossed up by an ancient tide. The sea had eaten away much of the cliff, and the shore was a mixture of sand, rocks, and splintered stones.

Fred was thirsty. The pubs weren't open, but the post office by the village green advertised ice cream and cold drinks. He paused in the doorway and watched the party take the path round the castle to the beach—all eleven of them. Then he turned away into the dark interior of the post office.

When he had finished, he realized the afternoon was wearing on. If they were to complete their itinerary, it was time they moved. He strolled towards the castle, feeling inexplicably tired and out of touch with reality. No fit condition to be driving a bus, even a small one.

From the low cliff he could look down on the shore.

There they were, larking about like a crowd of kids. Four of the men were digging with their hands and throwing up a mound of sand. But there was no laughing and joking: unless it was lost under the rustle of the tide beginning to splash in across green-slimed rocks.

They seemed to be playing a silly game, burying one of their number in the sand, like he had done when he was a kid. Or maybe not one of them, but a rounded rock they had picked up somewhere—rounded and unusually smooth, quite distinct from the heavier whalebacked rocks.

Fred called. They all stood up and looked at him. He waved, beckoned. Obediently they began to return, following him to the bus. All ten of them. He counted as they got in: eight, nine, ten.

"Everybody aboard?"

Harold Wright settled into the seat beside him. "All present and correct."

Fred drove back the way they had come. The silence was almost solid within the bus: as solid as the woman sitting complacent and contented behind Mr. Wright.

Until he heard that odd little, half exasperated sigh he remembered so well. And she was asking: "Could we stop at the next garage with a café?" And at once there was a murmur of agreement.

A mile along the main road, and Fred pulled in. As he opened the door, she moved past him and he heard it again, the sigh: winging away into infinity, a last whisper and a last laugh.

Mocking them; and releasing them.

Mrs. Brearley blinked across the aisle at Mr. Armstrong.

"That's odd. I could have sworn . . ."

"Where did she *go?*"

And Mr. Wright was looking round, puzzled, as they got out of the bus and leaned over, rubbing their knees and bending their legs against the pain of returning circulation. They were all stiff and weary, and all suddenly aware of it.

Mr. Wright said: "Where's Madge?"

"Funny. I don't remember her getting on the coach."

"And I don't remember her *not* getting on."

They stared accusingly at the driver. Surely he ought to have been responsible enough to ensure that everybody was aboard before driving off? Responsible enough to have known how many there ought to be. Lucille would have known.

Fred said: "Look, there's ten of you . . ."

They all turned towards one another and counted.

Without Fred, there were nine.

"She got out."

"But where's Madge got to?"

Gradually, incredulously, they began to remember. They all saw in their mind's eye, miles behind them, the picture of that little rounded ball like a head above the sand, packed in, imprisoned by their impressive sandy fortifications.

Fred was the first back into the bus. They bundled in after him, and he swung the wheel and twisted the bus round and began to race back the way they had come. But when he looked at his dashboard clock he realized how little point there was in hurrying.

By now the tide would be in.

R. A. Lafferty

The Funny Face Murders

R. A. LAFFERTY IS QUITE INEXPLICABLE, BUT HERE ARE A few facts. He was born in 1914 and worked most of his life in the electrical wholesale business. "The most interesting part of my life was the four and a half years in the US Army in WW II, mostly in the South Pacific. I began to write in 1959, at the age of forty-five, a time when most writers are about finished. I quit work except writing in 1970. I have never written very hard and I loaf a lot. I am a Catholic, a political Independent, a fiscal conservative. My hobbies are history, geology, languages, writing, and travel."

Never written very hard? Why, besides a hundred and sixty stories (some of them collected into three books) he has written at least twelve novels, including The Reefs of Earth, Okla Hannali, Fourth Mansions, Arrive at Easterwine, *and* The Three Armageddons of Enniscorthy Sweeny. *But then he suggests in an interview that stories choose their authors rather than anything resembling the reverse.*

Perhaps "The Funny Face Murders" is comic relief, or perhaps not. It reminds me (very slightly!) of one of Chesterton's nightmares, say The Man Who Was Thursday, *without the theological reassurance. Beyond that, you're on your own.*

1

Judy Kingfixit filled a large paper sack with bundles of paper money and went down to Broken Bench Lane on the outskirts of T Town. She had a need to see whatever new face the Lane presented this morning.

"What we do on Broken Bench is look at the world and reality out of new faces," Judy's husband Harry often said, "and that's another name for the Science of Invention. And we who invent, we see the world as wearing a new face every morning."

"I will have to find Harry," Judy told herself. "He cannot get along without me, and he will *have* to be on Broken Bench Lane. That's the only place he knows to go. He isn't much fun, but he's habit-forming and I live by habits now. I wasn't paying attention when he said what he was on to this time, but he's got to be down here. Now there's an idea! I'll try it."

There was a sign on a booth there that read *Trouble-Dissolver Ten Cents a Large Glass*. Judy got a large glass of it and drank it off quickly.

Two adventurous boys were coming to the Lane at the same early morning moment. They were coming at it from the woods to take it unaware, to ambush it and to be ambushed by it. To be an adventurous boy in the very early morning is even better than to be Judy Kingfixit with a large sack full of money. It was very much as though the boys came on a raft from those flowing woods. It was really a *Big Star Weed Rider* that they came on. But it is Judy on scene yet.

"This leaves me at loose ends," Judy said when she had drunk off the Trouble-Dissolver. "I hadn't expected it to work so quickly. My troubles are all dissolved and I become a balloon without ballast."

"It takes a little time," said the proprietor of the place with a happy leer. "But now that I am used of it this way, I wouldn't go back to having troubles again for anything."

Judy hadn't a whole lot of respect for Broken Bench Lane.

"I have an uncle just like this alley," she said out loud. "Disreputable, that's what they both are."

She really hadn't a whole lot of money that she could afford to waste here; but there was an attraction (besides trying to find her husband Harry Kingfixit who was usually somewhere on the Lane), there was a seeking and a shabby interest that got hold of her sometimes and drew her down to the Lane. Sometimes? It drew her down there just about every morning, just as soon as the morning began.

At just this time there was a terrific crash involving that least dependable of all aircraft, the *Big Star Weed Rider,* and two boys, Roy Mega and Austro. The fact that they were travelling very low, about six inches above grass-top, probably saved their lives and got them off with nothing more than grass burns. But the crash was damaging to their reputations as aircraft designers. You can't have something go wrong with the design of your ailerons and still keep a sound reputation on Broken Bench Lane.

Broken Bench Lane, that bright ribbon in a sea of green, was particularly verdant because of the great quantities of Great Heart Discovery grass that grew so thickly in the whole region that the Lane traversed. The grass was the discovery of Great Heart Harkte who had been an inventive Indian man of several generations earlier. He had invented a sod buster plough superior to every other one. He had invented a pokeweed harvester and a coon skinner. He had grown the first puffed wheat and the first Golden Day sand plums. And he invented Great Heart Discovery grass that did not thrive well until after Great Heart Harkte himself was dead and buried. Then it grew richly, with every primordial root of it coming out of Harkte's buried heart, and it covered a region of several miles. Wherever it grew, there was inventiveness supreme; and Broken Bench Lane had the lushest Discovery grass of the whole region.

Where else but on the Lane was there such a merry, early morning chirping going on at every hour of the day and night? The barkers and cardinals and meadow larks all seemed to sing together:

"Lookie, lookie, lookie! Invent now! Be a millionaire by noon!"

Broken Bench Lane was the gaudiest-appearing of all those little streets and ways that tumbled and twisted down the green slopes all the way from Standpipe Hill to the south edge of town till they disappeared in the verdant haze beyond which, in the misty distance, rose Beautiful Downtown Broken Arrow. There were not streets and arteries like these everywhere, not like this bunch: Jenks Road, Clown Alley, Harrow Street, Five Shill Road, Lollywaggers' Left-Hand Lane, Speckled Fish Road, Leptophlebo Street, Trotting Snake Road, Broken Bench Lane! And the brightest jewel of them all was Broken Bench.

(Yes, Judy Kingfixit will be all right for a while. What can possibly go wrong with anyone who has had all her troubles dissolved and who is wandering around with a large sack full of large bundles of money?)

These streets are not necessarily located in the order here given. There are many other streets, better kept and broader, that intrude between these. Half of these arteries are not even proper streets in the sense of accepting vehicular traffic; they are mere pedestrian walks or paths or alleys. (Broken Bench was in between the categories in that it accepted vehicles, but for only one hour a day.)

Quentan Whitebird, in his monumental work *Forgotten Lanes and Byways of Tulsa,* refers to this cluster of little streets (plus four others, and with Lollywaggers' unaccountably left out) as "dream streets." Well, there *is* a green haze over all of them that is very like a summer afternoon sleep. Even in the brightness and hustle of some of them, there is always this noddiness or nappiness. And there is the frightening snapping-out of it also, and the raffish terror at realizing that one hasn't quite snapped out of the spell after all.

There was a graffito on a wall that read "Who is False Face Flaherty?" That was the beginning of a doubt.

"Oh, what is there so weird about Harry disappearing this time?" Judy Kingfixit moaned, "and what is there so weird about me myself? And how has False Face Flaherty come into the thing these last several days?" The Trouble-Dissolver would really dissolve all troubles, but if new and different troubles should arise, it would require another glass of the stuff to get rid of them.

Broken Bench was the brightest and most hustling of all those little roads. What factories and shops there were there! What venturehouses! What money coining enterprises! What dreams that had taken flesh in solid crab-orchard stone with tomorrow-glass façades! There were bustling manufactories and tall financial empires and inventories (well, what *do* you call the studios where inventors work?). There was all the flowing lifeblood of newness. The Lane was so crammed with newness that those who visited it only once a day were always dumbfounded by the changes in it. Here were the waves of the future sold by the gallon or barrel or oceanful.

"Be on time," read another graffito on another wall. "The murders take place this morning at nine o'clock in Madame Gussaud's Wax Museum."

And here was something new! The Lane never disappointed. Judy Kingfixit was at a Mokka-Chokka stand where she was both attracted and repelled by the hot odour of something new.

"You look like a lady I know," Edith Thornbush said, and she was a bit puzzled. "You have ankles and wrists kind of like hers. Her name is Judy Kingfixit."

"And my name is Judy Kingfixit," Judy said, "and it's no more than eight hours since we were together last. What's the matter with you anyhow, Edith?"

"If you *are* Judy," Edith said, "and even if you aren't, it doesn't come well from you to ask *anybody* what's the matter with them. Just what *has* happened to you? Where did you get that face?"

"You *are* Judy Kingfixit, aren't you?" Ophelia Izobret asked in a pained way. "Didn't you happen to look in the mirror this morning?"

"No, the mirrors kept breaking," Judy said. "I never did get a good look at me."

"Well, sit down with us," Ophelia said. "None of us is perfect this time of day, but you miss it farther than anyone I ever saw."

"Thank you, Ophelia," Judy said and she sat down with them all in a booth in the Mokka-Chokka stand. Cornelia Falselove was there also. "You have to be Judy," this Cornelia said. "No one else would ever imitate Judy Kingfixit. Who'd *want* to?"

"Thank you, Cornelia," Judy said. She bought and began to drink a cup of hot Mokka-Chokka, the first time in her life she had ever drunk it or heard of it.

There was a new graffito on the wall: "False Face Flaherty is a Corporation Man."

Oh the drink was horrible! But, *oh,* it was sociable! Really, is there anything in the world so pleasant as to sit and drink hot Mok-ka-Chokka with friends?

"Oh yes, isn't it horrible!" Ophelia Izobret asked. "The inventor said that he worked for seven years to find something bad enough to be this good. But he had precedent to go by. When first introduced to the western world six hundred years ago, coffee was almost as horrible, so ancient writers have indicated. It was instantly terrible and it was an instant success. And it came with its own furniture, which we still have with us, up until this morning at least. With the coming of coffee, there was born in one blinding flash the coffee houses or cafés, the eating-out places of ever since then. There hadn't been any regular eating-out places before that, except in the Asian regions that already had coffee. Kitchens were changed, or real kitchens were born. They are all coffee kitchens now, or were up till this morning.

"Now there is Mokka-Chokka the totally new beverage, and it predicates totally new and different sorts of eating-out places and kitchens for the whole world. It is by such giant leaps or mutations that the world and its institutions change, but the changes are usually ascribed to lesser things."

"Mokka-Chokka franchises and distributorships are going to sixteen figures," Cornelia Falselove said, "and that's a lot of Mokka. I hope that my—what's his name anyhow?—George is able to get in on it. He's here somewhere on the Lane, if I can find him. I'd like to get in on it myself, but I could hardly raise an eight figure ante. And George, he couldn't even raise a one figure ante, but sometimes he thinks of something. Oh, there is so much that is new here this morning! Whenever I am about to give up I come here and find out just how stimulating things are. Say, are you *sure* that you're Judy Kingfixit? You are very funny-looking this morning, even for Judy."

On the wall, a writing finger wrote "Cornelia Falselove is a Corporation Woman," and, having writ, passed on. But there is nothing like Mokka-Chokka to get the morning juices to surging through one.

"Invest in Broken Bench Lane!" a fuzzy-faced boy was calling. "Ten cents a front foot!"

They all had dimes out to make deals with him when they heard that. Land on Broken Bench Lane usually sold somewhere between two dollars and a thousand dollars a front foot: ten cents a front foot was fantastic.

"I want eight front feet," Edith Thornbush cried out. "I'll set up my own little booth in the Lane, just eight feet wide."

But the fuzzy-faced boy hadn't mentioned front feet of land. They were front feet of rabbits that he was selling for a dime each.

"Aw, Austro, that's cheating," Judy Kingfixit said (the fuzzy-faced boy was Austro, that youthful genius of the Australopithecus race). "Give me two more though. Where do you get them?"

"I get them from the Sooner State Rabbit Fattery out on the Sand Springs Road," Austro said. "They butcher a million fat rabbits a week there. They've always disposed of the left hind feet to *Luck Charms Limited*. And there is a very peculiar industrial application for the right hind feet only (I cannot tell you any more about that: I am besworn). But the front feet of the rabbits were always thrown away until I thought of this grift. Ahoy there, folks! Invest in Broken Bench Lane! Ten cents a front foot!"

Austro made several other sales to people who came into the Mokka-Chokka stand. This was extra income that would be needed to carry the *Big Star Detective Agency* over a slack period. Austro and his partner Roy Mega, a youthful genius of the Milesian race, had just moved their *Big Star Detective Agency* to Broken Bench Lane that morning. Barnaby Sheen had made the two young geniuses move their agency out of his electronics laboratory; but the new Broken Bench location was only a hundred feet from that hole-in-the-woods where the laboratory stood.

A hundred feet, but a million miles distant in spirit. For the magic of enterprise and invention was everywhere in the Lane.

"Where are all the funny-looking people coming from?" Ophelia Izobret asked them all. "Some of them look even funnier than Judy does today."

"They get their faces at *Funny Faces Incorporated*, that little pill-pushing emporium over there," Austro told the ladies. "It's one of the hottest enterprises thus far this morning."

"Oh, do they glue the faces on to them?" Ophelia asked. "They look so natural for not, ah, looking natural at all. They fit so well that they must be glued on."

"No, it's a lot more scientific than that," Austro said. "Everything is very scientific now, especially on the Lane. That's why Roy and I have taken chambers here for contacts with our clients. The funny faces, they grow them on people with fast-acting pills. You pick out the face that you want to wear for a while, and False Face Flaherty who runs the pillory over there will engineer the pills to give you that face quick. He bought up all the assets and secrets of *Instant Physiognomists* and also those of the *Pow Nose-Shrinker* people. He has absorbed companies and he has absorbed people. He's put it together now with a line of the fastest-acting psychosomatic pills in the world. You pop them down, and your face begins to change within seconds. You will notice several people running around with faces like mine. They picked mine for a funny face apparently, I don't know why. But I can always tell the difference. I have a mark on me that none of them know about, and they haven't engineered a pill for it yet."

"Is all that the truth, Austro?" Edith Thornbush asked.

"What is truth?" Austro inquired, and he used his owl face when he asked it.

"But how do they get rid of the funny faces when they're tired of them?" Ophelia Izobret wanted to know. "How do they ungrow them?"

"False Face Flaherty asks the customer how long he wants to wear a face, an hour, a day, a week," Austro said. "Then he adjusts the pill (he says) to give that time effect. After that time, your own face will come back (he says), or an improved model if you wish. And there are no after-effects to the changes (he says). He lies though (everybody on the Lane lies till he gets a truth really rolling for him): none of the pills really has a time coefficient or a reversal effect. False Face doesn't know how long a funny face will remain. He never tried this line of pills before this morning, except on his wife accidentally last night, and the results aren't in yet."

"Poor wife!" said Judy Kingfixit. "I don't believe that I quite like that False Face Flaherty. And I don't believe that I can quite stay away from him. That is the ambivalence of my life."

"I think that I will get myself a false face to cheer me up," Edith Thornbush said, "and I really don't care how long it sticks to me." Edith left the Mokka-Chokka stand to go over to *Funny Faces Incorporated.*

"The implications of this are tremendous," said Ophelia Izobret. "Consider only the criminal aspect of the funny face movement."

"You are always *so* good at considering the criminal aspects, Ophelia," Judy said.

Really, funny faces were big. Oh the inventiveness of the people on Broken Bench Lane!

"Good persons, here are business cards of our main business," Austro said, and he passed the cards out to all the good persons who would accept them.

"Big Star Detective Agency," the cards were printed. "Mega and Austro, scientists and artists in detection and improvisation. Interesting murders solicited. Tedious murders solved grudgingly. Skip tracing done. We locate anybody or anything. Husbands found cheap."

"How cheap?" Judy Kingfixit asked Austro. "I wonder if you could find my husband. I wouldn't want him for more than four or five dollars worth, but I'd go that much."

"Find mine too," Ophelia Izobret said. "Complications, Austro? Oh, I'll pay for the complications also."

"Find mine also," said a funny-faced woman who just arrived there and who sounded like Edith Thornbush. "Oh, that was fast! How do I look? Yes, find mine, Austro."

"Yes, I guess so. Me too," said Cornelia Falselove.

"Remember also," said Austro, "that the *Big Star Detective Agency* is not concerned entirely with crime detection. We also detect patterns and tendencies and unborn facts in the ethical and sociological and scientific fields. Folks, we're good."

"But is your information and discoveries correct?" Judy asked.

"What is correct?" Austro asked, looking like an owl.

Three other Broken Bench widows, Hedwiga Pompey, Seraph Wideditch, and Lavinia Firstlight, gave Austro earnest money of one dollar each to find their husbands. The additional sums of three dollars and ninety-five cents each would be given on the actual uncovering or delivery of the husbands. This low price was extended to all of them except Ophelia Izobret. Ophelia had to pay one thousand dollars earnest money and gosh knows how much on final delivery (because of some complications in her case), but she paid the first payment cheerfully.

"Seven cases, carrock!" cried Austro with boyish satisfaction. "That's good. But they are all little husband-missing cases. Not an interesting murder among them. Not even a tedious murder so far. That's bad."

"That's bad, yes, Austro," said a half-familiar voice encased in a new funny face (apparently a man voice and a man funny face), "but you are wrong about there being no murder in the package. There *will* be a murder or several, and perhaps there has already been one. Whether it is an interesting murder or a tedious one will depend a little bit on the detective of record."

"There will be a murder," said Austro sombrely. "I will have to watch for that, and at the same time I will have to figure out where we went wrong with our ailerons this morning." (The *Big Star Weed Rider*, that most esoteric of aircraft, had crashed that morning with Austro and Roy, due to faulty ailerons. Fortunately for them, the elevation was only six inches when they crashed.)

"Are you my husband?" Ophelia Izobret asked the mysterious funny-faced man who had spoken of murders.

"Madam, that is confidential information," said the person, and he moved away and merged with other funny faces in the hustle of Broken Bench Lane.

"He looks a little bit like my husband with that not-quite-right face of his," Ophelia said. "It's going to be hard to tell now. My husband always had a not-quite-right face too. What do you think of the ethics of wearing such a face, Austro?"

"What is right?" asked Austro looking like an owl. "What is not-quite-right? What, on the face of it, is a face?"

But this isn't getting us into the early-morning wonders of Broken Bench Lane. Listen, travellers and natives alike, no other street anywhere has such sheer inventiveness as Broken Bench.

Clay-Eaters Enterprises! Could there be a company of such a name on your own street? This business had opened just this morning, and it had never been known before.

"Clay-Eating raised to an Art and a Science," a banner on Clay-Eaters' Building proclaimed. "Gourmets' clay from Georgia,

Florida, Louisiana, and our own Oklahoma," a sign announced. You know what? Some of the clay smells from that place were authoritative and they were nosy. Judy Kingfixit went and bought a hundred dollars worth of stock in *Clay-Eaters*.

"Get in on the ground floor of this, on the clay-dirt ground floor of it," another sign said. Judy got a hank (a long handful) of good, yellow, country clay. It didn't taste very good but it had possibilities. There must be a lot of clay in the world, millions of tons of it. This looked like a famine-proof industry. How could one go wrong for only a hundred dollars on one of the most basic foods of them all? Clay is even mentioned in Scripture, earlier than any other food that you can think of. It is the real staff of life. "Clay makes the Man," another sign there said. And it was easy to believe that this superior clay contained any number of rare earths.

Judy Kingfixit left them and went over to *Funny Faces Incorporated*. And False Face Flaherty who was the proprietor over there made more passes at her than a Vegas diceman.

"I love your face," False Face said, and he kissed her. "Is it your own?"

"I'm not sure," Judy said. "I thought you might know. I hadn't even known that I was wearing a funny face till my friends started to make remarks about it. I think now that my husband spiked my headache tonic last night before he skipped out. Are you my husband? He's an ambivalent man. Is your name as well as your face false?"

"Yes. But what did your husband spike your headache potion with? Is it possible that someone else knows my secret of physiognomenical freebooting?" False Face Flaherty asked. "No matter. He cannot be my equal. He surely does not have my unique talents. Oh my dear, I must have your funny face. It is a masterpiece. Is it a masterpiece that I did in a dream and then forgot about, or is it the work of a different master? It is primordial, it is prodigious! I will make copies of it for the rest of my life."

"Your voice reminds me of someone I know, but I can't remember who," Judy said. "And your hands remind me of someone I know. Oh yes, I'll buy a hundred dollars worth of your stock.

Make it two hundred. Oh, False Face, you do something to me! But I have ramblings to ramble and people to find on the Lane."

"My stock boy can handle things here at *Funny Faces Incorporated* for a while," Flaherty said. "He's already wearing a Flaherty Special False Face, so he looks like me anyhow. We will ramble together, my dear."

Hand in hand, Judy Kingfixit and False Face Flaherty rambled the Lane together. They were both buffs of these hasty businesses which required so much daring to launch and which, when once launched, were so much more likely to sink than to survive. They visited the *Hot Sauerkraut Sandwich Drive-In.* Hot sauerkraut sandwiches were something whose time had just arrived, and where should such a timely thing more likely show its head than on Broken Bench Lane?

They visited the *Dog Dirt Gasoline Company* with its compelling motto: "Our product alone contains volatile matter from high octane Great Danes." Dog Dirt Gasoline would fill a need and remove a nuisance.

They visited the *Old Original Flea Market,* a hold-over from the day before when it had been named the *New Original Flea Market.* Judy Kingfixit bought one male flea and eight female fleas. She got the papers on them too.

"Hereafter they will have to give me the flea-breeders' discount on everything I buy there," Judy told False Face, "regardless of whether it is related to flea-breeding. That is part of the Flea Marketers' Franchise Agreements, but they won't give it to you unless you insist on it."

They went to *Madame Gussaud's Wax Museum,* still going hand-in-hand; but each of them seemed to be carrying something in the free hand now. The Wax Museum was a very contemporary place. Funny faces, appearing on human persons by the pillatory magic of False Face Flaherty no more than fifteen minutes before were now displayed on wax figures at Gussaud's, by the magic of scientific reproduction and copying and the use of the new telestencils.

Gussaud's was rather a fun place. Everyone who came in there received free a Dirky Dave Rubber Dagger. It was a souvenir of the museum, for Dirky Dave was one of the most popular of the wax pieces. All the pieces were very lifelike.

One of them moaned horribly now as if it were death stricken. The figure that moaned was wearing one of the new Hamlet Izobret funny faces, the face that was a little wrong for the real Hamlet face. How did they make the figure moan so lifelike (or so death-like) as that?

Edith Thornbush was in Gussaud's. So was Ophelia Izobret and many other persons.

On display were the wax figures of all the T Town notables, past, present, and future, in living wax; but one had to look at their name plaques to be sure who they were. False faces were popping out on more and more of them, by the magic and science of Madame Gussaud perhaps, or by the magic and science of False Face Flaherty who had great influence on his surroundings this morning.

"Who *is* False Face Flaherty?" a wax raven croaked.

Oh, the same or another wax figure moaned horribly again, a death-struck moan!

There were the waxen images of all the great Evangelists of T Town, all the great Western Swing Kings, all the great Inventors. There were absolutely authentic reproductions of—

—but here there was a disturbance and interruption. There was another moan like a death râle from one of the wax figures, one of them with the not-quite-right Hamlet Izobret funny face. Then, moaning unnervingly once more, the figure fell heavily with that peculiar squashing thud that is given off only by a column of wax, or by a column of human flesh, when it falls.

"He is stabbed to death!" Judy Kingfixit cried in a sharp liquid voice. "There is a Dirky Dave dagger in him."

"But it's only a rubber dagger, Judy," False Face Flaherty laughed. "See the words on the handle of it as on all the rest of them: 'Dirky Dave Rubber Dagger, Souvenir of Madame Gussaud's Wax Works.' It must be some sort of joke about him being dead, if they use a rubber dagger."

"The rubber is steel-hard now," Judy said, "and steel-sharp" (and various persons were beginning to cry out "Murder, Murder!") "as a result, probably, of the all-pervading science of Broken Bench Lane. Who could have transmuted it so?"

"Oh, it was no great trick," Flaherty said. "There's a hundred different inventors of us on the Lane who could have done that at a minute's notice, without props yet."

"And the blood! Look at all the blood, Flaherty! Did you ever see so much blood come out of a wax man? Do you think that's wax blood or rubber blood, F.F.?"

("Help! Help! Murder! Murder!" other people were calling.)

"No, it's real," Flaherty said. "Get the police, get an ambulance, get a doctor!"

"Get Austro. He's a detective now," Judy said.

2

All those people were there quickly, the police, the ambulance people, the doctors, different laboratory crews, the detectives Roy Mega and Austro, a police detective named Otis Hardtack, honest citizens, and funny-faced rogues. They all milled around there, and they never did solve that murder.

"It's the funny faces that cloud the water," said that police detective Otis Hardtack when he finally got his brains stretched around the fact that most of the people there were wearing false faces and that they were living and flesh faces that wouldn't come off easily. "This dead man looks like Hamlet Izobret the con-man and inventor whom we have up often. He looks a lot like him, but not quite enough like. Hamlet is a pest that we all know down at headquarters, for the crime-solving inventions that he brings in as well as the quasi-crimes and frauds that he commits. Being an almost-Hamlet, this dead person is *not* Hamlet Izobret. Hamlet already had the original Hamlet funny face, and it was as good and authentic as any original could be. The one this dead man is wearing is not very accurate. It just isn't good enough to be the original, so the dead man can be anyone except Hamlet. What's behind this funny false face caper anyhow?"

"What is 'funny'?" asked Austro in his owlish way. "What is 'false'?"

"What we do on Broken Bench Lane is look at the world and at reality out of new faces," False Face Flaherty was saying with the

160

air of one who had often said it before. "And looking out of new faces is another name for the science of invention. And we who invent, we see the world as wearing a new face every morning."

"This man here, the dead man, told me that there would be a murder or murders," Austro said. "I wondered then how he knew about it."

"Are you sure it is the same man?" Otis Hardtack asked.

"What is 'sure'?" Austro asked. "It was either this man, or one of those wax figures that were on each side of him when he fell. They have the same faces as he has, and they look as if they were ready to fall also. Why couldn't the man have told me who would do the killing and that it would be done to himself? He was thoughtless."

"The one who did it took a little thought," Otis said. "This rubber-turned-into-steel of the dagger won't take prints. I always hate trouble anywhere in this Lane. There are always freakish elements to it."

There was a horrible wail as of a demented siren.

"The murderer is identified," Austro said. "That is a new machine that my partner Roy Mega has perfected within the last five minutes. It will sniff out a recent murderer by the aura that he exudes, and it will not be silenced till he is apprehended."

There was a second and a third siren wail that joined the first. And then a twelfth and thirteenth wail.

"The new machine is multi-voiced," Austro said. "That is for just such contingencies as this. The murderer *did not work alone*. He was part of a conspiracy. I hope that your men are apprehending the murderers as the machine directs them, detective Hardtack."

"More likely they're trying to shut off that damned noise machine," Hardtack growled. "Oh, how could anyone ever come up with noises like that?"

And now there were about twenty separate wails coming from the machine as it identified target after target.

"My partner, Roy Mega, set out to discover the most irritating noise in the world," Austro said, "the noise that nobody could possibly ignore. We call it the murder-will-out noise, and that's it."

"But, Austro, even you must realize that something has gone wrong with it," Hardtack said. "It's howling for at least fifty separate targets now. There can't be that many people in on this murder. Even in Broken Bench Lane that isn't possible. Something's wrong!''

"Well, there *was* one slight thing he hadn't corrected yet. He decided, because of the immediacy of the murder, to go ahead and put the machine into action anyhow, is that not true, Roy? It seemed so unlikely that the case would arrive."

"Uh, it's like the man who sold the horse to the other man," said Roy Mega who had just returned to the wax museum after setting his machine into action. " 'I will acknowledge that the horse has one fault,' the seller said. 'He sits down on grapefruit. He cannot pass a grapefruit on the ground without sitting down on it, but otherwise he is an exemplary horse, and he is patient with children.' "

"So the man bought the horse and started to ride him home," Austro said. "He went fine until the man rode him through a little creek, and the horse sat down in the middle of it and would not budge. Cudgels and calumnies would not move the beast, so the man walked back to the seller with his complaint."

" 'Oh hell, I forgot to tell you,' the seller said, 'he sits down on fish too,' " Roy Mega finished it off.

"So???" police detective Otis Hardtack intoned, and everyone listened silently. Even the howling murder detector was quiet now, having been incapacitated by men with hammers and wrecking bars.

"It's the same with my new machine," Roy Mega said. "It howls when it comes on to a recent murder. It also howls (this is one of the quirks in it that I hadn't had time to take out yet) when it comes on anyone who had apple wine for breakfast. I didn't realize that there would be so many or even any of them."

"It was likely those advertisements on the air last night," detective Otis said. " 'Apple Wine, Apple Wine, Start Your Day with Apple Wine.' A catchy tune and your loss. You have no idea what a sense of security you two boys give me. Police detectives sometimes are worried by their competition from outside the lines. That situation sure doesn't obtain here."

There was a little slight-of-body business here. Laboratory men were working over that dead body in bunches, but the confusion could be channelled. The attention of all was called away several times. Hypnosis was used, and misdirection. Austro and Roy somehow got the dead body over to their *Big Star Detective Agency*, and the police finally loaded an unscathed wax figure with a similar funny face on to their morgue wagon and took it down town with them.

Madame Gussaud was one of the few people who noticed that the switch had been made.

"But, in spite of it, I'm not short a wax figure," she said. "I'm two wax figures over! It's those damned false faces that have been popping out on them. How is anyone to keep them straight?"

Several of the folks gathered in the Gift Shop, the Wax Museum in the wake of the murder having attracted a number of persons of the grosser sort.

"Do you have the Gift of Second Sight for sale?" False Face Flaherty asked the Gift Shop proprietor.

"Oh certainly," the man said. "We have every sort of psychic and mental and personal gift for sale. We have the latest and most scientific things along the Lane. My own second sight tells me that you should have sought the gift of second sight yesterday and not today. My own uncanny-intuition gift tells me that you are in a jam. Sir, you are now in a room with only two doors leading out of it. The name of one of them is 'Too Late' and the name of the other one of them is 'Never,' but either of them is better than staying where you are. For five thousand dollars I can give you the gift of second sight. Just put your head into this helmet, bite down on the bullet of your selection, and remember that pain has no memory."

"It's cheap enough, I suppose," False Face said. He paid the five thousand dollars and put his head in the helmet. For the next few minutes he went through numerous contortions as though he were in extreme pain. Austro and Roy Mega and a few others went next door to the *Air-Skate Rinkarama* so as to miss the sufferings of False Face Flaherty.

"Item," said Austro, as he watched the air-skaters skim along two inches above the top of the grass of the rink, "we have a dead man not yet identified by ourselves, though the police may have identified him by his prints. They don't tell us everything."

"Item," said Roy Mega, "over in the Wax Museum there are

two dead wax figures that are similar in face to the dead man and are similarly stabbed with rubber daggers turned to steel. Those two are in addition to the unscathed wax figure that we substituted for the body. This business of *three* of the rubber daggers being transformed into steel is what puzzles me."

"Oh, I've solved that part," Austro said. "One in six of the latest bunch of Dirky Dave Rubber Daggers (apparently manufactured during the night just past) was made of steel and honed to an edge. This is something that even Madame Gussaud doesn't know. But the junior underground along the Lane has been putting out the word all morning that *Dirky Dave Roulette* is the new In game in the neighbourhood. So it would be easy for three different persons to select the heavier steel daggers out of the souvenir dagger baskets and then plunge them into the intended victim, and mistakenly into the two adjacent wax figures that were funny-faced exactly like the victim."

"Dirky Dave Roulette sounds like a childish game," Roy Mega said, "but I can see where it would be fun. 'Stab your Bosom Buddy in the Bosom! One chance in six that you will kill him or wound him.' Do you want to go by there and try it, Austro? We just reach in the basket blindly and take out the Dirky Dave Dagger that comes to our hand. And then we will have at it."

"We will go by the Museum and maybe we will do it and maybe we won't," said Austro.

And they didn't do it. They were diverted by crowds of scoff-laws, hitsters, and hooded-crows. They were buffeted by these hurrying persons in the Lane, and they forgot all about playing dagger roulette.

The newcomers were visitors, from Kansas City and Memphis and Dallas, of the woolly sort. They had apparently come to town on the mid-morning planes, and they had headed for the Lane at once. News that a new wrinkle might be found on the Lane had travelled fast. The scoff-laws wanted the funny faces that could be worn for either long or short times as ruddy and living flesh disguises. ("We get so damned tired of wearing those ski-masks when we make a hit," one of them said.) They wanted whatever variety of funny-face pills might be had. They spotted False Face Flaherty instinctively as the Factor in Faces. They dragged him out of the helmet in the gift shop and began to shove money at him. So False Face went back to his base at *Funny Faces Incorporated* to attend to business.

"We really don't know who False Face Flaherty is," Austro remarked, "even though he seems to have a leading role on the Lane. It seems to everyone that he has been here for ever, but he had never been on the Lane as late as yesterday. There's almost too much of him for one person, and there's a lot of things missing from him that even the poorest person should have."

"Who is Cornelia Falselove?" a wax raven in Gussaud's Wax Museum was heard to croak.

"The mistake we are making is in dealing with surface or apparent persons rather than with psychological persons," Roy Mega said. "We might, for instance, inquire about the apparent person of False Face Flaherty: we would find, I suspect, that there is no such person at all. Ah, but let us examine the psychological persons that hover about this Flaherty, though not about him exclusively: the corporate *Substrate Lord*, the *Shadow*, the *Anima*, the *Animus*, the *Ego*, the *No*, the *Hemeis*; aye, and the *Id*. I believe that there is a corporate, but not a personal, personality behind those false faces of Flaherty."

"I know a little bit about that corporate personality myself," Austro said. "I have just obtained a copy of the Articles of Corporation of *Funny Faces Incorporated*. The articles state that False Face Flaherty *is* a corporate personality that may be inhabited by Harry Kingfixit or Edgar Thornbush or by Hamlet Izobret; it states that all three of these have equal rights to this personality, especially the rights of entering it and leaving it."

"Well, I wonder which one of them is inside Flaherty at the moment?"

"Oh, I'm sure that it is Harry Kingfixit," Austro said. "It could hardly be one of the others since Judy Kingfixit seems to have such a lively affection for it. It must be her husband Harry Kingfixit."

"Hey boys," said Cornelia Falselove as she came to them. "Those two dead wax figures that were on each side of the dead man back at

165

the wax works, well, it turns out that they aren't dead wax figures at all. They are dead live human people is what they are."

"Who knows about this?" Roy Mega asked in his conspiratorial voice.

"I do," Cornelia said. "I have a sensitive nose and it says that they are people and that they are getting a little bit ripe already on this warm day."

"Can you get the two figures for us without anyone catching on?" Roy said.

"Oh, I can buy them as wax figures I guess."

"Do it. And bring them to the *Big Star Detective Agency* at its new location in its special *Two-Guys-in-a-Garage Invention Kit and Utility Building.*"

"All right," said Cornelia Falselove who was an agreeable woman also. She went to buy the two figures who were actually dead human persons according to herself.

"Who *is* this Cornelia Falselove?" Roy Mega asked.

"What is 'is'?" asked Austro looking like an owl.

Roy Mega and Austro went to their *Two-Guys-in-a-Garage Invention Kit.* All that morning they had been fooling around with that kit that was both a building and a business, and they hadn't been able to put it together yet. This was strange, because they were the ones who had invented the *Invention Kit.* But it did take a lot of invention and genius to put one of those things together. Now, about those *Two-Guys-in-a-Garage Invention Kits:*

T Town Oklahoma had always been an inventive place beyond all others, and Broken Bench Lane had always been the heart of that inventiveness. The *Two-Guys-in-a-Garage* syndrome was the most common form of T Town inventive enterprises. It was the companies and factories started by *Two-Guys-in-a-Garage* that had kept T Town afloat and thriving when big oil companies and big aircraft factories and mobile home factories moved away or closed down. You get a couple thousand of those *Two-Guys-in-a-Garage* going and you have burgeoning diversification. And pretty soon some of those companies will have grown to a thousand guys in a garage. But the accommodations of the *TGIAG* syndrome had been left to find their own blind ways—until just two days before this.

Then two boys, or under-aged young men, Roy Mega and Austro, had begun to market prefabricated module kits to house and equip *Two-Guys-in-a-Garage* set-ups.

They procured a quantity of odd-shaped and odd-length boards from the *Elite Lumber-Rippers and Board and Price Cutters Company* that was near by.

They procured a quantity of imperfect building blocks from the *Honest Goof Concrete and Select Seconds Building Stone Sales Company* that was also near by and was run by Honest Goof Gomez.

They procured small kegs of mixed nails, bolts, screws, turnbuckles, and odd angle iron fittings from Junky Joe's. They got mounds of old automobile accessories that one could spread around and make it look as though this had been a garage indeed.

They fixed up, in an imposing envelope, assembly instructions that read in full "If you are real inventors, you will find a way to make a building and a business out of this kit. If you are not real inventors, then you shouldn't have bought an Invention Kit in the first place. It's lucky you find out now that you don't have what it takes."

With each of their kits they included another envelope titled "Three Red Hot Inventions Just Waiting to be Invented."

Roy and Austro had sold two of the kits the first day and four of them the second day. All six pairs of purchasers had groused a little bit at the skimpy assembly instructions; but all of them, being real inventors, had gone ahead and built fine buildings out of the stuff, each of them different, each of them distinctive and effective.

So, on the morning of the third day, Austro and Roy tried it themselves with one of their own kits. They intended to build a home for that most inventive and begeniused of enterprises, the *Big Star Detective Agency*. And they sure had been having a lot of trouble making anything at all out of it.

Cornelia Falselove and several persons she had dragooned into helping her arrived with the two additional human bodies from the wax works and unloaded them at the *Big Star*. They stretched them out beside the first body that the boys had got by a slight-of-body trick that they played on the police.

"Wonderful, wonderful, wonderful," Roy Mega said. "We will just see what kind of flies these three bodies will draw here.

167

And I will turn on my newly completed Confession Compulsion Machine and see who rises to the tainted bait.''

"That isn't the same thing as a Guilt Machine, is it?" Cornelia asked. "I feel a little bit guilty buying human bodies for wax prices that way."

"A guilt machine? Oh no, that would complicate it too much to have a Confession Machine and a Guilt Machine in the same unit," Roy Mega said. "I should scatter myself as someone else seems to have done. I have to activate my Confession Compulsion Machine, and at the same time I have to contemplate these three sets of remains here."

"And at the same time figure out what went wrong with the ailerons of the *Big Star Weed Rider* this morning," Austro said. "What really crashed this morning was a part of our reputation. You turn on the machine, Roy, and I'll contemplate the remains, and we'll both think about the ailerons."

The two boys set themselves to these three tasks. There came the ghostly humming as Roy Mega turned on the Confession Compulsion Machine. The ghostly humming had nothing to do with the *operation* of the machine. It was for effect. It was a good and impressive sound and the boys used it with all their machines when they put them into operation.

"Well, Austro?" Roy Mega said. He meant how was Austro doing with his assigned task.

"The most noteworthy thing about the remains is that they *are* remains," Austro said as he looked at the three dead fellows with affection. "That is to say, something, other than life, has been removed from them, and what remains of them is most incomplete. Something's lacking in these three. We come back to the same question: who is False Face Flaherty?"

"That man over there," said Cornelia Falselove, "the man with all the money and all the women."

"But who is he really?" Austro asked.

"He really is the man with all the money and all the women," Cornelia insisted.

But Flaherty lost one of his women just then. Judy Kingfixit left him and his group and came uncertainly towards the *Big Star Detective Agency*.

"The second thing about the remains is the now-you-see-it-now-you-don't syndrome," Austro said. "I keep taking blood out of these guys, and it keeps changing. Besides being too fluid for fellows who are dead almost an hour, it keeps flip-flopping. Sometimes it seems to be good *anthropino haima* or human blood. And then it tests as *kaoutsouk haima.*"

"And what is *kaoutsouk haima*, little fuzz-faced boy?" Cornelia asked.

"Rubber blood," Austro said.

"Who is Cornelia Falselove?" croaked a wax raven that had somehow followed them out of the wax museum.

Judy Kingfixit, a bit dazed, arrived at the *Big Star Detective Agency*.

"I have this compulsion to confess that I killed Hamlet," she said. "Why ever would I have a compulsion to confess such nonsense as that?"

"Have you a feeling of guilt, Mrs. Kingfixit?" Roy Mega asked.

"No, of course not," she said. "What a question!"

"The question, for you and for my machine," Roy said, "is how there can be a compulsion to confess without a feeling of guilt. My machine says they don't go together, and you say they don't."

"The real question," said Austro, "is whether there is any criminality in crime."

Somebody left them then like a cork plopping out of a bottle.

3

"Who was that?" Austro asked.

"It was that stringer from the International Universal World Press," Roy Mega said. "Nobody ever notices him when he's around with his pulsating ears; but he always makes that cork-out-of-the-bottle exit. I wonder what sort of story he got a lead on here that he's in such a hurry to spill it to the world?"

"I have this compulsion to confess that I stabbed Hamlet Izobret to death," Judy Kingfixit rattled off with unseemly passion. "Oh, I feel so much better for having confessed it!"

"But did you in fact kill Hamlet?" Austro asked.

"That is information I am unable to supply," Judy said. "The main thing is that I have confessed it. The confession becomes the act and the happening. It is like taking off from a dull rock and soaring into flight. The flight is what matters. The rock is an accident to be forgotten."

"Why did you, in the context of the confession anyhow if in no other context, kill him, Mrs. Kingfixit?" Roy Mega asked.

"Oh, he was trifling with my affections, I think. And he was after my husband to put more money into their things and not let me loot it all."

"Ah, he was a threat to your paper-sack-full-of-money syndrome," Austro mumbled. "What do you call it?"

"I call it 'Diversified Investment Procedure According to Educated Whim,' and it works if I can really keep it diversified, a hundred here, a thousand there."

"Can you say which of these three figures that are lying here is the Hamlet Izobret that you killed, Mrs. Kingfixit?" Roy asked.

"No, they all look alike when they're spread out like that with the same false faces on them all. They were already getting to look alike anyhow since they associated together so much."

Several persons came in and gave Judy Kingfixit large sums of money for the investments that she had made in the various industries earlier that morning. When a person invests in enterprises along Broken Bench Lane, the harvest (before noon usually) will be thirty and seventy and even a hundredfold.

The *Plant Engineering Company* was right to the left of the *Big Star Detective Agency*, between it and the *Hasty-Wasty Planned Obsolescence Company*. They did some amazing things at *PE*. They engineered plants for every need and botany. They had a nutty tree or bush that grew nuts so fast that a prize was offered for anyone who could ever pick them all. The bush had a capacity of only twelve nuts, but it would regrow them faster than any two-handed person could pick them off. The bush would have solved the hunger problem of the world, if only the nuts had been edible.

But a half dozen other plants that *PE* had engineered *had* solved the world hunger problem. They had done this more than a week before, but the word hadn't got to remote areas yet.

And they had engineered, at *PE*, plants that would walk and talk—really—and these had been used (one use among very many for them) by Madame Gussaud at her wax works as scaffolds or armatures to build wax columns on. This accounted for the flexibility or liveliness of some of her creations.

Wait a minute! Someone else is coming into the *Big Star Detective Agency*.

Edith Thornbush burst into the Agency, and a rush of words burst from her as she came.

"I have this compulsion to confess that I stabbed Harry Kingfixit to death!" she burst out. "Say, confessing is fun, isn't it? Is it generally realized that confessing is one of the great creative acts? I believe, if I just let myself go, that I could confess to such a flood of things as would knock the ears off you."

"Did you actually kill Harry Kingfixit, Mrs. Thornbush?" Roy asked.

"Oh, there's no way of telling," Edith said, liplessly as it were, and as if it were someone else using her voice. "There is no sharp line between kill and not-kill. I banged a dagger into one of those gawky look-alike people that were hiding among the wax figures in the wax museum. It might have been Harry I knifed (I hoped it was, I still hope it was), or it might have been one of the others, or nothing much at all."

"Can you say which of these bodies is the figure that you banged the dagger into?"

"No I can't. They're all alike," Edith said without moving her mouth. What was this business of her talking without seeming to talk?

The *Animal Engineering Company* was right across the Lane from the *Big Star Detective Agency*. The *AE* had formerly been named *Dog Designers Incorporated*. They did some amazing things at *AE*. They had branched out a long ways from their old *Dog Designer* days of the week before. Now they were into everything.

They had designed the Basic Ape that, with a bit of further creative tampering, could pass for any new-departure simian or bear or human. Madame Gussaud at the wax works had been using Basic Apes for two days now. She used them for her living wax figures as they were patient and would accept infusions and grafts. They would pose well. They would also work well and could do simple tasks like sweeping the floor or pouring wax; and they would (this was something that had been discovered within the last hour and a half) readily accept the new false face patterns that were so prevalent about the Lane this morning that they seemed to infest the very air.

AE had been using rubber blood in its Basic Apes for several hours, and this, blinking on and off, will simulate other bloods, animal or human or whatever, and will function well in many conditions.

"Oh, here they are," False Face Flaherty cried and he strode into the *Big Star Detective Agency*, "the three figures that were swiped from the wax works. Swiping, as some people don't seem to realize, is a form of theft. I'll just take them along back to my place as I have an agreement with the wax works."

"I own them now," Cornelia Falselove said, "and you will keep your body-robbing hands off of them. I may be able to make something out of them, or use them for receptacles."

Ophelia Izobret burst into the *Big Star Detective Agency*.

"I have this compulsion to confess that I stabbed Edgar Thornbush to death," she burst out. Ophelia looked dazed and these words had come out of her mouth with very bad synchronization. It almost seemed as if Cornelia Falselove had been speaking the words for Ophelia.

"Well, that accounts for all three of the knifed figures," Roy Mega said. "And I'm not sure just what else it accounts for."

The *Human Engineering Company* was just to the right of the *Big Star Detective Agency*, between it and the *Cat-Rat Fur Company*. They had been doing some amazing things at *HE*. One of the mottos at *HE* "We can change the colour of your eyes in nine minutes" will give you a pale blue idea of what they were doing there. "See us, and you will never be the same again" was another motto a bit on the chilling side.

HE was able to supply Basic Persons, coordinated humans with the personality and brains denatured. These went beyond the Basic Ape. They could not only perform simple tasks such as sweeping floors or pouring wax, but they were able to complain about them while doing them. Madame Gussaud used many of the Basic Persons at her wax works, and countless other firms along the Lane used the product.

"Are you trying to peddle these waxwork glories as our husbands, boys?" Judy Kingfixit asked of the three murdered figures on the floor that may or may not have been wax. Then Judy's face changed a bit and she said in words that were badly synchronized with her mouth, "Oh, I guess it will be all right then. I'll accept whichever one you say is mine if this is the state he happens to be in." Then her face changed back to its first case and she spoke again in her regular voice "Damnit, Cornelia, you are *not* spokeswoman for us. I, at least, will speak for myself. Get out of my mouth and get out of my voice."

"Oh, I believe that it will be suitable for Cornelia Falselove to be spokeswoman for the three involved ladies, just as it is suitable for me to be spokesman for these three incapacitated or dead gentlemen," False Face Flaherty said. "Connie and I will settle whatever needs to be settled. And then we will inform the six of you of the settlement, or else we will *not* inform you of it."

"Find out who False Face Flaherty really is," one of the dead wax-or-flesh men said hollowly.

"How?" Roy Mega asked that length of stuff on the floor.

"Take him apart," the figure said. So Roy Mega and Austro began to take False Face Flaherty apart.

"Find out who Cornelia Falselove really is," Ophelia Izobret asked.

"How?" Austro asked her.

"Take her apart," Ophelia said. So Roy and Austro began to dismantle Cornelia Falselove just as they were dismantling False Face Flaherty.

Ahhhh! Zombie Plant, Basic Ape, Basic Person with denatured brains and personalities, rubber blood, wax work (hexagon) structure modules, consensus figures and artificial figures! That's what False Face Flaherty who had all the girls and all the money was. That's what Cornelia Falselove was also.

Did False Face Flaherty really represent Harry Kingfixit and Edgar Thornbush and Hamlet Izobret as a corporate person?

What false process had put together such corporations?

"We leave it to you our clients whether you should pay us or we should refund to you," Austro said. "Have we located your husbands for you? I don't know. That's a question in semantics, and palaeonthropologists say (from the shape of our skulls) that we australopithecines were probably weak on semantics. What we have here are three boxes that your husbands have been in now and anon, and likely they are in them presently to a limited extent."

"What if we insist on having all there is of them?" Edith Thornbush asked. "We didn't contract for you to locate only pieces of our husbands. What if we insist that you produce them completely?"

"I suggest that the demand be lodged by all there is to you then," Roy Mega said. "You here present are only three boxes that three ladies have been in now and anon, and likely you are in them yet to a limited extent. But essential elements of you are missing or are hiding out somewhere."

A harried little man came into the *Big Star Detective Agency*.

"Have you heard about the Murders of Speckled Fish Road?" he asked, speaking in a very apprehensive voice.

"Ah yes, interesting case," Roy Megan said. "Do you wish the investigation to be reopened? Ah, let's see, just when was it that the Speckled Fish Road Murders took place?"

"They are likely to take place this very afternoon or night unless I can get expert help in preventing them," the nervous little man said.

"Ah yes, we will put you on hold for a while. Please be patient. We are winding up a triple-murder case now with our famous dispatch and efficiency."

"See how busy we are," Austro said. "Let us now move to a consummation of the Wax Museum Murders. All we need is good faith from all parties, and we have not been getting that. There is hanky-panky somewhere in that you three ladies slew the figures of each other's husbands and not your own. This is related to what is known as the fooling-around syndrome. As to the stabbings or 'murders' themselves, they really don't amount to very much."

"It was slicker than going over an alley fence to a 'little game' (in the old comic-strip context of that situation)," Roy Mega said. "The three men slipped out of their skin and bones and left them behind. Every man needs a hiding-place, and the trail to it should be crossed by as many false clues as possible. The men delivered their empty skin-and-bone boxes over to a corporate person of their own creation, False Face Flaherty. That was the second stage of their evasive trail to their hideout."

"Why should they want to evade us when they love us so much?" the box that Edith Thornbush had been in now and anon asked.

"Why should *they* want to evade us when they love *us* so much?" the waxwork box in which Hamlet Izobret had lingered now and anon asked. "But the dames have their hide-outs slicker than anything we could devise, and they spend a lot more time in them."

"You are so tedious sometimes, that's why," Judy Kingfixit said.

It was what is sometimes called a Mexican Stand-off. The boys of the *Big Star* had solved the disappearance of the husbands (and the technical murders of them or of the carcasses that they used now and anon), but they hadn't solved any of it very resoundingly. And the ladies might have made a case that nothing had been solved, "but it would be like opening a can of crocodiles," as Ophelia Izobret said. Nobody was very proud of the outcome.

There had been this very decadent influence (an unreal influence, really) along Broken Bench Lane for several days, and now the shattered fruit of that decadence had come to market. Simplicity had gone from the Lane.

It was decided that all should go to the *Hot Sauerkraut Sandwich Drive-In* for lunch and to discuss the financial aspects of the thing over hot sauerkraut sandwiches, try to resolve the who-owes-whom question.

And then the murderous malarkey-men of the media broke over them in wave after smelly wave!

"Which one is the illustrious Professor Austro who has made the 'Quotation of the Season?'" a half dozen of those flashpans bayed the question.

"*I* am the illustrious Professor Austro," Austro said. "Ah, which 'Quotation of the Season' is it, boys? I get off a lot of good stuff.''

"The illuminating statement 'The real question is whether there is any criminality in crime?', that is the quote that has rocked the country for the last six minutes," said one of the media men there. "Who else but the Great Professor Austro would have the temerity to phrase such a thing? The whole world must have skipped a second to hear an utterance so utter.''

"Everybody change watches one second to pick up the skip," said Roy Mega ungallantly. "I never remember whether we set them up a second or back a second.''

"Is there any particular childhood influence to which you might attribute your brilliance, Professor Austro?" a reporter-in-depth asked.

"What is 'brilliance'?" Austro beamed like a beacon. "Ah, we always ate a lot of rock soup when I was a kid on the Guna Slopes." Austro liked the adulation.

"Would you care to tell us, Professor Austro, what brand of rock soup it was?"

"Ah, we're on live and nationwide, are we? It was *Rocky McCrocky Rock Soup!*"

"I will just take two hundred dollars worth of stock in this *Rocky McCrocky Rock Soup,*" Judy Kingfixit offered, and Austro had the money out of her hand before she finished.

"The news services are running five minutes behind in trying to supply data on you," said another newsie. "There hasn't been such a single-quotation stir since Tuesday.''

"Professor Austro," a back-up analyst interposed. "There are two disassembled bodies here on the floor—" (They were those of False Face Flaherty and Cornelia Falselove: the three stabbed figures had risen and were waiting to go to the *Hot Sauerkraut Sandwich Drive-In.*) "Are they some of the debris of your murder investigating trade?"

"Oh certainly, certainly," Austro bubbled the words out. "You can't have a murder investigation without breaking a few bodies. These last three murders we just solved, though, weren't our most successful ever. There's loose ends hanging out of them everywhere. We did solve them, and we contributed solutions to the nature of reality at the same time, but we didn't solve them with our usual verve and style.''

"Professor Austro, what would you say was your most towering characteristic?"

"My modesty."

"Are you *sure* that this monkey-faced kid is the Great Professor Austro?" one of the reporters-in-breadth asked Roy Mega.

"He's the only Austro there is," Roy said, "so he has to be the Great Professor Austro. *The Great Professor Austro?* Oh, what a wet nose he's become now!"

"A wet nose, sir? What do you mean?"

"He's drinking the first of the four wine cups. It's enough to turn any kid's nose wet."

"What is the first of the wine cups, sir?"

"The cup of adulation. It's sometimes called Monkey Wine. He's sure going to be hard to get along with from now on."

"Do you solve any of the murders yourself, sir?"

"Only all of them."

"And who are you yourself sir?" the newsie asked. "Are you someone important?"

"Of course I'm important. I'm the Great Professor Mega."

"Ah, cut it out, Roy," Austro begged. "You're poaching on my rock pile."

"The Great Professor Mega!" another newsie gasped. "You're, you're even newer than the Great Professor Austro!"

"Let me tell you about that—" Roy Mega began to unroll his tongue.

Marianne Leconte

Femme Fatale
(Translated by Mlle. Alexis Kischkum and John Brunner)

MARIANNE LECONTE WAS BORN IN NANCY IN 1944 BUT WAS
*on the move at the age of four, to the Congo and Mozambique,
while her father searched for uranium. She married when she was
eighteen, and has two daughters. From Paris she edits anthologies, including* Méduse, Femmes au Futur, Les Enfants du Stur-
geon, *and* Les Pièges de L'Espace. *She is the editor of a French
publisher's science fiction list.*

*"I am not a quick writer," she says, "and an idea must linger a
long time in my mind before being written." She brought "Hyra
La Rousse," one of her infrequent stories, to the Milford writers'
conference in Britain. Everyone liked it, but where could she sell
it? A chorus (Priest, Brunner and Rob Holdstock, I believe) cried
"Ramsey Campbell!" They were right, and I'm doubly grateful to
Mlle. Kischkum for rendering the story into English for Milford
and to John Brunner for the energetic translation you are about to
read.*

Elle portait des culottes,
des bottes de moto,
un blouson de cuir noir
avec un aigle sur le dos . . .

From Edith Piaf's song *L'Homme à la Moto*

In the fogbound streets beyond the old fortifications she roamed at random among the shadows of a moonless night. Her motorcycle throbbed and quivered under her like a mettlesome thoroughbred. For hours on end she devoured kilometres of asphalt, climbing narrow streets, rushing down the slopes of the hills encircling the decaying and tumbledown city of Paris.

And then suddenly she spotted, alone on a street corner, the girl-child. Now motorcycle and rider began their seductive dance. The huntress passed and repassed the teenager, scanning her pale face which under the neon signs fragmented into streaks of orange, green, red, as though it had been lifted straight from a painting by Fernand Léger. It was a small face with immature features, new from the sculptor's touch, but on it might be read the hopes of hot young blood.

The dream, clearer and clearer, more and more detailed, harbingered awakening, rebirth, return to life.

It was time. It was her time. It was the hour when children of the war might emerge without fear of being recognized for what they were. The sleeper roused and stretched herself. Night was falling. Now, as at every dusk, red-headed Ira could go hunting.

She wore motorcycle gauntlets
and boots and pants of black,
and a big leather jacket
with an eagle on the back . . .

Her motorcycle reared like a spirited horse before rushing away. Ira knew where she was heading. From the Montmartre cemetery with its gutted tombs which nobody had bothered to rebuild—those who lived on couldn't give a damn about the dead who were resting in peace—she went down towards the wasteland of the Place

Clichy, turned left, sped past the countless sex-shops which like overripe and rotting fruit spewed forth clusters of men and girls ready to sell themselves for a mouthful of bread: a foul hangover from the days of Before. From the wreckage of the Moulin Rouge came a nauseating stench of broiled mushrooms and fried soybeans.

For a moment Ira, with her red hair, her wilful, almost emaciated face, her hollow cheeks and her pointed chin, was tempted to begin her search in these stews of debauchery for hayseeds. But her taste for a more challenging quarry gained the upper hand. In this district she would only find a few flabby tarts, overweight, halfcut, bloated with their unwholesome diet—livid-skinned creatures not at all to her liking.

So without hesitating she made a wide turn and entered Rue Fontaine. From there she continued to the ruins of Notre Dame de Lorette, then opposite the former Protestant church in the Place Kossuth took Rue Drouot straight towards the Palais Royal.

Behind her altuglass visor her feverish green eyes, dilated by fasting, watched the rutted roadway with hypnotic fixity. Inside her shining black helmet her temples throbbed. Her pressing natural need was making itself felt more and more keenly. Twisting the throttle wide open, she accelerated violently; her machine roared onward with a fusillade of farts that roused the whole of Rue de Richelieu. In the few apartment blocks which were still habitable despite the vast cracks across them, babies woke up howling, while their fathers once again cursed that fucking machine and their mothers crossed themselves in case it was the devil.

Now stabbing pains, as yet weak but nonetheless insistent, were shooting through her head. Desire was goading her on more and more, wearing out her patience—and the sickle was taking the brunt. Her wild and powerful steed seemed to be tuning itself to her suppressed complaints as it screamed along the road.

Suddenly Ira sighted a slender girl with an intersexual body: a barely sketched bust, a trim arse moulded by jeans so tight one could discern her pubic mount, a flat belly—a little pussycat pretending to be a liberated woman. Oh, her type was vulnerable, yes—once the hard veneer was flayed away.

Yet that kind would never quite give in. Right to the end they would clench their teeth and seal their lips. They would rather die than cry for mercy. They would never admit that the machine was going too fast, that its rider was frightening them.

It was very hard to make the children of Afterwards suffer.

Once more the motorcycle tore away at the behest of Ira's hand. Body welded to body, they flew as one on to the Carousel Bridge. Tyres screamed as they made the sharp turn into Rue des Saints Pères. Already Ira could feel against her back a tense and supple body, pressing close, hanging on to her as to a life-buoy . . . But they never broke down. They were quite something, these end-of-the-twentieth-century teenagers. They never even gasped, let alone cried out . . . An extraordinary kind of courage, almost inhuman, a wild refusal to give in . . . As though, once having risked a lift on a motorbike, they must put up with the consequences at all costs, for the sake of bravado. Perhaps I'm picking them too young, the redhead thought for the first time in her life. Perhaps the generation left over from Before are not so brave? Shrieks, screams, fists beating at her back while a frantic voice wails and howls . . . panic growing and growing, communicated from one body to the other along with the vibrations of the machine. Maybe I should try it at least once—a novel and different sensation.

Under the excited grip of its rider the motorcycle cavorted with joy.

The urge which had seized her would not go away; she wanted to hear someone shouting, moaning, begging, weeping. But whom to choose, and how? She must not be too old. A grimace of distaste twisted the red-haired Amazon's fleshy pink lips. Best would be a wealthy woman from an expensive district, in her thirties, with a firm, healthy body. But how to approach a woman like that, who would not be at all impressed by a motorbike, having seen too many in the old days?

The huntress crouched in her saddle to take the curve of Rue de Rennes. She sped on, disregarding the admiring whistles and lewd jeers of a small group of boys who every evening at this time turned out to await her split-second appearance—or rather, her motorcycle's, for it was one of only a few still on the road. No doubt they imagined that one night she would relent, stop long enough to pick one of them up and carry him away. But what did they think they were, these fashion-plates from well-to-do homes slumming on Boulevard St. Germain? Their wealth kept these sons of the middle class from rotting away like other people; they had no need of the expedients she, Ira, was driven to.

You've got another think coming, chums! Me, I go for your naughty little sisters, the ones with the boyish looks who hang around Montparnasse. What sort of girl to choose tonight? Above all, how to make her get on behind? A woman in her thirties is not the daredevil type . . . unless . . .

An idea took hold of her little by little. With her tomboyish air, her short hair, a fringe over her eyes, her jacket and her motorbike, she was fully equipped to seduce that type of female. To hell with her usual habits. Tonight she was going to allow herself something different, a victim to frighten, to terrify—a real treat. With a connoisseur's tongue she licked her gilded lips, swollen with lust. Sheathed in supple chestnut-coloured kid, her thighs tightened on her broad black leather saddle. The machine's vibration coursed through her body, rising up her belly, quivering in her loins, massaging her breasts. Flat out, she drove her steed towards the stunted, warped penis which was all that remained of the Montparnasse Tower. Only its concrete framework had endured. What had once been the boastful phallic symbol of a decadent society, a stiff, hard, black penis, was nothing but one more ruin. But Ira had never given a damn about it, even before the rain of fire and ashes. Men weren't her trip, nor were blacks, and pricks didn't turn her on . . .

She pulled up smoothly before the Nouveau Sélect, mounted the edge of the pavement and stopped a yard from the tables on the café's terrace. She closed the throttle. After jolting and snorting a bit, the machine quieted. Ira remained astride it, disregarding the lustful looks she was attracting. She, or the sickle? A black-clad silhouette with a scarlet eagle on her back: a disturbing, a demonic shadow.

Without moving, as though leafing through a book, she began to survey the customers sitting at rickety tables on this terrace littered with debris, chunks of broken wall, scraps of plaster which no one had bothered to cart away. This was the moment she loved most, and she didn't want to spoil it by being over hasty, despite the unsated desires which tormented her, made her belly churn and her head buzz. Unearthing a quarry always made her excited. She raised herself upright, her bust as square as if it were reinforced by plastic, her waist neat and tightly belted, her buttocks round and high, moulded by the leather garment that fused with the leather of the broad saddle.

On the pavement near by a tall crazy number was parading up and down. She had long skinny legs, such narrow hips that her shiny pants hung in creases around her thighs, a wide gold belt, a mauve lace blouse with a huge open collar falling on her unformed bosom, rings on every finger. Under the fascinated gaze of lustful males she simpered and gestured and showed off. She was there every night, turning the Nouveau Sélect into her personal theatre, spending her life on an imaginary stage, dedicated to offering the passers-by free entertainment. Her heart was in her *métier*. She came over as a genuine artist, who could enter honestly and entirely into her role.

Ira switched her attention back to the customers at the café. Glistening under the neon signs, her black blind helmet reinforced the mysterious aspect of the equally romantic character she was playing: the vamp, the *femme fatale*.

A brunette with slant eyes like an Oriental caught her interest: a little white Chinese shirt with a stand-up collar that set off her matt complexion, black hair cut page-boy style, dark eyes made softer by a stiff square fringe. It was a shame that too close to her sat a hail-fellow-well-met type with a beard, no doubt full of inhibitions, psychological hangups, sexual energy and the power to dominate . . .

Not for me, that kind of girl.

But they were all there, the midnight losers, those who in these artificial paradises among the company of friends sought refuge from visions of despair, boredom, depression. Survivors, almost healthy—healthy in body, if not in mind.

And then suddenly Ira snapped out of her brown study, snuffing the air like a hound. Among the three women in the second row . . . Smouldering under ashes, sharp remarks and bitter answers. The crestfallen air of the tense blonde with hair like an angel's; the cunning expression of her very young and very slender rival; the calmness of the butch one, well past forty, with her short hair, a cigarette in her mouth, cool, intelligent and oh-so-reasonable! Ira shivered. Over and over she had witnessed such a scene, and she knew how it would end. Diamonds, hearts and clubs, reproaches, sneers and sobs. The inevitable flight of the loser, while the new girl, pretending to be unaffected, moved in and over.

She would have her victim in a few minutes.

Her machine roared as it leapt back to life. People jumped. Startled boys shouted angry insults or propositioned her. But Ira was already on the far side of the street, taking station beside the other pavement. It was time to start stalking her prey. From a distance she kept watch on her quarry, her betraying movements, her gesture that grew more and more jerky, her bowed shoulders, her arms crossing on her chest as though to protect her against a violent blow.

At last the girl jumped up and ran into the road. Prepared for the event, Ira had already moved gently away. For once her accomplice the motorcycle made no noise. Together they closed on the blonde shadow crossing the street, heedless of what went on around her. At the last moment the machine bucked to avoid hitting the miserable girl, who uttered a cry. Ira caught her by the arm, held on to her, saved her from crumpling to the ground. Lifting her up, she supported her with one strong hand while with the other she raised her visor and revealed herself: smiling, beautiful, her red hair cut like a boy's, her green eyes shining firefly-bright against her pale skin: beautiful, calm, reassuring.

Neither spoke. Ira pressed the weeping girl against the warm, purring motor, then gently stroked her head as though to soothe a great sorrow. She rocked her thus for a few moments, brushing her fingers over her soft and satiny flesh; then she firmly ensconced this stray kitten on the long one-piece saddle. The girl complied like a helpless child. As soon as she was seated she huddled against her rescuer, drawing comfort from the warm contact between them.

The motorcycle seemed to be taking wing as it bore away the girl and her misery. Closing her eyes, she forgot the despair which had beset her when she saw her lover smile at her new partner. She forgot her rival's dark eyes, her teenage figure. Little by little she forgot all her troubles. They were borne off by the wind which tousled her hair and smacked it against her cheeks, salty with drying tears. She pressed even closer against the body of her new companion, to keep warm. She did not smile—not yet. But her memories of the evening grew fainter and fainter, drowned out by the throbbing purr of the engine, which had settled to a relaxed cruising speed.

She let herself be carried along, steered, directed, just as she had done all her life, relying on the strength of someone else, yielding up her life with no more resistance than a boat caught in a westerly gale and sinking before she has time to react. Intoxicated by their speed, dazzled by occasional lights, she felt herself drifting. With a very slight shift of her hips the rider brought her rounded bottom closer to her belly; she hollowed it to make a snugger fit. The thrumming of the machine surged back and forth in the very depths of her body. She began to regain normal physical awareness; she grew aware that the lips of her cunt were crushed against the black leather, that it was hot and moist under her slinky silk dress. She pressed her thighs tight on the slippery surface of the saddle, making them clasp its supple cover with a sigh of pleasure. The machine and its woman were carrying her away on a wild ride to nowhere. But she was not afraid.

Well, not really . . .

Really not? But she had a strange feeling. There was a prickling at her nape, shivers were running down her spine, her heart was in her mouth. Why had her belly suddenly tightened so, leaving a gap between her and the rider's back to be filled at once by a blast of icy air? Why this terrible giddiness? Suddenly she wanted everything to stop. She felt sick, as though she were riding one of the switchbacks of her childhood, before the war. She felt sick—sick—she wanted to throw up. Because of that dreadful parting—because of her misery, her anguish, all these curves, the way the machine leaned into the bends. But how could she warn the girl who was driving? It was useless to whisper in her ear, and just as useless to shout. Now the motorcycle was moving far too fast. Walls rushed by on either side, walls of light or of solid concrete, threatening walls, forming an alley that grew ever smoother and more featureless, with no way out.

185

Now she really began to be afraid, and with numb fingers tried to pinch, to bruise the strange woman to make her understand that everything was going wrong and she must stop. But there was no response; she was too well protected by her jacket to notice her passenger's frantic signals.

Accordingly she tried to take her hands from around the unknown's waist, but at this speed it was no longer possible. She clung on, panic-stricken. The motorbike seemed to have turned into a cannonball which nothing could stop, short of a wall of steel. She was terrified by the idea. That was what was bound to happen if this madwoman didn't slow down, if she did not at once get off this deadly projectile. But how? The driver seemed so intoxicated by the run that she might as well have forgotten she had company.

But she was wrong. True enough, Ira was relishing her onward rush, the speed, the power of her mount, but above all she relished the fear which little by little was invading every fibre of the young woman hugging her waist. She felt her body tauten with anguish, slacken with terror, yield to despair. She was aware of it all, because her passenger was flattening herself against her, against the machine, and all her feelings and all her agony were conveyed and amplified by the shaking and quivering of the motorcycle.

Lust seized her again, crescent in the hollow of her loins. But her victim was not yet ready. She accelerated faster still, pretending not to notice her terror which nonetheless came through to her in ever-increasing waves. Delight too mounted within her, mounted in precise proportion to the tightness with which the girl clung to her, mindlessly. The blood of her trophy was growing chill. By now she no longer knew how to attract the attention of her kidnapper.

The sickle tilted from side to side more and more often, whirling its two riders into a demonic maelstrom. It leaned over as though from now on there would be no more roads, as though they would turn and turn for ever, almost horizontally, on a wall of death. The girl had no idea where she was. She no longer saw, no longer felt anything save her anguish and the wind. Chilled to the bone, she endured in an unreal maze of dark and terrifying colours, the shades of cold and fear. Unable to endure her plight any longer, she sought in vain to utter a few words to comfort herself, to speak at least so she might hear her own voice and make herself believe she still existed. But the sounds would not pass the threshold of her lips.

Ira could guess that a scream was burgeoning in the chest which swelled to emit it—and suddenly it came, louder and louder and louder. Taken aback by its violence, shaken by the madness which was exploding in the misty brain of their passenger, rider and machine straightened up a little, but without slowing.

The girl kept on screaming for a long time, no longer capable of judging how much time was passing, nor how many kilometres they had covered. The dance went on. Pressed close, both tight against the motorcycle, one of them showed the face of a woman about to come, the other of a woman about to die in agony. One was tormented by overwhelming desire, the other by now was almost resigned to her pain and terror. Little by little the screaming became fainter, mingled with the noise of the motor, turned into a gentle moaning, much like the sound of a newborn child rocking itself to sleep by humming, always the same tune, always in the same key.

That wearied the red-haired Amazon, who was leading the dance. But once again lust rose within her, commandingly. It was more than simple desire which possessed her. It was a need.

The motorcycle slowed, sputtered, as though it too were tired. It seemed to gasp for breath as it used up its last reserve of fuel. Time to sound the mort. Ira too was worn out by the rush through the night, by the pleasure she had taken when she came, and by lack of food. Both of them needed a respite. Soon it would be time for the false dawn. They had travelled all night.

Letting go of the handlebars, Ira let the machine carry on by itself and drew off her black leather gauntlets. The girl behind noticed nothing. She was wiped out and could not react to this further recklessness. She was still lulling herself to the near-African beat of her rhythmical refrain.

A cruel smile turned up the lips of the red-haired she-wolf. Unfastening her jacket, she exposed her bosom; it was milky-pale, dotted with freckles, as though it had never seen the sun, had always been wrapped in leather. It was as pallid as the morning twilight, or as a corpse bled dry. It looked almost diseased.

Slowly she tucked her gloves in the hollow of her breasts, then eased free her companion's hands from their death-grip around her waist. She was obliged to pry them loose, first from each other, then from her belly.

With vast gentleness she took one soft white wrist, pearly, alive, silk-smooth, turned it palm up and bore its unprotected surface to her lips. Blue veins pulsed beneath the near-transparent skin. Deferentially Ira ran her moist mouth over the cool hand, up the length of the arm, down again. The young woman let herself be kissed without resisting. Ira inhaled the scent of this slender blonde. It filled her nostrils, it affected her like too deep a toke of grass. Her head spun. She could control herself no longer.

The sickle uttered a pitiable choking sound.

"There, there!" Ira murmured, speaking for the first time. She straightened from the hips, thus releasing herself from the other body still clinging at her back. Feeling her support suddenly removed, the girl desperately tried to regain contact, and warmth. She slithered close again across the saddle. Ira moved her hips further forward. The girl groaned, but followed her, matching the slightest of her movements. The motorbike, which had slowed down, nonetheless kept on rolling, level and dead steady, and without a sound.

Aroused, the girl stopped humming, fascinated by the lack of noise, by the perfect silence of the engine. Everything stood still; then there came a squeaking, and a sliding, and slowly, slowly, she felt a hard, cold, metallic object pressing against the lips of her bare cunt, parting them against her will, entering her carefully and gently, but irresistibly. This—what was it?—this piston, as it were, began to quiver, to vibrate, to make her moisten. Suddenly running wet, astonished by what she was feeling, she dared not move—dared not so much as think. She was too shocked. Lust she did not comprehend arose in her, climaxing in a fireball of heartbreak which expanded and expanded until a final outburst made her entire body feel as though it was exploding, along with her consciousness, in a brief and brutal howl of orgasm.

Whereupon, like a river of rubies, the lovely nourishing liquid flowed down into the complex works of the motorcycle, pouring over every part and portion; then, once it had spread over every bit and bolt, the red blood seeped up towards the black leather saddle and was greedily absorbed by the body of Ira, the beautiful Amazon who was inseparable from her bike. They were two unnatural beings that made a monstrous whole: in fact, a machine invented because of and to meet the needs of the war.

Gorged with its fuel again, the sickle bucked under the vigorous grasp of the rider who was also its Siamese twin. The movement dislodged a limp puppet which flew through the air to land on the asphalt with its arms outstretched, making a cross.

Without even glancing at it, fiery-eyed, Ira—the vamp, Ira—leapt onward like a demon, bound for another of her nighttime haunts.

Margaret Dickson

Can You Still See Me?

MARGARET DICKSON COMES TO US COURTESY OF STEPHEN King, who read this story in his creative writing course at the University of Maine and sent it to me at once. "He's been a good teacher, a meticulous reader of my work, full of encouragement," she says. She had already written poetry for the Maine Review *and the* Maine Times, *and a three-act play that won first prize in a University of Maine contest. As I write, she is working on a novel. She writes copy for a Massachusetts advertising agency. She and her husband have two children.*

Her story, which says a great deal in a few words, can speak for itself.

Mason will tell you now that the dead do not rest no matter how flat you lay the marker to the ground, no matter how dust blows out of the cloud it makes in the air or how far you fling the cup that held the dust. A funeral is the acknowledgement of a physical fact, but the mourners don't believe it. They sit and listen and watch the coffin. How does he breathe, shut in there like that? A door opens or closes in the parlour and the relatives look up once, twice. Whom do they expect? The truth is, Mason will say, that a funeral does no good. When Merle Thompson died, Mason will say, he wasn't finished. No one is finished for ever.

Merle Thompson had a plaid jacket made of wool, black squares and green squares. The right front pocket had torn off the welt, snagged on a nail. His hat was blue with a visor and a grease stain around the bottom, softened with wood dust and grains of gypsum.

Once, home tough and fresh from college, Mason had gone straight to Merle, not to embrace him, but to take his hat off him and use a hatchet on it right in front of his eyes.

Merle had been dumbfounded. "What you want to do that for? What you want to do that for?"

Mason, wiry with the energy and sparkle of this joke he'd been planning for days, separated the hat into neat quarters and laid them out on a sawhorse. But then he looked up and saw the old man's face. It was grey. Mason reached into his back pocket.

"In order to give you this," he said quickly, and handed Merle a new hat, identical to the old one.

Merle had taken the new hat and turned it around and looked inside it.

"I lost you there for a minute," he said. "But your heart's in the right place." Merle did not smile, but he put on the hat and looked Mason over. "Your heart's in the right place, after all. Ain't it."

The old blue eyes, Mason still thought. Looking right through the joke at me.

And then Merle had turned and gone back to work.

He went through his whole life and his pants never fit him. They were baggy and patched at the knees. Doris, who was too fussy to allow the hat and jacket in her house—they stayed on a nail outside in the shop—worried over the pants and washed and mended them and his flannel shirt and the insulated underwear he wore from November to May. On Sundays she made sure Merle wore his respectable black suit. But even those pants rode low on his hips and bulged out around the ankles.

He had a scar at the base of his head from an operation that removed a blood clot. He'd lost one finger on his left hand. Two fingers of his right were permanently bent from what he called "an argument" with a rip saw. He'd had a prostate operation. His skin rumpled down his stomach and when he lay for three months waiting, breathing with a sound like a gurgle under water, he developed bed sores. Mason, who often lifted Merle on to the commode for Doris, thought the sores looked more like bruises on a bottom as innocent-looking as a child's.

Dying, Merle choked. It took him ten minutes.

Doris would say later, "He worked at it, didn't he? On and on."

His choking frightened her so much she left him and ran to the back door and screamed for Mason.

"Mason! Mason! Help me! Help me!"

Mason saw her and climbed off his tractor and raced across his newly manured field. Then he'd stopped at the door long enough to take off his shoes. Also, he was scared. When he went to the bedroom, Merle was struggling, gasping, weeping. Doris wept, too, and kept saying in a tight voice,

"Now, Merle. You're not going to cry. Don't cry. You're not going to cry." Tears streamed down her face. She put one arm under Merle's shoulders. "Help me, Mason!"

Mason went to the bed and lifted Merle.

"Sit him up! Sit him up!" Doris said. "Sometimes it works . . ."

Together they held Merle up. But it didn't work. His body arched and flung them back. The eyes rolled up. The mouth pulled open over the teeth. Then he seemed to fall away from them.

"Now, Merle, Merle." Doris wept and pulled back her hair and tried to lift him again. "Come on now. You're all right."

Mason felt sick. He leaned against the wall.

"I think he's gone," he said.

Doris looked up. Her hair stood up around her head like grey fire. Her mouth stopped quivering. She touched the body lightly with one hand. "There," she said. "Is he?"

"Yes," said Mason, lowering his voice in case Merle should hear them and it would kill him, "I think he is."

Doris laid her hand on Merle's. She watched the body. It was still.

"Yes," she said. "Mason!"

He went to her then and she hung on to him. She seemed too small and old for this.

After a while, Mason patted her shoulder and said, as gently as he could, "Should we cover him?"

Doris looked at Merle.

"We should," she said. "I can't! I can't! Let's call Lin. We'll call Lin."

They left the body and helped each other to the living room. Doris sat in her chair, opposite Merle's chair. Mason went to the phone.

The relatives gathered. There was a funeral. It was a cold spring day and rained hard. Lin Howard, the undertaker, held two black umbrellas, one for the minister, one for himself and the coffin. The service was short; Doris did not believe in what she called "a public display." After everyone left, Lin Howard's assistant dug the hole. Just as if Merle was dead.

Lin Howard, heavy and florid, who sang deep true bass in the church choir, would have said that he buried Merle, or that his helper, Little Mick, had done it. It was Lin who snapped Merle's body into the plastic cover and rolled it out of the house on a stretcher. Then he came back and sorted through Merle's clothes and found his respectable suit, a shirt, a tie. Doris went through the bureau drawers and sorted out some underwear. Lin agreed that he had to have that.

Would they come and view the body?

"No," Doris said, "I don't know if I could. It wasn't pretty, Lin. It was awful. Mason will tell you. It was awful."

Lin looked at Mason. Mason nodded.

"This cosmetic business, Lin," Doris said, "we would know you had done it. It wouldn't really be Merle. Would it?"

Lin looked at the floor.

"Well, it's just as you like." Quiet, his voice was still deep and melodic. "But I'll fix his face up anyway. I always do. I don't charge for it. It's easier that way. You never know. I've been doing this a long time. Somebody has to. Sometimes people don't want to see the body again. Sometimes they do. Sometimes they change their mind between the death and the services. I always fix the faces up. It doesn't hurt. Sometimes I'm glad I did. You want to come see him, you call me. He'll be ready tomorrow."

Lin Howard fixed up Merle's face and he was glad because the next afternoon Mason called him and made an appointment to come in with Doris and Mason's wife Nancy, Merle's daughter. They did come. Lin had fixed a peaceful look on the corpse's face. He left them there, but on the way out Doris came to find him.

"It's better, Lin," she said. "Thank you."

The minister's wife, who got to the corpse even before Lin, had gone in to wash Merle, knowing that Doris would want him to go clean. But she looked Merle over and came out saying that Doris had kept Merle so beautifully there was nothing for her to do. On her way out of the house, she smiled and nodded to Lin who had just driven up. She was a practical, not a theological, woman. But she felt that death, which she saw often and did not fear except for herself, was an instance in which nothing could make something. Of course, if anyone asked her, she would say, in her practical way, "It's over. He's in there with Lin. Doris kept him immaculate." But she did not keep from smiling.

By the third day after the funeral, the relatives have been and sorted out all Merle's personal belongings. At Doris's request, they have taken them out of the house. When she has slept one night at Nancy's without a sedative, Doris moves back to her own home. It's important to her to do it alone. The room where Merle was is now completely empty. To oblige her, the relatives have even removed the hospital bed and apparatus. Old bills, letters, records—all have been sorted. Clothes are gone.

"After all," she says to herself, "what need does he have of them?"

Alone in her house, she nerves herself and goes into the empty room. The tiny dishes are gone, the ones too large to hold what he would eat. She opens a closet door. Everything is empty, even the coffee cans that held his wool socks rolled with mothballs. The windows have been opened, there is no smell.

Perhaps, she thinks, I could do something in here. A guest room? No. Not yet. From the window she can see the door of the shop. But Merle's jacket and hat are not there. They took everything, she thinks. Was I right to tell them to? I'd like to see his jacket there. It would remind me that he's not out on a job . . .

Where is he? Where is he? Nowhere. She shuts the bedroom window. The slate, she tells herself, is clean.

She moves out of the room and closes the door. She is alone. Almost to prove it, she begins to hike up her dress on the way to the bathroom. Holding it with her elbows, she opens the bathroom door. She starts in, stops on the threshold, screams a little to herself although she knows it's silly to scream, comes out, shuts the bathroom door.

Later she tells Nancy, "There's a snake. A big old black snake, coming out of the register. I know it's silly, but I saw it. Could you come?"

Mason and Nancy both go down with her and go all through the house. They find nothing. Mason closes the register. Nancy smiles a little on the way home.

But Mason is not immune either. At night, the snake bothers him. Merle bothers him. He waits for what he was told would happen, but it is too soon.

"Does it hurt you?" he'd asked.

"Yes," she'd said. "It hurts."

"Then why do you have them?" He didn't know any better.

"You forget," his mother said. "By the time the baby smiles, you've forgotten."

"But you yell when it hurts?"

"I yell like crazy. And when it's over I forget it. That's the way our minds work, Mason."

But Merle is still there.

Sitting up at night, Mason thinks he is a little boy again, playing in Merle's living room. He would have liked to live there, if he could. He and Nancy line blocks up across the living room in a long, black train. Each block smells of the dark oil Merle has rubbed it with. The smell stays on the fingers. Merle stands outside the window and peeks in at them and grins. Mason and Nancy love it.

Then Mason thinks that he and Nancy are newlyweds and Merle has built them a house and knows where their bedroom is and forgets they're grown up. He comes across the lawn, leaving a wavy track in the dark grass. He thinks they are still children, sleepyheads late getting up. He comes to the bedroom window and stands outside it and grins and does not think and presses his nose to the glass and waves at them.

Nancy and Mason look up quickly from where they are lying, naked, on the bed. Nancy reaches for the covers and cries towards the old man,

"Go 'way! Go 'way!"

Merle looks horrified and is too ashamed to go near them for days afterwards. Eventually Mason and Nancy catch up with him and they all apologize.

"I should have thought," Merle keeps saying. "I should have thought."

Nancy's voice comes to Mason now, as if he's hearing it through Merle's own ears and it hurts. A low-pitched, ragged sound. It coils in Mason, but he is helpless. What can straighten things out now?

The next day, Doris calls them again.

"Our friend is back," she says to Mason.

"Oh?" He smiles, but something inside him plummets.

"I don't know how he gets in here," Doris says. Her voice is shaky. "This time I was getting up from my nap, and there he was, hanging from the ceiling fan. Could you come and look?"

Nancy and Mason both go. Mason cleans out the fan and closes it off. He checks the bathroom register. There is nothing. But Doris is trembling.

"It's getting so I don't dare move," she says.

"Mother, come home with us. Please," Nancy begs. "You don't need to be alone."

"No!" Doris says. "This is my house! I am going to live in my house. I told Merle . . ." But the formula that worked does not work. "A little old snake," she says quietly. "Haven't had a chance to be lonely yet. You go home."

Mason sits in his living room and does not sleep. Nancy has gone to bed. He thinks he can hear her breathing. He watches the air. There is something about the spaces around the furniture. His eyes strain looking into them.

Merle Thompson is not dead. He appears. He has the face Lin gave him, smooth, younger. Merle's eyes are open. The forehead has slipped somewhat towards the chin, but the eyes are there and it is Merle. He is wearing his respectable black suit.

"Merle!" says Mason.

The fallen forehead nods.

"Is it you?" Mason cannot move.

"Are you afraid of me?" It is Merle's voice.

"Afraid of you! Merle, I . . ." Mason looks at him carefully. "Merle? Have you begun to decay?"

Merle holds out his hands. They are black, round. The fists have begun to sink into the palms.

"It doesn't matter, Merle!" Mason says. "It doesn't matter! You're here! You're alive! Don't you care about the hands, Merle! I don't care about them!"

Merle's hands come closer. The round black hole in the circle of the fingers is like the hole on a swan's beak. No. That is not it, Mason thinks. They're more like diamonds, black diamonds. He looks into the holes for a moment and then pulls himself back.

"Merle? Can you stay? I'd give anything if you could!" Tears sting Mason's eyes. "Or as you were, Merle! I miss you! Trade hats with me, remember? And make faces! Come to any window you want, Merle, I don't care! You knew what I was. It wouldn't matter! Any window! Any window!"

Merle shakes his head. "Can't do that, Mason." It is not the air or the sound of breathing, but Merle's voice. "Can't do that."

Merle's blue eyes blink. Or do they have colour, so near the sides of his face? The arms move close to the body. Merle's knees buckle, he floats, sinks.

"Merle?" Mason cries, half-rising from his chair, "wait!" But is there anything, a snake, anything, on the floor, in the fan, at the register, anywhere? "Merle, where are you? Are you still there?"

Yes. It is Merle's voice that drifts to him from the spaces.

"Can you still see me?" Merle asks. "Can you still see me?"

Felice Picano

One Way Out

FELICE PICANO WAS BORN IN 1944, AND STILL LIVES IN New York. He graduated with honors from New York City University in 1964, and off he went to be (briefly) a teacher, a social worker, a graphic arts magazine editor, a Rizzoli bookstore manager. Most of the time, he says, he was a layabout and sixties hippie type. In photographs he looks mournfully pensive and bearded. He writes charmingly formal letters.

His novels include Smart as the Devil, Eyes (which has nothing at all to do with the film Eyes of Laura Mars, despite what the film poster would have you think), The Mesmerist, and Lure. There is also a book of poetry, The Deformity Lover. It's an impressively varied bibliography, and one never knows what to expect from Picano, as you will see.

Bay threw down the apple core and stomped it into the soft loam until only a little mound of dirt was left. The bells from a distant steeple—the highest point of a tiny village nestled in the New England hills—were just striking twelve. It was Sunday. That would mean even less traffic than usual, less chance of truckers and easy pick-ups, especially as this wasn't a highway, only a double lane country tar road.

He tightened the straps of the knapsack over his shoulders and loped off the ridge down on to the road. He tried to adjust his mind and body for a long afternoon walk, trying to stay off the frayed edge of the road and on the dirt as much as possible, to make the walking easier on his feet.

After ten minutes or so, he still hadn't seen a car. Everyone must be at home, having dinner. The dark grey of the road shot away from under his feet down a long incline, rising up to another ridge half a mile away where it hid from sight, then rose straight up to another ridge, rising and dipping, again and again into the spine of hills—like a ribbon grabbed by the wind.

Bay was just bracing his legs for the long incline when a rush of air and force slashed past him. Swop, swop it went, knocking him to the ground amid a flurry of dust and small pebbles.

Whatever it was, had been too fast for him to catch sight of it. He picked himself up, brushed off his denims, looked back in the direction he had come from, muttered a few curses, then started off again. Then he noticed something.

Ahead, like mechanical insects rapidly climbing down a wall, were two small, very fast vehicles, moving towards him down the ribbon of road. They fell out of sight for a second behind a ridge, and as they did so, two identical vehicles appeared at the top of the road, beginning the drop down.

They were going so fast that as he refocused from one pair to another, they seemed to change places. Then he saw the effect was caused by a third pair of identical vehicles which had now appeared at the top of the ridge.

They flashed so much in the noontime sun, that Bay could scarcely see them coming at him. He could make out that they were low, squarish and painted a metallic green. But what was so odd after seeing no cars at all, was that these seemed so regular—each one side by side, covering both lanes of the road, the second and third pairs exactly as far away from each other, as if in formation. Bay was reminded of a slot-car set he had once played with as a child.

Then the first pair were up to him. Then passing him. As they went, they made the same sound: swop, swop.

That left no doubts. An earlier pair must have knocked him down. This time he was braced; even so, he could barely stay on his feet in the dust and blast of their passing. He followed their squat retreating figures down the road, only a double blur now in all the dust they lifted, following them like little cyclones.

He couldn't help feeling there was something odd about the vehicles. He braced himself against an overhanging shelf of rock, and shaded his eyes, trying to catch a better look at the next pair as they passed. When they did, he was even more unnerved.

They were unlike any vehicles he had ever seen. Low flat boxes, angled towards some indefinite apex three-quarters of their length. No lights. No chromium decoration of any sort. And no glass—and therefore no way to see inside them, if they had an inside. He had thought they were painted a metallic green, and that was the closest he could come in describing their colour and material to himself, but it wasn't metal, and it wasn't green. It was both more and less than that. An unknown substance refracting light in a way he had never seen any material do, and a colour that seemed to absorb as much light as it reflected. Worst of all, as the vehicles had lifted over the ridge of road, they had lifted off the ground—going approximately 150 miles per hour any vehicle would have—and they had no wheels!

Bay was thinking whether he had noticed any military base in the area—on the filling station map he had carried with him. None. Could this be a testing ground for an automobile company? Might they be experimental cars of some sort?

The last pair finally shot past him, interrupting his thoughts, and making that dull, swop, swop sound again. He turned to see if any more were coming. None. Then he turned to watch the last pair speed off, and was amazed to see they were slowing down, and then almost stopping before quickly swerving off the road on to a pasture very close to the ridge where he had spent the night.

All the curiosity and vague discomfort he had felt came to a head. He had to see what these vehicles were. He turned around and ran after the last two.

It was only a few minutes back to the craggy ridge he had left so shortly before, overhanging the open meadows. But in the short while, the occupants of the vehicle had got out and had transformed the area.

What had been a dry grass pasture, now seemed to be a cleared area of some hundred feet in radius. Dark-clothed, helmeted figures moved about stiffly, but quickly, carrying strange tools. Two of them went into the open backs of the vehicles parked at the circle's edge.

Two other figures were setting up a hollow-looking platform exactly in the centre of the circle. From a long-snouted tool one of them held, a pressurized liquid shot out on to the ground and hardened into a concrete-like substance almost the instant it touched the dirt.

As they worked, the first pair edged a canister-like object out of the vehicle and on to the ground. Although Bay was concentrating on the object and the figures, he could see the insides of the vehicle were artificially lighted—half pink, half yellow.

The canister must have been extremely heavy or very fragile, as the figures carrying it moved very slowly, in exaggerated mechanically dainty steps. At length they got the canister into the centre of the cleared circle, and sunk it slowly into the cement material. Another shower from the spray instrument covered the canister completely.

The four figures retreated to beyond the edge of the circle, then one of them pulled a little hand-sized cartridge out of a deep pocket in his suit, adjusted one or two buttons on it, and the trod-down grass began springing up again in the clearing, so quickly and so completely that even from his bird's eye view, Bay could scarcely make out the exact location of the platform and the sunken canister.

Then the figures were inside the vehicles. The doors closed with two gurgling pneumatic slaps, the vehicles spun around as if on invisible axes, and were tearing down the main road in the wake of their companion vehicles as quickly as they had come.

The entire operation had taken perhaps ten minutes. All of it had been hidden from the road by the ridge of rock where Bay had watched them; even if there had been a traffic jam on the road to see it, no one would have noticed. And where the canister had been sunk, it now looked like nothing at all had happened.

That was when Bay started feeling a tingling along the back of his neck. He had had the feeling once or twice before in his life. Once when he was being followed down the dark, deserted streets of a Midwestern city, another time when he had heard prowling, heavy steps outside a tent he had pitched in the Rocky Mountains. Both times before it had meant danger, and now he knew it meant whatever was in that canister was about to go off, and go off big. Without stopping to ask why or how, Bay knew something momentous had been sunk in that meadow. He had to get away fast, now!

He almost stumbled running down the ridge on to the roadway when he remembered he had taken off his knapsack and left it on the rock. Leave it! Go! he thought. Then: No! I have to have it! I have to get away fast! In a car! That thing's going to go off any minute now. I need a car to get away from it. The knapsack will get me a ride.

He was still tying on the knapsack when he reached the road again. No cars. He started to walk as fast as he could, following the direction he had started towards earlier.

Why this way? This is where the vehicles came from. They might have laid a whole chain of these things. They might even be laying more at this moment, behind him. He had to go north. North.

There had to be a northern crossover ahead. He had to get to it. But first he needed a lift. Still no cars. Damn. He felt a little calmer now as he strode along the road, knowing he had a direction now, a way of escape. The thin hot trickle was still burning a network into the back of his neck and his shoulders, and he was beginning to feel a sharp little pain in his side from his exertion. He was sure the first was adrenalin rising, and the extrasensory fear of whatever was going to happen.

If it was? Just supposing it was what he thought it was, what could its radius be? Two miles? Five? What had been the radius of the last nuclear test? Five miles? Ten? Or was that only the radius of total destruction? And if so, what was the radius of the fire storms? Another five, another ten?

He turned to look behind him. No cars. As he turned back, one coming towards him passed by—but it sped on, and he scarcely had the chance to flag it down he was walking so hard, straining to keep up and yet stay in control, to keep himself from running ahead blindly, breaking out totally. No. He had to stay in control. To let go meant to invite the end. Survival lay only in holding on. Holding on.

And still the burning of his nerve ends. It seemed stronger the further he got away from the canister. And still no cars.

Then there was one, behind him. Dark and sleek, coming up to him. Bay almost fell, as he stumbled to a stop, and thrust his arm out dangerously over the edge of the road.

The driver made a great show of screeching to a halt, braking so fiercely that half the car was under Bay's outstretched hand when it came to a full stop.

He ducked down to open the door.

"Haven't asked you yet?" a voice said.

Bay stopped. Oh God, no! Not a joker! Not now!

"Sorry," Bay said. "C'n I have a lift?"

"Sure."

Bay got in, closed the door. The man faced ahead. Nothing but profile.

"Where you headed?"

"North," Bay said with a determination that surprised him.

"This way's west."

"There's a crossover a few miles up. I'll get off there."

"No need to. I'm going north there."

Bay was still undoing his shoulder straps as the car took off.

Finally the knapsack was loose and he swung it on to the floor and sat back, watching the v-shaped hood lap up the dark road.

"Nice car," he said absently.

"It's all right."

Thank God he's not in the mood for company, Bay thought. Imagine having a conversation about the weather now. Not now. It might slow him down. Just drive.

"You seemed to be in a big hurry there," the driver said, "almost as if you were running away from something."

203

Did he know? Was he connected with the vehicles? Was he a scout, a clean-up man, to get rid of any possible witnesses?

Bay said nothing.

"Of course," the driver went on, "there's nothing there to run away from. Is there? Just a coupla nothing farms." He laughed, and Bay looked at the driver. His own age. Good looking in a slick way, like the car. Heavy straight dark hair. Moustache, beard. Sultry lids over dark eyes. Tanned. Spoiled looking. But otherwise all right. Like a hundred others.

"Nothing farms and a coupla cows. Eh?" And he laughed again.

Even if he didn't know anything about the canister, he still might be a little off. Christ! Just what I need, a loony.

Before Bay knew it, they had come to the crossroad and the driver flicked the wheel and spun across the other lane right on to the crossroad.

"No!" Bay shouted. "That's wrong! We're going south!" He almost jumped out of his seat.

"What?" the driver said, and cupped one hand to his ear, as if he were hard of hearing. Bay began frantically repeating that they were going the wrong way. But the car was already in a sharp U-turn, then across the crossroad of the east-west road.

"A little nervous?" the driver asked.

"Yeah," Bay mumbled, collapsing into the bucket seat. But he felt no relief. This guy was a joker. And who knew, maybe insane too. And the burning fear from the knowledge that he was still within range of the canister was getting worse, pricking every nerve of his skin.

How in hell had he got into such a situation?

All he knew was that he was hitching east. Yesterday he had got a ride out of Albany, and into Kingston. There, he had eaten a hamburger and malt shake at a roadside Friendly's, had been picked up by a sharp-faced woman and her two silent children, had driven through the Berkshires, been dropped off in a small town called South Egremont, had been picked up by a truckdriver, and finally had allowed himself to be dropped off where he had spent the night. And before yesterday he had travelled. Hitch-hiked.

Through mountains, plains, cities, deserts—all of it blurred and vague now, unimportant, unreal.

He was certain it would go off soon. Why and who had done it were no longer questions. But he knew that being there and seeing it sunk into the ground had connected him to it, and that he carried the knowledge of it like a time bomb running out of time.

"How far do you think we are?" Bay asked.

"From where?" Suspicious.

"Oh, I don't know. From Boston? How about from where you picked me up?"

"About three hundred from Boston. Sixteen and a half from where I picked you up," he tapped a dial sunken into the leather plush of the dashboard, "according to the odometer here."

"That's all?"

"That's pretty good time," sounding offended. "That's about sixty-five an hour."

"Can't you go any faster?" Bay asked.

"I'm in no hurry."

"The speedometer goes up to 140. Or is that just numbers?"

"It'll do that. These roads are lousy. You want me to rip the underside up, just so you can joyride?" Already the speedometer had tilted up to seventy mph.

"Car like this was probably built to cruise at 120," Bay said, very wise-guy. Seventy-five now.

"I usually cruise around 100. On good roads." The speedometer tilted 80 mph.

"I was told that if you don't open them up every once in a while, the oil lines clog up." 85 mph now.

"Of course that could be be talk, too," Bay added.

90 mph. Then 95 mph. The car seemed to be slipping along the road. It was taking the dips so fast it was getting Bay queasy. The landscape was shooting by, trees going flick, flick, flick so fast they bunched and blurred. A stream alongside the road snapped and jerked past like kids shaking a dark rope along the ground playing snake.

100 mph.

And Bay's nerves were on fire. He could hardly keep still in his seat with the twitching. Soon. Soon. Any minute now. He had to get away. Out of the car. Soon. Soon. Throw himself clear. Or get the guy to stop and find cover. But where? Where?

There! In the stream. In the water. The water would protect him, keep him from being badly burned. Now. Now.

"Stop! Stop! I get off here. I get off here!"

"What?" The car sped on.

"Stop! Stop. Now!"

"You're crazy. There's nothing here!"

"Stop! Stop." Bay rose in his seat, opening the window.

"Sit down! You'll get killed!"

The car swerved into a stop like a slingshot twanging.

Before it was stopped, Bay felt an agony all over his body. He threw the door open, ran to the side of the road and fell to his knees beside the stream. He thrust a hand into its brackish murk, up to his elbow. It would have to do.

Behind him, he heard the driver muttering and closing the car door.

Grabbing up two hollow onion-bulb stalks, he broke them off at both edges, and put one open end of each in his mouth. He breathed in one, out the other, then slid into the stream face sideways, hearing the rev of the car as it sped off.

The tubes worked. The minute he felt the cool sludge around him, he was calm. Then he twitched all over once, from head to toe, from every nerve and muscle and cell of his body, and was blinded by a whiteness of light that surpassed any white he had ever known, went into depths and subtleties of sheer white light, grasping at the edge of every inch of him and totally enveloping him. It grew, increased, and as it did the sludge around him grew tepid, then warm, then very warm. And still the white blared on, even whiter, like a thousand brass instruments, white and soundless. The sludge was receding from his head, and the reeds in his mouth were hot and useless, and he couldn't breathe the hot air through them anyway, so he dropped them, and turned over on to his face, filling his lungs with air from dark oxidizing pockets of dank around his face, while the universe went white white white.

Then orange, then red, then dark, then a vague, flickering colour.

But the twitching was over. And the pain. And the fear. His hair no longer felt on fire. The sludge stopped bubbling around him. It was dried, encrusted on his head and hands and clothing.

Cautiously he rolled over. Cautiously he breathed a little. It was warm still. Acrid, with the smell of burning. But breathable. He took more breaths. They hurt his nasal cavities and throat, and he swallowed once or twice. Better. Then he sat up, and flicked the crusted dirt off his fingertips, then delicately picked the dried crust off his eyelids.

The sky was pink. Not quite: purple and orange and pink. All around him, the countryside was in sudden blackened desolation. Ahead, a grove of pines burned like a huge torch. In the distance, across flat charred fields, firs shot sparks from a ridge of hills. The air was still hot. But the worst was over.

Shakily, he reached his feet and got up, then fell weakly to his knees, and retched, vomiting chunks of his breakfast into the thick, cracked bed of what once had been a stream. He immediately felt lighter, and stronger. He wiped his mouth with the damp underside of his sleeve, then stood up again, and lumbered forward along the half-melted, disfigured road.

Everywhere the fires. Then the showers of ashes descending all around him. God knew from what. Like rain. But he was all right. He had got through it.

He walked on, just looking. Then, around a slight bend in the road, and through burnt trunks of trees, he saw the dull metal shine of a car. It was stopped dead in the middle of the road, as if its driver had just stopped a minute to go for a leak on the side of the road and would be back any time.

As he came closer to it, Bay saw there was no glass.

Even closer, most of the outside of the car—sheet metal, bumpers, fenders, roof—seemed intact, but as if heated and pounded in by a hundred thousand tiny hammers. Then he saw that it was the same car that had picked him up before, and he made out the back of the man's head, erect, sunk into the backrest.

And, if it weren't for the millions of gently trembling shards of glass splinters covering his head like a delicate lace helmet, and the red trickles staining their edges, the driver would have looked as if he were alive—just staring ahead, a little bit surprised.

Even the seats and floor and dashboard were rimed with glass shards. But the dashboard dials were still on, and the motor was still idling in neutral. The driver must have been suddenly blinded by the light, and by reflex stopped the car. And then the glass hit him and who knew, but probably the fire too that had seared all the leather inside the car and his skin and flesh too, until they were all the same mottled half brown, half bright pink.

Bay opened the car door, swept a drift of glass shreds off the metal with his foot, then gently pulled at the corpse's back, until the body fell over. Another push and it was out on the road. The burn smell was stronger now. Awful.

He swept off the front seat, reached into the glove compartment where he found a piece of chamois to wrap around the still hot, half-fused steering wheel. There were still a few remaining dangerous-looking pieces of glass left in the windshield and side vents. He knocked them out.

When he was ready, Bay sat in the driver's seat for a minute wondering that instinct was not telling him what to do next.

"I'll go north," he said aloud. "North."

He switched into first gear. The car whined, then leapt forward.

An hour later, he ran out of gas.

He had been surprised and even a little alarmed that there were so few cars on the road. Where had everyone gone to? Were they all dead? In hiding? Or what? The further away he drove, the less there seemed to be any damage, even any signs of what had happened. But everything seemed abandoned. Everything meaning the few clapboard dinettes and gas stations he had passed. If he had only thought to stop and get some gas.

He left the car on the shoulder of the road, and began walking, again north—always north. Every once in a while, Bay would turn around and look behind him, seeing the sky still pink, with clouds of ashes falling in the distance, and one particular area to the southeast—could it be Boston?—bright red and orange, as if the air were consumed by flames.

He reached a large clapboard house off the side of the road, behind a wickerwork fence and gate. Several sedans and a pickup truck were parked on the grassy side lawn. There must be someone inside. They might have some gasoline. Or even be able to drive him to the next gas station.

Aside from blown-in windows, the house didn't seem at all damaged. The front door was swinging open. Bay called "hello" and when he had got no response, walked in.

The place seemed deserted. The kitchen had been in use—food was half cooked in pots on the big double stoves; two cups of coffee were set out on the table. Bay called out again, still got no answer, and half absently picked up one cup of coffee.

Was it all right to drink it? Would it be radioactive?

He went to the sink instead—an old-fashioned pump and basin—and pumped out a glass of water. It was cool, slightly minerally, but good. He had another glassful.

Was that a noise behind the door? Voices? Or one voice, droning on and on?

"Hello," he called out to whoever would be on the other side of the door. "Is anyone there. My car ran out of gas down the road."

No answer. But the droning seemed to go on.

Bay went to the door and tried it. Open. He carefully turned the knob and half stepped aside, not knowing what to expect.

A steep, well-lighted stairway, leading up.

As he ascended, the hard, cracked old voice he'd first heard became clearer. Bay thought he made out the words "And behold, there came up out of the river seven well favoured kine," followed by a pause, and what seemed to be the shuffling of several pairs of shoes on bare wood.

At the top of the stairs he was in a long corridor with several closed doors and on the floor, a worn, multi-coloured knitted oval rug, looking like a faded rainbow.

One door was ajar. Behind it the old voice took up again. Bay approached and slowly pushed the door open enough to see in.

His first impression was a room filled with people: men, women, children, old folks, all sitting or standing behind chairs, leaning against the side and back walls, all of them facing a corner of the room where because of the angle of the wall, all Bay could make out was the shadowed figure of an elderly man. Bay stepped into the room quietly. The old man was still in obscurity, although now Bay could make out a dark leather bound, frayed edge book, open on a lectern in front of him, out in full view.

"So Pharaoh slept and dreamed a second time," the old voice repeated, tonelessly. Neither the reader nor anyone else in the room turned to look at the doorway, at Bay.

The old man paused again, and there was a murmur from the group assembled. One little boy no longer able to hold back his curiosity, peeked out at Bay from behind a woman's shoulder. As Bay noticed him, the boy darted back into hiding, then timidly edged back into sight.

Half of the child's pale blond hair was gone, the remaining scalp a purple splotch with large brown blisters and smaller broken pus pink sores, as though he'd been raked from the crown of his head down over the closed congealed eye and reddened-black chin with an acetylene torch. It took Bay a great effort to look away from the boy, and to fix his sight on the worn natural grain of the wood floor.

"And behold, seven ears of corn came upon one stalk," the old man read on, "fat and good."

Everyone murmured their approval. Bay looked up at the boy again. He was hidden again by the bulk of the woman, his mother?, who turned out of profile towards Bay. She too was burned and mispigmented, as though a swathe of intense fire had been whipped across her face and breast.

Bay backed up against the door, holding tightly to the dry wooden moulding behind him, spreading his feet apart for support, as he surveyed the others in the room.

Everyone else was blasted, discoloured, bleeding, suppurating.

"And behold, seven thin ears and blasted with the east wind sprung up after them," the old man intoned, his voice as dry as the planking that Bay gripped so hard it was flaking into his fingernails.

A woman closest to Bay, her arms crossed over her cotton print housedress, turned to him as though first seeing him. Purple splotches mantled all but a tiny triangle of her face. Her lips were charred lines. Her teeth almost glowed green as she smiled. Only a few clumps of glossy auburn hair were still held in place by her blackened hairband.

Bay had to look down at the floor again, but he also couldn't stop himself from looking up again, now at one, then at another listener, all of them quietly, attentively listening to the old man's reading, monstrously ignoring what had happened to them.

"And the seven thin ears devoured the seven fat and full ones."

The people were animated by these words, moving about, gesturing, revealing new facets of their horror. One scabrous-faced man with only a projecting bone of nose leaned over to whisper into the blasted shell of what should have been another's ear.

Bay shut his eyes, then, held on to the door, the floor, for what seemed a long time, fighting down what was in front of him, declaring that he wouldn't open his eyes again.

He was out in the corridor again.

"And it came to pass in the morning, that Pharaoh's spirit was greatly troubled."

Bay shut the door, held it shut, knowing that they would jump up from their chairs and smash it open on him. His skin felt like every pore was bursting with poisonous filth and infection.

When nothing happened, and the voice went on behind the door, Bay leapt down the stairs, stumbling over his own feet to get down, almost tearing the open stairway door off its hinges as he careened out, through the house on to the roadway, running.

When he stopped running, his body aching with the sudden exertion, he was far from the house. No one followed him. The house seemed deserted. Ahead, over slightly rolling country, he couldn't see another hamlet in sight. What was the difference, if the people there too would be as mutilated, as unconcerned as this group?

Then he came up to a local delivery bread van parked on the edge of the road. No driver, the key still in the ignition. Had the driver, too, been struck by the blinding glare, burned to the bones of his skull, and staggered off mutilated into the high grass, or even more likely back to that house?

When Bay turned the key on, the tank light on the dashboard showed half full. Ought he siphon it off? Or should he just take the van?

Before he could make up his mind, the ignition was on and he had thrown the clutch. All around him he smelled the fresh bread. He reached for a loaf of pumpernickel, tore the plastic wrapper off and ate three pieces, gulping them down. Then he threw the gear and took off.

He hadn't realized how hungry he had been. He ate the entire loaf, and part of another one, as he drove.

The van couldn't go anywhere near as fast as the car had gone, but it was taking him up north all the same. He couldn't help but think that there were going to be more bombs, more trouble, and that he'd be safe as far north as he could get.

He had reached the deep humps of the Green Mountains when he realized that the buzzing he'd been hearing since he'd got into the van came from the radio. The driver must have left it on when he stopped for a cup of coffee in the old geezer's house.

Bay tried tuning it. For a few minutes all he got was cracking and popping. Then he had a voice, distant and faint and high.

". . . to report to their local distrib . . . eleven oh seven two four . . . all battalions followed by code J, H, R and S . . ."

Then it was off.

He fumbled some more, leaning across the side of the high dashboard to tune it, until he got another station, this one more clearly.

"Minister and the Parliament declared full neutrality in the sudden, total conflict between the Government of the United Sta . . ." then it drifted. Bay tried tuning it again. ". . . a participating member of the Geneva Convention, the Commonwealth of Canada has opened all borders to evacuees from the United States. Emergency centres, food, and shelter are offered to all evacuees. Repeat. Emergency centres . . ." it had drifted, and was gone.

So that was it. Nuclear attack. Full attack on a massive scale. Another world war. But Canada was neutral. There was food, shelter, safety there. He had been right to go north. Instinctively, Bay pressed down the gas pedal as far as it would go, then turned back to try to tune in the radio.

After fifteen minutes of nothing but hisses and words isolated in a radio drift, Bay pressed one of the buttons on the front of the set that said "emergency." For a long while there was nothing but more hisses and pops. He turned it down lower, but left it on in case it did catch radio signals. Then he drove on, thinking.

He had been lucky. Close. Too close. But lucky. If he had still been in Albany, been in any city, it would have been all over. That was certain. And he had been lucky to be so close to Canada. He could visualize evacuees from the cities trying to reach Canada over hundreds of miles of melted throughways. Horrible. It would be easier for him. Only another hour or so, and he'd cross the border. That was the value of hanging loose, travelling, being on your own. Nothing to hold you back. Always in the right spot when you needed it for survival. For survival.

He paused once on the top of a high ridge of mountains, and got out to look back, feeling like Lot in the Old Testament seeing the destruction of Sodom and Gomorrah. The skies south were still orange, fading to pink. The sun itself seemed contained within a flaming, new corona. A flock of birds were rushing northward over the mountains. They knew. They knew where it would be safe. He got back into the van and started off again.

Then there was static on the radio station. He raised the volume and tried catching the station. The static was unnerving, dizzying. Then there were voices. Calm voices. Men. Two men talking. He turned up the volume even more.

It didn't sound like emergency news—more like a private conversation overheard. Had he picked up a ham operator's conversation? And if so, why were they so calm? He turned the volume up full, and shut the van window, cutting off the wind current noise.

"So far the case exactly parallels our graph of reaction," were the first words he made out. Then it was louder, clearer. "Really quite extraordinary. Almost classic." The voice was so calm it was annoying. Didn't they know what had happened?

"And you're certain the sudden communication will not be too much of a shock," another voice said. "I mean given the intensity of applied reality." This man was less confident. What were they talking about?

"The shock is precisely what we want. By eliminating the possibilities to only two—one a total nightmare—the patient invariably will opt for the other. Voluntarily. Willingly even. The knowledge that there is a choice overrides any shock from the communication itself."

There seemed to be a static storm over the radio and Bay fiddled with the dial. He was back on the channel again, but it was silent. He left it there, and continued driving, his thoughts divided now between the strange conversation he had somehow overheard, and the image of the country completely destroyed submitting to an invasion by . . . by who?

"Bay! Can you hear me?"

He almost jumped out of the seat. Then he realized the voice came from the radio. One of the two men who had been talking. He repeated his question.

"Bay, this is Dr. Joralemon. Can you hear me?"

What the hell was going on?

"Dr. Elbert is here with me too. You remember Dr. Elbert, don't you? Bay, if you can hear us and understand us, then shake your head from left to right. Do you understand? From left to right. Slowly."

Bay did as he was told.

"Very good. Now, Bay, do you remember who I am? Dr. Joralemon. Again, Dr. Joralemon. If you remember me, shake your head again."

The name wasn't familiar. But the voice was. Or was it?

"Bay, did you hear what I just said?"

Bay nodded from left to right, thinking what the hell am I doing? where are these voices coming from? He opened the window and flipped the mirror all over the road, to see if someone was following him. Nothing. Nothing at all but forest: sparse, mountain forest.

"Now, Bay, do you remember Dr. Elbert?"

"Bay?" the other voice came on. "This is Jim Elbert. I'm your doctor. Or, at least I was. Do you hear me?"

Yes. Yes, Bay thought. "Jim," Bay said. "How can I hear you through the radio?"

"Bay!" Elbert's voice interrupted his own. "If you remember me, just shake your head. I see you're trying to talk, but we can't hear you."

Bay nodded vigorously. What the hell was Elbert doing on the radio? Where was he? How had he located Bay?

"Do you remember me, Bay?" It was the other voice. The one that called himself Dr. Joralemon. And now Bay did recall the voice. Not like Elbert's, pleasantly, like a friend, like growing up and playing stickball and going around driving together, but differently.

Dr. Joralemon repeated his question, and Bay heard rooms in his voice. Rooms and doors. Far away rooms in pastel colours. Venetian blinds half-closed. The murmur of someone's muffled crying.

Bay nodded slowly.

"Good," Joralemon said.

"Bay?" It was Jim Elbert again. "Now that we've communicated, you must understand that what I'm going to tell you is fact. Do you understand that? Will you believe me? Do you have any reason not to?"

No, Bay thought. I don't. He nodded, then reversed the motion of his head.

"All right. Some twelve hours ago, you underwent a new approach in psychic surgery. It's only used in the most hopeful of . . . well, of extreme cases. Dr. Joralemon invented the method. He calls it the dreamprobe."

"And so far we've had 100 percent effectiveness," Joralemon interrupted to add in.

"What it does, Bay," Elbert said, "I mean, what it is is a combination of a drug that operates on the cerebral cortex, and a series of timed electrical shocks. What it does is to channel all of your fears and anxieties into one area, into one major fear and anxiety. Your unconsciousness then takes over, and makes that one fear and anxiety into a dream of a tremendous catastrophic experience."

Bay didn't understand.

"You're asleep, Bay," Dr. Joralemon said. "You may think you aren't, but you are. You're fast asleep."

Bay gripped the wheel. What the hell! Sleeping? The trees were whizzing past the van window, clumps at a time. There were still no vehicles behind him, and he hadn't seen one coming his way at all.

"That's right, Bay," Jim Elbert said. "Sleeping. Dreaming. Everything that has happened to you has been a dream."

"Not an ordinary dream," Joralemon said. "That's how the drug works, it doesn't approximate reality with symbols and foolish inaccuracies the way most dreams work. It has seemed very real to you. Intensely real."

"You must realize that it was a desperation measure, Bay. I was against it at first, but your increasing catatonia, and Dr. Joralemon's persuasion forced me to accept this way."

"Do you understand this, Bay?"

Understand it? It was insane.

"Bay?" It was Elbert again. "Can you still hear us?"

He nodded, yes.

"Can you understand what we're telling you?"

He half nodded.

"I know it's difficult to believe," Joralemon said. "Because it was all so concentrated, every aspect, every impression seemed completely accurate."

"In effect," Elbert said, "it was another reality."

"An alternative reality, really. Can you understand that?"

Bay couldn't. Whoever these jokers were, they must be off their rockers. He looked up to see if there was a helicopter or plane above him. He even looked out the window. Still nothing. How were they in contact? How were they tracking him? With radar? Sonar? Should he shut off the radio? Did that activate the beam on him?

"Fine," Joralemon said. "Everything is going to be all right now, Bay. You don't have to run any more. You've seen an alternative reality. You've faced up to the worst that you could ever have faced up to, and you've survived. That was the furthest you could go in the direction you had been going in all these months. And now you're going to be all right and you're going to come back."

"And we're going to help you come back," Elbert said.

"Right. You see you don't really have much of a choice, do you, Bay? Because if you don't come back, then you'll have to continue living in a nightmare state. You're over the worst, but given that, what can you expect to follow: a catalogue of horrors, each one worse than the next—that's the logical extrapolation of the monumental trauma you've just experienced."

"Now, Bay," Elbert said hurriedly, "in order to get out of your state, you must merely be able to move your right hand."

Bay drove lefty. The right hand hung by his side.

"Move your right hand so it reaches over to your heart."

216

Who were these guys? And why were they trying to stop him? Were they the enemy? The same people who had planted the bombs, killed so many people? Almost killed him?

Bay would string them along for a while. He must be getting close to the Canadian border soon. He moved his hand to where they had directed him.

"Now, you should be touching a pocket. Do you feel it?"

Of course, there was a pocket.

"Now, there's something very important in that pocket, Bay. We want you to reach in and take it out. Can you do that?"

What the hell could be in his pocket? Bay reached in, felt around, and touched something smooth and flat. He pulled it out—it was a plasticine packet. When did that get in there?

The road was beginning to dip now, out of the mountains. This must be the last stretch before the border.

"Open up the packet, Bay."

He did. Inside were two small pellets. Like pink barrels.

"Good," Elbert said. "When you take those two pills, you will appear to fall asleep. But only to you. What really will happen, is that you will wake up. Do you understand that, Bay?"

Sure, sure, Bay thought, and black is white. Whatever these pellets were, how did they get in the pocket? He hadn't put them there. Had somebody? While he was sleeping? And what if they were what this guy who sounded like Elbert said they were? Where would he be then? Inside a hospital? An asylum, that's where. Probably tied down. No, sir.

"Can you understand us, Bay?"

He nodded.

"Fine. Just pop them into your mouth. All at once."

Bay rolled them in his fingers.

"Is there anything wrong, Bay?"

"It will be all right, Bay." Elbert again. "If you aren't in a position to take them, if you're walking, or driving or something, just stop. Because you'll go to sleep with them."

What if they were cyanide? Planted there as he slept?

"It will be all right, Bay. I assure you. In a few days you'll be fine. Fine enough to leave the hospital. The recovery programme is the finest around. You'll be proud of yourself. You won't be afraid any more. Not of anything.''

Afraid! The far away rooms. Hospital green and blue and canary yellow. The walls converging, tilting, falling in on him. The crying. No one ever coming. No one, except for a quick look and lying words and another syringe. Murmurs of soft crying all around, constant, interminable. His crying, his own crying, as if heard twenty rooms away. Through locked doors.

"Now, Bay, we have great faith in you," Joralemon said, sternly. "Great faith. That's why you were chosen for this dreamprobe over other patients. There were many who . . ."

"Is there a reason you can't take the pills, Bay?"

Bay nodded. Of course there was. He had to get to Canada. He'd be at the border any minute now. There might be other cars there already. He recalled that several major roads converged there. Others would be ahead of him, safer than he was. There might even be a wait. The road was going down more sharply now, he must be close.

"Whatever it is you're doing, you have to stop, Bay. These pellets are the antidote to the drug we gave you. Do you understand that?"

"Bay, no one will hurt you."

Pastel rooms and medicine smells. Shadows squatting and burblings and murmurs and screams cutting through the walls. Shadows vomiting and screaming, colliding; and always the distant crying.

"Please, Bay. This is all a dream. A bad dream. It will be over just like that. Don't you want that?"

"You have to, Bay."

"Bay! Bay!"

But Bay wasn't responding. Ahead, along the road, he could see the curve up, the converging of two other roads, and at their centre, the wooden log cabin building belonging to the Canadian Mounted Police.

"Never had to inject the antidote before, Elbert, never! We simply don't know where that will leave him."

"You mean it won't bring him out!"

"We've never had anyone opt for the alternate before."

"Inject it."

"I'll need authorization."

"I'll give you authorization. Inject it."

No you don't, Bay thought. He lifted his foot off the accelerator as the van coasted down to the border, and kicked the radio hard, once, and then again. It crumbled and the voice jumbled, got mixed in with static, then died.

There were no cars down there, just a Mounted Policeman waving at Bay.

Bay waved back, laughed out loud. In his hand were the pink pellets. He threw them out the window, clear into the pine trees, and slowed down at the station.

"Welcome," the Mountie said. He had no face. But Bay didn't mind. He would be safe in Canada.

M. John Harrison

The Ice Monkey

M. JOHN HARRISON WAS BORN IN 1945. HE SUFFERED FROM *education in Rugby, work in a fox-hunting stable, and studentship at a teacher training college, before (presumably) deciding he had suffered enough and moving to London and writing. These days he lives in the Holme Valley, where he writes and climbs. He can often be found at a typewriter in the comics department of Bookchain in Manchester, making sure that he doesn't lose touch with urban seediness.*

His books include The Committed Men, The Pastel City, A Storm of Wings, *and as I type this he is threatening to write* By Gasmask and Fire Hydrant. *Now that Robert Aickman is finally gaining the reputation he deserves, in America at any rate, Mike Harrison is probably the most underrated living British fantasy writer; he is certainly among the most original. For seven years he was literary editor of* New Worlds. *Reactionary science fiction fans might call that a contradiction in terms, but in retrospect* New Worlds *is one of the most distinguished magazines of imaginative fiction. It published his superb story ''Running Down'' (also to be found in his collection* The Machine in Shaft Ten) *which was about the occult power of apathy. So is this.*

When Jones turned up he was dressed to see his wife. Clothes were meaningless to him. He had no taste, and needed none until occasions became "official." This distinction, vestigial of a middle class upbringing, caused him great pain. He drew the line between official and unofficial himself, by some process I have never understood; and on the far side of it, where the habitual no longer offered its comfort and common sense no alternative, lost his nerve and fell back on the usage of a red-brick university youth—that is, he tried to make himself look as much as possible like the ghost of some young Kingsley Amis. It was a dim and propitiatory instinct and today it had also advised him to shave and have his hair cut, a process which, while it threw his harsh cheekbones into prominence and emphasized the aggressive boniness of his jaw, yet made him seem young and vulnerable and silly.

I knew what he wanted but I hadn't the heart to pretend to be out.

"Look, Spider," he said. To hide his embarrassment he fiddled with the handkerchief he had wrapped round his knuckles. "Could you do me a favour?"

"I'd like to, Jones," I said, "honestly—" Then I remembered that because of his performance that afternoon he couldn't very well ask Henry. And no one else he knew was in London, so I put on my coat and went with him to the tube station. "It's my turn anyway, I think," I said, trying to make light of it. He shrugged and stared at the platform. This was habitual too. "I don't want another set-to," I warned him as we got on a Metropolitan Line train: "I'll have to leave if it's anything like last time." But my voice was drowned by the hiss and thump of the doors closing behind us. At the other end the wind had dropped and a thick rain fell straight down on us, and on London E3, in rods.

"I quite liked Maureen, you know."

They—by which I really mean Maureen and the child, since Jones rarely lived there even when she allowed him—had a small furnished flat on the second floor of a house somewhere between Bow and Mile End. For five years or more it had been scheduled for demolition, and now it stuck up with two or three others out of a contractors' waste land a mile across, the enormous floor-plan of a slum, full of lazy fires, silent bulldozers, and trees which seemed naked and doomed without the garden walls they had once overgrown. We forced a route through the rutted clay and piles of smouldering lath, and when we got there a plump West Indian girl put her head round the front door. She winked. "He's here, Maureen love!" she called up the stairs. "Don't you forget what I said!" She grinned defiantly at us, and stage thunder rolled over the Mile End Road, but I think the effect was wasted on Jones. It was more than a game to him and Maureen: neither of them had seen E3 until the age of thirty, and their failure to deal with it was ground into the stairwell walls along with all the other dirt.

"You aren't half going to catch it, Mr. Jones," the West Indian girl said to me.

Maureen was standing at the front window of the flat, nervously smoking a cigarette and staring out across the waste as if measuring it against some other landscape she'd once seen. Her shoulders were at once rounded and tense. At her feet the child was playing happily with an imaginary friend. "About time," she said distantly to Jones. She was thinner than the last time I'd seen her, a short, harassed blonde in paint-stained jeans and an unravelling Marks and Sparks sweater, the flesh carved off her originally heart-shaped face by anxiety and loneliness, her voice dull and aggressive. "Oh my God," she said, "what *do* you look like?" She blew smoke fiercely down her nostrils and jabbed the cigarette into the bottom of a glass ashtray. "Just look at yourself!" Instead Jones stood in the centre of the room like a marooned sailor and let his eyes roam helplessly over the open makeshift shelves stuffed with baby clothes, the brown carpet, the yellow plastic potty. He was already desperate and puzzled.

"Twenty years on," Maureen told the fires and silent, shrouded bulldozers. "Christ, it's still 1958 for you, isn't it?"

"*Up* the hill and *down* the hill," chanted the child. It had rubbed chocolate into its hair and clothing.

Jones lifted his hands slightly. "They're all I've got," he said. "Have you been decorating? It's nice."

Maureen laughed. She compressed her lips. "Sit down," she told me, giving up the security of the window. "Your turn this time was it? How's trade, Spider? How's Henry? It'll have to be tea. I can't afford coffee." She went into the kitchen, scrupulously avoiding Jones still aground there in the middle of the room, and began knocking things about in the sink. "Which of you decided to get his hair cut?" she called. She came back with a tray. "It's not all that bad for 1958. Have a ginger nut, Spider. Where's my maintenance, Jones? You owe me three months and I can't get by without it any more." She made her way quickly back to the window as she said this, and gazed out into the rain, measuring, measuring. Round her neck she was wearing a little silver monkey on a chain. The tiny hoop that attached its head to the middle link had broken, so she had wrapped the chain round its neck to hold it on. Jones cleared his throat and drank his tea. There was a silence. The child looked up at its mother. Suddenly it squatted down and made a loud farting noise. "Up the hill and down the hill," it said. A horrible smell filled the room. "They knocked the pub down," Maureen said, "so I've got no job. This place goes next month and the council still haven't rehoused me. You've *got* to write to them about it this time." She picked the child up and dropped it in Jones's lap. "There's your daddy," she told it. "Ask him to change you." It stared up at him for a second then set up a startlingly high-pitched whine. Jones stared back.

"Can't you see you're going to be in trouble with the maintenance? Tansy says they can easily make you pay—"

"Tansy!" yelled Jones suddenly into the child's face. "Tansy?" he laughed wildly. "Oh great! Who's bloody *Tansy?* That silly cow downstairs? Of course they can bloody make me, you've got your own brains to see that!"

"She's all I've got!" shouted Maureen, and burst into tears. "Oh you rotten bastard, I've got nobody else to tell me—"

The child waved its arms and whined. Jones put it roughly on the floor and ran out of the flat calling "Tansy says! Tansy says!" and laughing desperately. When he'd gone I took refuge in the kitchen, which was less smelly, and made some more tea. "You don't have to stay, you know," said Maureen. "He'll be kicking about out there on his own." She dabbed hopelessly at the child, found a clean nappy. ("Up the hill and down the hill," it went, looking up over her shoulder at some invisible friend.) "I don't know what happens when he comes here," she said. "I can't be any more reasonable." And, "Remember Swansea, Spider. It was all different then. I did Art. I loved his hands. Look at them now, they're all

223

scabby." She sipped her tea, staring past me out of the window, recalling perhaps the times when she'd been accustomed to wear a white two-piece and swim, while Jones made his name on the heroic Welsh sea-cliffs of a distant summer, and the water was the colour of a new blue nylon rope.

"His hands were pretty scabby then, Maureen," I reminded her gently.

"Get stuffed, Spider. Fuck off."

At the door I offered her a job serving in one of the shops. "Get in touch if you need help with solicitors or anything," I added.

She said: "I'd believe you really wanted to help if you just made him come on his own for once."

He was out among the smoky contractors' fires, his thin silhouette appearing and disappearing mysteriously as he moved from one to another in the rainy gloom, kicking at the embers and, I thought, trying to get up the nerve to go back inside again. It took me a while to attract his attention.

"They're the only good clothes I've got," he kept saying as we sat miserably on opposite sides of the tube carriage. "Why does she keep picking on them like that?"

It would have taken too long to explain it to him, so while the train roared and swayed its way back to the civilized areas west of Farringdon I let him stare dumbly at himself in its dark windows, touch curiously the sore shaved pink cheeks of his furry inaccurate reflection, and fuss (puzzled but on the edge of resentment and already taking advantage of the self-righteousness that would enable him to stay away for another month or two) with the mustard-yellow knitted tie, the tobacco-brown corduroy jacket and the white shirt with the thick chocolate-coloured stripes he'd had since the last proud birthday of his adolescence.

While I imagined Maureen, in E3 where all horizons are remembered ones, dwelling on vanished freedoms: how on Monday mornings in the summer term, after two nights toothbrushless in Llanberis, in a barn or cheap cotton tent, she would hurry down the long polished corridors of the teacher training college eating burnt toast, late for History of Art, still slightly crumpled and sleepy and hungover in one of Jones's unravelling Marks pullovers and pale blue jeans, focus of all interested, jealous eyes.

"I bought her that thing round her neck," said Jones peevishly. "I notice she's broken it."

"Come on, Jones," I said.

Preoccupation is easily mistaken for helplessness. This was how Jones survived in a world which didn't understand him, although I don't think he employed it often as a conscious device. His obsession with climbing was genuine, and had begun long before Swansea or Maureen. Five weeks after the maintenance fiasco, in the middle of the coldest February since 1964, I took him up to Scotland. I was going to see my parents who have retired to Bearsden, a comfortable suburb where they own a garage. The motorways were covered in black ice: there were extensive detours, and I ended up driving all through Friday night. Jones slept in the back, and then ate three fried eggs in a café straddling the road, watching with his head tilted intelligently to one side as the sparse traffic groaned away south and a kind of mucoid greyness crept into the place through its steamed-up windows. He talked of the time he had fallen off a famous limestone route in Derbyshire and broken his nose. His chalk bag had burst and his face had been daubed with blood and chalk. He had a photograph which someone had taken at the time. "The worst bit was a feeling of not being able to breathe," he said. "I thought I was dying." He repeated this two or three times with what seemed at the time a superstitious enjoyment.

He told me he wanted to do Point Five Gully on Ben Nevis that weekend, and asked me to go with him. "Henry won't come," he said. "I suppose you know why." He sat there pouring tomato sauce on his plate.

"I can't go, Jones," I said. "They're expecting me." I hadn't been ice-climbing for years; neither of us had. After Bridge of Orchy I let him drive, hoping to get some sleep. He put us into a snowdrift in Glencoe; I watched the carnivorous bends of the A82 gape open all the way to Fort William. (Sitting on the back of his motorcycle ten years or more before, I had driven a tent pole straight through the rear window of a Mini as he tried to overtake it on one of those bends. I can't imagine why I had it under my arm, or how he persuaded me to carry it at all.) When I next woke up he had the van in a car park somewhere and cold air was spilling into it through the back doors. He had put on a pair of filthy stretch breeches and a Javelin jacket completely threadbare in the forearms from climbing on gritstone. An ancient Whillans harness flapped between his legs like some withered orange codpiece. He was talking to somebody I couldn't see.

"Excuse me," he said. "Would any of you have a cigarette?"

Giggles answered him, and I went back to sleep.

We walked up to the climb early on Sunday morning. It was still dark, and the weather was appalling. "Come on, Jones," I said: "Nobody bothers with it in conditions like this." When you could see it, the Ben looked just like a mountain from a fifties film about Alpine guides: not pointed, true: but just as cardboardy, dioramic, painted on. Powder snow blew about like fog on a bitter east wind, cutting at our faces. We set out with some other people but got separated from them as we blundered about on Tower Ridge. For a few minutes we heard their voices thin and urgent sounding against the boom of the wind: then nothing.

Jones made me lead the first pitch.

With front-point crampons on your feet and one of the new short axes—their acutely-angled picks like the beaks of pterodactyls—in each hand, even overhanging ice can be climbed. Waterfalls are the most fun: suspended up among the huge icicles which have grown together until they look like a sheaf of organ pipes, balancing on half an inch of steel two hundred feet up on a sunny morning, you can quite enjoy it all. *Chunk!* go the axes, as you drive them into the ice. I couldn't hear myself think on the Ben that day. Eddies of wind exploded continually into the gully. In places there was hardly enough ice to take an axe—it starred and flaked away under the pick; while elsewhere the route was choked with powder snow like a laundry chute full of Persil. After a bit I couldn't see Jones below me any more (or hear him singing), just a greyish space boiling with ice particles, the two nine-millimetre ropes vanishing into it. I could only go up—chopping, floundering, front-pointing delicately on black verglas while the wind first pushed me into the gully-bed then sucked me out again, forcing spindrift down my neck, under my helmet and into my eyes . . . Eventually bulges of good ice appeared. I got up on to one of them, smashed in a couple of ice screws for a belay, and gave Jones a tug on the rope to indicate he should climb.

By the time he joined me on my little melted ledge, conditions had improved. The wind had dropped; we could see each other, and hear each other talk. The next pitch turned out to be a fifty foot bulge, curving out above us fringed with short twisted icicles and showing up a greenish colour in the growing daylight. It looked like good firm ice. Jones lit a cigarette, rubbed his hands together and moved off up it at a terrific rate, showering me with chunks of ice. He quickly got up to the difficult overhanging section, beneath which he put in a tubular screw and had a rest. I could just see him if I craned my neck, a dark figure dangling from a bright orange sling, turning gently from side to side like a chrysalis in a hedge. The sound of singing drifted down. "Come on, Jones, we haven't got all day." "Bugger off." We had begun to enjoy ourselves. I flexed my fingers inside my Dachstein mitts; checked the belays; whistled. When my neck got stiff from looking up at him I rested it by peering out of the gully. No view. "I'm moving off again," called Jones. "This is easy." Rope ran out through my hands. He stuck both axes in the ice above the overhang, jabbed his front points in. The whole bulge exploded like a bomb and he tumbled backwards into space above me.

He'd been catapulted right out of the gully. His protection screw failed the moment his weight came on it and he hurtled down past me screaming. Thirty feet of rope slid through my hands before I braked his fall; even then the impact pulled my belays like rotten teeth. I fell a hundred feet, mostly through clear air, turning over and over. I was thinking "Christ, Christ, Christ," in a sort of mental monotone. Part the way down I landed feet first on something solid, tearing the ligaments in my legs. For an instant or two I was sliding down a slope: I tried to use the one axe remaining to me as a brake, rolling over and digging the pick into the ice: it ripped out. I fetched up at the bottom of the gully in a foetal position, gasping and groaning and choking on the powder snow which had saved me. My legs hurt so much I thought I'd broken both of them. I could see Jones a few feet away. He was kneeling there in a fog of spindrift making a queer coughing noise. I lay there thinking about

227

being crippled. This gave me enough strength to get up and help him.

The ropes had wound themselves round him as he fell. One turn had gone round his neck and was supporting his whole weight. I couldn't get it off him. The rope was snagged on something further up. His tongue was still moving but he was black in the face and he was dead. He would have died anyway in the time it took me to crawl down the hill.

The funeral was awful. It was held a few days later in one of those places trapped between Manchester and the gritstone moors (Mottram, perhaps, or Stalybridge where nothing is clear cut and there is neither town nor country, just a grim industrial muddle of the two), in a huge bleak cemetery on the side of a hill. Jones's open coffin was displayed in the front room of the terrace in which his brother lived. When it was my turn to file past I couldn't look at him. His relatives sat dumbly drinking tea; each time one of them caught my eye, my legs hurt. We always blame the survivor, I suppose. The funeral cars took what seemed like hours to crawl through the grimy wet streets behind the town: and at the burial plot some old aunt of his teetered on the edge of the hole in the wind, so that I had to drop my stick and grab her upper arm to stop her falling in. Under my hand her bones felt as fragile as a bird's. We tried to talk to one another but the wind whipped the words away.

Afterwards there was a dismal meal in an assembly room above a baker's. It had wooden panelling, and the lukewarm roast lamb was served by local women wearing black dresses and white aprons. I was alone there. (Some of his other climbing friends had turned up earlier, but left after the ceremony in a group. In any case I didn't know any of them very well.) When they served him, Jones's brother jumped to his feet suddenly and said: "No meat! I told them, no meat!" All the old women looked at him. He was much older than Jones, a tall thin man with lines of tension round his mouth that might have been vegetarianism or pain; he died himself a few months later, of cancer of the bowel, which just left the women. After they had persuaded him to sit down again he burst into tears. The place catered for functions of all sorts. Someone had left a crude little monkey, a tourist souvenir with limbs plaited from jute and a wooden head, hanging above the serving hatch; and there were faded Christmas decorations up in the ceiling.

I stayed the weekend in a hotel and before I left on the Sunday afternoon went over to the cemetery on my own. I don't know what I expected to find. The road outside it was littered with satin ribbons and florist's cellophane which had blown off the graves during the night. When I wound down the window of the van there was a smell of wet moorland, and I thought of how Jones had begun to climb here as a child, coming home ravenous and sore late at night from the outcrops near Sheffield. In the summer, as he inched out across the big steep gritstone faces, there would have been the sudden dry odour of chalk-dust; the warm rock under the fingertips; a laugh. The grave looked unfinished, and his brother was standing over it with his head bowed. He had heard me limping along the gravel path so I couldn't very well leave. I stood there and bowed my head too, feeling at once intrusive and intruded upon. After a few minutes he blew his nose loudly.

"She didn't come, then. The wife. You'd have thought she'd have made the effort."

I pictured Maureen, staring out of the window at the ruins of east London, the falling rain.

"I think there was some sort of strain," I said.

"Strain?"

"Between them."

He obviously didn't understand me, and I didn't want to explain. I tried to change the subject. "He'll be missed," I said. "He was one of the best rock climbers in the country."

He looked at me.

"You'll all miss him, will you?" he asked bitterly. "You should have had more sense than to encourage him."

Maureen remained at the back of my mind but events kept me away from E3. The shops were doing well: in anticipation of a good summer season I went to New York and California on buying trips, coming away with a line of lightweight artificial fibre sleeping bags and the English agency for a new kind of climbing harness

229

which I thought might compete with the Whillans. When I got back the weather in London was raw and damp, and it was late March. My legs ached intermittently, like a psychic signal. It was quite a sunny afternoon when I got off the eastbound train at Bow.

The mud of the contractors' battlefield had frozen into hard ruts, and only two houses were left standing, saved—if that is the word—by a temporary withdrawal of labour in the building trades. I couldn't remember which one it was. I chose the one without the corrugated iron nailed across its ground floor windows; I waited for someone to come and answer the door. Bulldozers lay all around me hull-down into the earth as if exhausted by a lengthy campaign, a hard winter. Grey smoke drifted between the little beleaguered aluminium huts which dotted the waste. Some attempts had been made to begin building. I could see trenches full of cement, piles of earthenware pipes, and here and there a course of new brick waist high above the ruts. They were fortifications already doomed: a kind of reversed archaeological excavation was taking place here, revealing the floor plan of the slums to come. "Oh, hello, Spider. It's a bit inconvenient just now," said Maureen.

"I'd ask you in," she said, "but I'm waiting for someone."

She'd had her hair cut short and was wearing clothes I'd never seen her in before. Her fingernails were varnished a curious plum colour, the varnish chipped where she had bitten them. She saw that I didn't quite know how to react. "I'm a bit smarter than usual!" she said with a nervous laugh. "Oh, come on up." Upstairs she lit a cigarette. "Coffee, Spider?" There was some new furniture in the kitchen—cupboards and a table with clean Formica surfaces, little stools with metal legs; while in the front room the makeshift shelves full of baby clothes had been replaced. In a bookcase with a smoked glass front were a few paperbacks and a dictionary. The flat was somehow unchanged by all this, resisting, like her fingernails, all her attempts to normalize her life. It still smelt of the child, which was squatting on its yellow potty looking vacantly up into the opposite corner of the room and whispering to itself. "You must have finished now," Maureen told it.

She looked at me anxiously. "I would have come to the funeral but I just didn't have any money. They wouldn't give me social security that week." She stubbed out the cigarette. "I got a letter from his brother," she said.

"You can always go up there later. I don't think they understood the situation, that's all."

"I don't know when I'll have time now," she said. "I've got a job."

It turned out she was the secretary of a local business man. I asked her how she managed with the child. "It goes to a crèche," she said vaguely. She was looking out of the window at a car making its way round the perimeter of the battlefield, a big European thing rolling on its suspension as its front wheels dipped into the holes left by the contractors' plant. As if the arrival of this thing, with its overtones of comfort and prosperity, were a signal, a reminder, she turned round suddenly and said: "Spider, I expected that police car day and night for bloody years. They came in the middle of the night and they weren't sure which of you was dead. They got the names all wrong." I tried to say something but she rushed on. "I cried all night, what was left of it. For him, for you, for me, for all of us. What we were at Swansea. Oh, if only he'd just once earned some bloody money!" She started to cry and dab at her eyes. The car outside came to a halt under the window. A man in a leather coat got out and locked it carefully. He looked up, smiling and waving. Maureen went down to let him in.

His name was Bernard. He had a dark suit on, blue or brown, I forget; and neat, longish hair. He used some sort of after shave, and seemed ill at ease. He was decent enough but I gave him no help. "How's the little chap, then?" he said, picking up the child. "Oh Christ." Maureen went to make him some coffee. "Bernard's a computer programmer," she called through, as if this might encourage us to talk. "It's systems analysis, Maureen," he corrected: "systems analysis." They held a whispered conversation in the kitchen and I thought I heard him say, "But we were going to the *film* theatre. It's *The Exterminating Angel*. You said you'd love to see *The Exterminating Angel*." When he came back it was to excuse himself and take the potty to empty in the lavatory. While he was out Maureen said defensively, "We're getting married, Spider."

After that we talked about Jones's climbing gear, which I had held on to in case she wanted it.

"I don't think it would be good for her to have all that brought back, do you, Spider?" Bernard appealed (certain perhaps that it never could be). He sipped his coffee which he took without milk. "While she's still on her own, anyway." He looked at his watch. "Is it about time we were moving, Maureen love?" Maureen, though, sat forward and rummaged through the bag I'd brought the stuff in. "There's a pair of double Alpine boots here," she said: "Quite new. Could you sell them in one of the shops, Spider?" Bernard looked irritated. "I don't think we're that badly off, Maureen," he said. He laughed. "Could you, Spider?" Maureen said. I told her that I'd try. (I sent her the money for them a couple of months later, but it can't have been forwarded from Bow because I've never had an answer.) There was an awkward pause. They invited me to the wedding, which was to be in May. "I don't think I can make that," I said. "I have to go to America on a buying trip. A range of sleeping bags I'm interested in." The child crawled round the floor breathing heavily. "Up the hill and *down* the hill." As I got up to go it was trying to climb the side of the bookcase, its little feet slipping off the shiny new melamine.

Bernard saw me to the door of the flat. "I hope I can make her happy," he said, and thanked me for coming. Maureen, I realized, had already said goodbye.

It was getting dark as I went down the stairs. The landing windows showed a waste land; fires. Further down I met the West Indian girl Tansy. She was wearing Maureen's little silver monkey and chain. They glittered against her skin in the brownish gloom. She hadn't bothered to have the monkey repaired, and the chain was still twisted round its neck. Maureen must have given them to her, I suppose.

"Cheerio," she said; and smiled.

andrew j. offutt

Symbiote

ANDREW J. OFFUTT HAS LIVED MOST OF HIS LIFE IN A PLACE called Funny Farm in Kentucky. The first time I met andy (as he likes to be printed) at the World Fantasy Convention in 1975, he asked me to cut about 4,000 words from a 15,000 word story, and it must say something for his charm that I agreed, to the benefit of the story. (For much more about him, his equally charming wife Jodie, and their daughter Scotty, not to mention a splendid tale woven around them, see Harlan Ellison's anthology Again, Dangerous Visions.*) andy has published over twenty novels that he admits to (including* The Undying Wizard, Ardor on Aros, Conan the Mercenary, The Iron Lords, Sword of the Gael), *dozens of short stories, and erotica under a pseudonym which friendship prevents me from revealing. He edits the* Swords Against Darkness *anthologies.*

Nothing else in his career prepares one for the following piece of unmitigated nastiness, but when I read it I received another kind of shock: in several ways it was unnervingly similar to "The Depths," the story I had written for this book. It wasn't the first time I'd experienced this kind of thing—once I wrote, scene for scene, a Henry Kuttner story which I'd never read—but I agonized

233

for months over including "The Depths," until I wrote "The Fit" (which appears in New Terrors) *and my wife Jenny suggested that was an ideal story for this anthology. Of course none of us knows where story ideas come from, but "Symbiote" has a dismaying suggestion to make.*

It had talent and power, the parasite Philip had named Joe.

The power, for one thing, to control him, totally. The power, for another, to "cloud men's minds" (for that was the way Philip, remembering *The Shadow* of the old days of radio, thought of it). The clouding of men's minds was handy and indeed necessary to Joe's purposes. It protected Philip from witnesses and police and the like. It covered his tracks. Made him not invisible or invincible, but unlikely to be discovered. That he was neither discovered nor suspected was necessary to the lives of both Philip and the parasite living on him, with him. Directing him. The police would have taken Philip's life. That would have inconvenienced the parasite Joe, for he was now dependent, he told Philip, on Philip's life.

Thus, he explained, they lived in symbiosis.

Symbiosis. A biological name for a mutual-trade agreement. An interdependence. True exchange and true justice: tit for tat, value for value. For Joe could live only as a parasite. He had no arms, no legs, no eyes. (Or mouth, or voice either; he spoke in Philip's *mind,* where he lived.) Philip was necessary to his existence. And at little cost; at no cost, really, since Philip profited so greatly. (Unless you insist on being moralistic and thus incur the scorn of a vastly superior life-form, Joe.)

Joe lived on emotions. More specifically, mental emanations of a violent nature.

Humankind, Joe had explained to Philip after he had chosen him and set up housekeeping somewhere in the neighbourhood of his Central Control, had long ago discovered that the human brain was, in a manner of speaking, electrical. Its activities generated recordable electric "current." This was food to Joe. And Joe was a glutton. He preferred engorgement on the richest of foods to a steady but less exciting diet of mental hamburgers. He preferred the current, the emotions, the excitement generated in Philip's mind by criminal acts. Violence.

Just having Philip break laws, Joe explained, was lovely: mental steak. This was because engaging in prohibited activities excited humans, thus generating strong mental currents. (A lie detector indicates this, in another way, though it is by Joe's standards an incredibly crude device.)

After two robberies and an arson, Joe tried a (briefly) premeditated murder.

It was far nicer.

Philip was greatly excited, and Joe was dizzy with delight as they approached the house. Joe told Philip there'd be no outcries to betray them; he'd see to that. Should the intended victim be on the point of endangering Philip—and thus Joe—he'd see to that, too.

The man did not make an outcry. Nor did he endanger Philip/Joe's life.

Heart slamming, adrenal glands working at capacity, Philip went silently through the little house and found his victim. He was right where Joe had said he'd be. (Joe had talent, and power.) The old man stared with enormous, terror-filled eyes. His mouth worked desperately and his Adam's apple bobbed like a fisherman's cork. No sound emerged, though, for Joe had hold of a nerve somewhere between the man's larynx and his brain.

Philip stabbed him thirteen times and staggered at the explosive reaction in his head. He returned to his apartment—with Joe clouding minds along the way—and slept for thirty hours. Joe was sated, and when Joe was sated he lay up and slept like a smug jungle cat with blood on its whiskers. And when Joe slept, Philip slept. Joe was sorry, but it was necessary. Once Joe had gone to sleep and aroused to find his host on the way to give himself up at the police station. Joe turned him around and directed his feet home and punished him by not letting him eat or drink for a day and a half.

After that Joe turned Philip off when he—Joe—slept.

You mustn't, you see, be too hard on Philip in your thinking. Once Joe had moved in, Philip really wasn't Philip any more.

After killing the old man and sleeping thirty hours, Philip awoke ravenous and he and Joe discussed the adventure, reliving it. Thus Joe fed again. He made it last three weeks.

During those three weeks Philip wrote nine short stories and retyped them for submission. (Joe helped, of course, or rather dictated; each story was his idea, as were the plot and the wording. Joe couldn't be bothered with Philip's having to spend a large part of each day working to earn money. So they wrote the stories.) Joe planned them to sell, and they did. (Joe had talent, and power.) Two sold to the highest-paying magazine in the nation and two more to the second highest. Each editor but one mentioned that she or he would look favourably upon more submissions from Joe Philips.

After collecting the nine cheques, Philip gave up the post office box he had rented as Joe Philips. He banked the money so that he had collateral, and he and Joe bought a house, which was more convenient and private than an apartment. They also traded Philip's car on a station wagon and made some adjustments.

By that time Philip's recounting of the murder had become a tedious, repetitive hash, and Joe felt the need for more steak.

This time it was a woman, about thirty-five, who had been divorced exactly three weeks. (The murders were in the papers, of course, and investigated. But there is so much crime, so much murder in Los Angeles, that one more killing now and then was far from being a *cause célèbre*.) (Besides, Joe clouded men's minds, and there were no clues.)

After that second killing—Joe had Philip strangle her first, then stab her a few times, experimenting with various techniques—Philip and Joe exchanged observations, which is only normal and fair in symbiosis.

"I notice that murder is the source of your greatest excitement," the symbiote Joe said. Or whispered, or thought.

"Of course," Philip said. (He usually spoke, at first.)

"And this time you were more excited than before."

"Yes."

"Because this one was female."

"Of course," Philip said, remembering and thus giving Joe a nice lunch. (He had dessert when they read the papers, particularly one reporter's picturesque line, "The young woman lay huddled on a carpet which appeared to have been painted with the same scarlet brush with which her nude body had been smeared.")

"Thus," Joe said, "the sensible, logical course is for us to forget other activities and concentrate on murder. Specifically, females."

"Sensible," Philip said, and the thoughts that rushed through his brain provided Joe with a nice snack. "By the way, I think we'd be smart to leave some clues or something. I mean, if we're going to go on with this, some of the murders had better be solved."

Joe explored Philip's mind and saw why this was true. "Very clever, Philip! We'll do that. Now though, let's write. We need plenty of money. You have to keep your strength up."

"Yes," Philip said, "and we really should buy insurance on the house."

During the next three weeks Philip went through a great deal of paper and two all-black typewriter ribbons of the first quality. He also developed some trouble in his lower spine. Joe found it, and fixed it. The novel concerned a secret agent and government officials talking importantly and beautiful women and sex and of course one of the women was tortured to make her talk and the whole world was menaced; Joe wrote (or dictated) only material designed to sell, and sell well. Joe was pleased with Philip's delightful emotional response during the writing of the two torture scenes and the slow hanging of a government tax official. The symbiote snacked.

"Killing another human is the highest crime," Joe observed. "And humans like to kill. So killing is the most exciting and thus satisfying crime to me. Men are ruled by reproductive urges, and so killing a female is even more exciting and therefore more satisfying. Men like to torture, too. Mostly women. You know that, from Freud and Havelock Ellis and Krafft-Ebing. Those who make movies certainly know it, too.

"So—in future we will kill females, and slowly."

Somewhere, way back in a dusty and dark corner of his mind, Philip was horrified. Joe noticed, but he wasn't disturbed. Joe was in control.

They were astonished when the novel returned from the editor—male, unusually—for the publisher they had chosen. He evinced unhappiness with what he called its "sadism" but indicated he would be happy to publish it, with a few changes. Joe laughed in Philip's mind.

" 'Disturbed at the book's sadism,' is he? He means by what he calls sadism—but he doesn't know what that means. The innate cruelty of humans has nothing to do with the psychopathological term 'sadism.' He also doesn't know himself, like most humans. The scenes excited him, Philip, be sure of that. And that is exactly why he sent it back! He thinks it's wicked because he feels guilty at being sexually excited. You humans really are ludicrous life-forms."

"Shall we change it?" Philip asked.

"Of course not."

They made a market study. They compiled a list of three publishers and mailed the novel to the first. She sent them a contract and later some money called an advance—to Joe Philips, Box 21372—and assured them that royalties would be forthcoming. During the time thus consumed they wrote another story and an article and sold them to two magazines for several thousand dollars; Joe chose to write only for the best-paying publications. They also killed a twelve-year-old girl by stabbing and Joe did some other things so that her father would be accused. (He was, and convicted too, although that was much later.)

"The older female excited you more than the younger," Joe said grumpily. "What if she had been much older?" Before Philip could reply, Joe had the answer from his mind. "I see. Human reproductive urges again. Let's look at some magazines." For Joe was not, after all, infallible. Philip remarked that, somewhere in a dusty and dark corner of his mind. Joe noticed, but he was not disturbed. Joe had talent, and power.

Joe found that the pictures in fashion magazines excited Philip very little, even when Joe prompted thoughts of torture and death. Old women too, and just-nubile or pre-nubile ones were quickly ruled out. They narrowed the researches. Joe considered it strange that Philip preferred pictures of women wearing some clothing, rather than totally nude ones. They refined the researches.

Joe learned that he would dine best when Philip's victim was a full-haired young woman, preferably with clearly defined hips and sitting and walking apparati. Also, he discovered with a puzzlement he admitted, the more pronounced the female's baby-feeding apparatus, the more delightful would be his repast.

They made some purchases and remodelled the house, particularly the basement. Philip found carpentry as easy as writing, with Joe's help. He had long ago been shown that he was capable of tremendous activity and exertion for long periods of time, although Joe was forced to let him sleep—totally relaxed, naturally, and very deeply—for long periods afterwards.

"The body is the temple of the mind," Joe said once, "and must be well looked after. Trust in me."

Philip finished the remodelling job and bought the cameras and recording equipment Joe suggested. (Joe did not give orders. Joe suggested, pretty much on a "Let's . . ." or "Suppose we . . ." basis.)

The young woman was a dancer, if you're not particular about terminology. An ecdysiast, if you cherish a fondness for fancy-Greeky words. A stripper. Beautiful, of course. That is standard in LA, which leaves the tired ones and the homely ones to Chicago and Cincinnati and the rest of the country. Los Angeles teems with beautiful women and girls, most of them consummately shapely and possessing pronounced baby-feeding apparati (not that they'd dream of using them for that purpose). They flock in by the bus load, these beautiful girls and young women from all over the country, attracted by Movieland as butterflies are by flowers—or as lemmings are, by the sea. Naturally they are not all Discovered, and even that tiny fraction that does Make It must do something for rent—sometimes for months, oftener for years, frequently for keeps.

They model, dressed and undressed.

They do other things.

It was not unusual, then, that the stripper Joe and Philip found was a real winner. She danced. Danced and undressed. In that order. When first they saw her she wore an ankle-length dress of something black and shiny-slinky, with long side slits. A few minutes later it was gold lamé underwear—that was her *schtick*, the gold metallic cloth, and the mass of black hair rippling to her waist. Next it was sparkly gold pasties and an elastic string equipped with a couple of sparkly gold triangles.

Joe took note of Philip's excitement—merely an *hors d'oeuvre*—

and noted that it heightened when the pasties departed their precarious perches. Joe asked, "Will she do?"

"Perfectly," Philip said. Something stirred in that dark and dusty corner of his mind, but neither he nor Joe took notice.

Not so strangely, if you know anything about most strippers and about Los Angeles, the young woman left alone when the place closed. (According to the papers a few days later, she probably had some studying to do. She was a Junior in University.) She did not study that night. The plan was to observe her habits, follow her, make a plan. Instead, a fine opportunity presented itself along the way and she became the first passenger, not counting Joe, in Philip's new station wagon. She became his—their—first houseguest.

Philip did not want her totally voiceless, so Joe obligingly paralysed the necessary nerve or nerves only partially, giving her what approximated a mild case of laryngitis. She could still plead. Quietly.

Philip found that there was more work involved than he'd expected in wrestling the unconscious guest to the basement and up against the wall where he had bolted the new leather straps. He held her sagging body with one arm while with the other he buckled her wrist. Then he secured her other wrist. She hung against the stone wall with her knees bent and her head hanging so that all that hair floated down like a rippling blue-black waterfall.

Philip shot some footage with the movie camera, then took several photographs from several angles.

"Would you like to begin," Joe asked, "or wait for her to become conscious?"

As Philip started to admit his impatience, the prisoner stirred and moaned a little. She moved her head and Philip went to her. She tried to scream, found that she could not, and whimpered. He had made artistic use of her hair in his pictures and she could barely see him, if at all, through the black curtain of it.

Erect, she stood shivering against the wall. The gooseflesh of fear and chill marked her skin, and Philip frowned angrily at the tiny eruptions. Gazing at her, he decided to fix two belts together and bolt a ring of some sort into the wall, high up. That way he'd be able to pull a guest's arms straight up and perhaps, were she short enough, force her to balance on tiptoe. It would display her to better advantage, be more interesting, and please his aesthetic sense.

Next time. Not this guest. The next one.

She pleaded. Pleaded and winced and tried to scream (in vain; Joe had both talent and power). She pled with him in the most piteous little voice Philip had ever heard. It gave him a tremendous, surging feeling of power. (Joe ingested it happily.) She pled and she bled.

He used a box cutter. It is a simple device, about the size of a pocket comb and only a little thicker. Stockboys in grocery stores insert a single-edged razor blade in one and use it quickly and usually skilfully to slice the tops of packing cases. It is extremely sharp, of course, this razor blade with a handle, and sometimes it slips and perhaps you find a slashed label or box on the shelf. Usually, though, the grocer saves the slashed package for the salesman representing the manufacturer of that product.

It opened human flesh, Philip found, with equal facility, leaving a slender little line that looked as if it had been etched with a pencil. A red pencil.

Joe supped with gusto.

It was an orgiastic meal he enjoyed, in an orgy of blood that lasted through the night and the next day and most of the following night. Then Joe, completely stuffed, fell into a sated sleep. Philip's sleep was that of exhaustion. Their guest's was that last long one.

Naturally they did that again, quite soon, with a few aesthetic refinements.

After several months and several young women Philip noticed that Joe's appetite was increasing.

"Perhaps we should move to another city," Philip said, as they drove home after leaving most of the eleventh victim in a fruit truck whose driver had parked to take a nap. "New York's bigger. That would be safer."

"Why?" Joe asked, in that lazy, sated way. "I'm not worried."

So they stayed in Los Angeles, and wrote some more stories and drowned a nightclub hostess in the bathtub, slowly. Philip found her irresistible.

"That was interesting, Philip. Your reproductive methods are

241

crude, but they certainly do excite you nicely! You should have done that with all of them."

"How do you reproduce, Joe?" Philip asked, rather embarrassed.

"Impossible to describe so you can understand," Joe said. "But not so exciting. Parthenogenetic."

A few days later, reading about the nightclub hostess in the paper, Philip asked, "Joe: how can you say you're a symbiote, rather than a parasite? You—you force me to do these monstrous things, so you can . . . eat. But symbiosis means *mutual* benefit. In god's name—what's *my* benefit?"

"In god's name? Nonsense," said the symbiote. "In Man's name! For all that Man has achieved he has thanked god; for all the evil men have done they blame 'human weakness.' Unfortunately that leaves guilt. It is not truly satisfactory, the man-god relationship, since god is not visible and man cannot be sure that god accepts the blame. I don't force you, Philip. I *let* you. I am your excuse. I am here. You know it is my fault. I accept the blame and the guilt. You are free of it, human—while you do what you as a man truly want to do."

"You are . . . god," Philip said.

"Of course. Now think about the hostess again."

A week later Joe was hungry again and Philip tried to dissuade him and Joe punished him by making Philip hit his thumb with a hammer. Thus Joe learned something new. It was a lovely banquet. And so simple! So little bother; no travelling, no witness minds to cloud. Joe dined at home, and thought about it. He put Philip to sleep and thought about it a great deal.

Then he woke Philip and made him cut off one of his fingers.

When the two medical examiners received the body, Robert groaned. Paul sighed. The creature the papers had dubbed the LA Slicer had been at work again, and had branched out. And only two weeks after that hostess; the killings had become steadily more frequent. Now it was a man. This one was minus all his toes and fingers save the thumb and index finger of his right hand. His left leg had been sawed half through. He was a mess.

242

"Shock," Robert said, bending over Philip's body. "Or loss of blood. What think, Paul?"

Paul also bent. "God. Looks that way, yes. It's up to us to—"

He jerked at a sudden sharp pain in his head. It was gone at once. He saw Robert jerk and clap a hand to his head.

"Hello, Paul," a little brainvoice said. "My name is Joe. I'm taking over."

"Hello, Robert," a little mindvoice said. "My name is Joe Junior. I'm taking over."

That was several years ago.

Be careful.

Charles L. Grant

Across the Water to Skye

CHARLES L. GRANT WAS BORN IN 1942. BEFORE HE MADE the leap into full-time writing several years ago, he taught for nine years in New Jersey public secondary schools. His photographs generally show him gazing mournfully through thin-framed spectacles. I met him first on a panel in Providence, at the World Fantasy Convention in 1975, where I was afraid of him because he was an officer of the Science Fiction Writers of America and he (he admitted a year later when we were on a panel in New York) was afraid of me, though I can't imagine why: a gentler, more saintly person never walked the earth. Presumably we stay in this business so that we can scare each other.

His dozen or more books include anthologies (Nightmares and the Shadows series) and novels: The Last Call of Mourning, The Sound of Midnight, The Hour of the Oxrun Dead, The Nestling. A short story, "A Crowd of Shadows," and a novelette, "A Glow of Candles, A Unicorn's Eye," have won Nebula Awards. Beyond the evocative titles you will often find stories as poignant as they are chilling. Certainly this is, and I believe it is his strangest story.

Labor Day; and so it is quite literally for some. But for others it marks the perennial end of a short-lived world, a frightening one bordered by bungalows and beaches fast deserted by backpedalling lemmings; a Lazarus world of wood and plastic fashioned into brightly tinted dreams from the stuffing of midnight nightmares. When the clown at the Fun House strangles its old woman's laugh, the firefly machines whirr to a dying, and life scuttles inland to lick at summer sun wounds.

For what it's worth, this is the substance of my mood as I lean against the peeling metal railing that separates the boardwalk strollers from the short drop to the sand. Of course, I do not deny I haven't felt regret myself when vacation ended. I hate being forced to return the sea/salt air to the nightwind, replacing it with the antiseptic shroud of the clinic. Not that I don't enjoy playing at healing, but I always feel somewhat older when I leave the lights behind.

And that regret is still there, but this time cloaked with a difference: I'm not going back. And, sadly, neither are the faces I see passing me by.

Which brings me to the beginning, to Danny sweet Danny and old man Ted; and also to a little-known riddle-rhyme my grandmother carried with her from the misted mountains she could see from the Isle of Skye.

> *Four old men sitting in a row*
> *Waiting for the black bird to take*
> *them in tow . . .*

Though I've tried to train myself not to count, not to count on the past, it must have been six or seven years ago that I finally came back to this what they used to call honky-tonk seaside resort. I had been casting for a way to exorcise a double memory: of a wife who hiked with me through the Appalachians every summer, and one day awakening to the enervation of a withering carcinoma; and of a son without a name who slid unborn into a surgeon's bloody hands. Twice in eleven months I had been clubbed to my knees, and only my Highland stubbornness made me stand up again. For balm the mountains were useless, and I even moved my bed so I could not see them from the window. Thus, a return to the sea. I refuse even now, however, to consider facile symbolism; it was, simply, a place where my wife and son had not been.

I wandered the boardwalk, staring at the faces of the children who shrieked the rides faster. Munching on cotton candy, candy apples, apple cider somehow frozen on a stick. I was braced for bitterness and an insane jealousy of the men who escorted their families from stand to stand and lugged the huge stuffed toys and carried the squalling babies. But there was nothing, nothing at all, and I found myself intently studying the faces, the hands, the late night shuffling of little girls' feet. I didn't know what I was looking for, and so found nothing. Not that year, anyway.

Except, of course, for Danny and Ted.

There is a carousel—you know the kind—that hasn't been moved or altered since I was a kid carrying dripping ice cream and exercising fat lungs. All manner of animals, some downright scarifying, others safe and lovely to hold. My favourite was, is, the llama: black, soft, whirling in the middle as if the rest of the universe did not exist. On the lion I got dizzy; on the llama I had dreams.

And beyond this spinning place that first time back, at the far end of the amusement area, was a freshly painted stand. Behind the counter an old man with an untrimmed black beard and battered yachtsman's cap sat on a stool and called hoarsely to the children to try out their luck. Flaccid and slick balloons were taped to a bewilderingly bright wall, and a hidden wheel spun lights across the playing area, turning concentration to frustrated tears. The darts were poorly balanced and dull, fraudulent and impotent, and everyone knew it and no one cared. The thrill was in beating the old man at his own game.

And if the wheezing challenge of the aged still wasn't sufficient unto the suckers thereof, there was the young girl in the loose black shift with sunset red hair and forest green eyes. She laughed when the old man scowled, enticed when he cajoled, while the bank sack on the floor filled with sticky quarters.

I found them around eleven on Sunday. No one else was around and damned if my grin didn't turn to a self-conscious grimace when I allowed myself to part with a coin and throw a few misses. The girl laughed and handed me three more. I missed again. The

246

old man lit a cigarette, leaned back and tapped the counter with a knobbed cane while I managed to pass four dollars, twelve quarters into his cloth strongbox.

"Hey, if I keep this stuff up," I said finally, "I won't have enough money to get me home."

"When are you leaving," she said.

"Tomorrow. Early. I like to pretend I can beat the Labor Day rush."

"Next year," she said, and with a quick look at the old man handed me a small doll from the far corner of the ledge holding the prizes. "Start on your first night down, and maybe you'll make it by the time you leave."

Annoyed because I felt a blush warming my collar, I ducked my head in a hasty farewell and fairly ran back to the car. It had been a long time since I'd felt so schoolboy foolish, and I remember trying to hide the doll until I was behind the wheel and could look at it in the green dashboard glow. She was no more than two hands long, with a plastic hula skirt and a drab lei painted over her breasts. Her hair was still and incongruously blond, and her face—I squinted, raised it close to my eyes and turned on the dome light. Staring. Then shrugging. It was a kewpie doll like uncountable others, but it was several uncomfortable hours before I was able to shake off the feeling that I'd seen that look a hundred times before.

I doctored, then, from fall to August, but I never forgot that boardwalk night. For a while I kept my prize on the desk, thinking it would be a clever distraction for the children. Unfortunately, they hated it, and their parents told me in no uncertain terms that they thought it highly inappropriate considering the surroundings. So I surrendered and dropped it into a drawer, forgotten until one afternoon . . . I was examining yet another in an oddly endless parade of housewives who complained of chronic listlessness and an inability to latch on to outside interests.

"You need something to pep you up, Mrs. Avaloni."

"Yes, Doctor."

"Why don't you get your mister to treat you to a steak dinner and a night on the town?"

"Yes, Doctor."

247

I tried not to sigh.

"All right, Mrs. Avaloni, let's have a look at those . . ."

I fumbled, pushing the examining stool back and hastily excused myself. In the corridor I grabbed one of my colleagues and got him to take over for me. Then I practically ran into the bathroom to hide.

Her eyes. Blank. The colour washed out as if soaked in salt water. Following my finger and the light well enough, but with all the animation of a still photograph.

I gripped the edge of the sink and stared at the reflection in the oval mirror, nodding even before I had thought the question: it was the same expression I'd seen on the kewpie doll, and the seaside faces.

Immediately, I launched into the tried and true pull-yourself-together-Simon routine. I dredged out coincidence. I blamed it all on a grief that continued to haunt me occasionally. I blamed it on stress, strain, the fantasies of the dart game girl that replaced the faces on my television screen.

And then I did some checking.

During the embryo days of the Cold War, tranquillizers became more than a fad—they were a national disease. Now, for a reason I wasn't quite yet ready to label, there was an abnormally high number of stimulant prescriptions, and in our clinic alone the youngest recipient was nine years old.

I did some asking and some listening.

"It's the Commies," the drug salesman said as he took the order for our resident pharmacist. "Stupid parents worried about the Bomb again, and the kids are worrying about schools and jobs, and the little kids are worrying about being big kids—have you ever seen the courses they make grammar school kids take nowadays? Hell, they might as well be in college. It ain't no fun being little any more, I guess. I'll say one thing, Simon, that doesn't make it too bad: it's sure been great for business."

"Technology, you know?" my bartender confided as he pointed with a towel at the crowded lounge, the crowded tables. "I mean, you got buttons for this and buttons for that, and what the hell kind of a life can you expect when you got nothing to do but push stupid buttons? Technology. Like television, for instance. Rots your brain. Take another drink, Doc, and take my advice: find yourself a dumb woman who don't ever read the papers and get yourself laid. It's the only thing you don't need a button for any more.''

I went to bed early every night because there was nothing to do.

> *Four old men sitting on the croft*
> *Waiting for the raven to take them*
> *aloft . . .*

The few years passed with parade-ground precision, and at least once a week in August I drove to the boardwalk and played with dull darts. I hadn't forgotten what I was looking for, but the urgency of those first few weeks somehow dulled into the background.

My mistake.

Generally, I couldn't stand the crowds that swallowed the public beaches. I spent most of my free summer days sitting on the porch of my ocean front cottage sleeping, reading, letting the breakers suck out the terrors of the city and the sick. I did meet a few women, I did wrinkle a few sheets a bit now and then, but it became more and more a mechanical thing and my middle-aged ego refused to settle all the blame on me. So my nights, then, from sunset to twelve, passed as I crunched through a candy apple and shot down the hours with Ted.

Ted. The owner of two dozen amusement stands up and down the Jersey and Florida coasts. He drifted with the seasons, bagging the tourists and filling his bank account against the day, he said, when apples would once again be hawked on the corners. Danny, his niece, laughed at his preaching economics but she drifted with him, and I never found the nerve to provide her with an anchor.

Until today, Labor Day.

Just three afternoons ago a patient of mine died of heart failure: he was seventeen years old. Worse, a cousin in a tightly meshed clan. The night before, last night, I asked Danny for her company at the funeral.

249

"Why?"

"To tell you the truth, I don't want to be there alone. A Celtic funeral isn't what it used to be, and I'll need an excuse to leave early without offending anyone."

To my surprise she accepted, and we arrived at the cemetery just before the first of the family.

It was grey, smelling of autumn, and a ground fog sneaked around the tombstones and climbed the dark trunks of the farthest trees. My cousins had kept close to the old ways, and as the coffin was lifted to rest on the straps that would eventually lower it into the ground, a piper began playing behind us. He was standing at the crest of a low hill, and when I turned I could only see his silhouette against the weaving clouds. A wind plucked at his kilt and dark tartan plaid, and carried over the words of the minister the mourning cry of "The Flowers of the Forest."

I looked to the others; I was the only one weeping. Danny pressed close to me and I put an arm around her shoulders. And still the piper called, and for a moment I could not remember who he was playing down.

As we drove back to the shore afterwards, Danny suddenly asked me why I'd never invited her out to dinner, to a picnic, for a drink at the orangeade stand. I was still hearing the music, still wondering who had died, but she insisted on an answer.

"Well, consider, m'dear," I said finally. "I, yours quite truly, am pushing so hard at forty-five that it's practically falling down. You, on the other hand, are not even thirty." Looking thirty-five, but I kept my mouth shut.

"Is that all?" she said. "I thought it was your wife."

"No," I said. "No, Danny, the piper played her down a long time ago. It's over in some ways, many ways . . ."

"Then please take me out, Simon, before it's too late."

I frowned. "Too late? For what, for crying out loud? Are you moving someplace permanent for a change? Don't tell me your uncle is finally giving up his wicked worldly ways." Unexpectedly, I was in a mild panic and babbled a bit more without giving her a chance to answer.

The traffic slowed, then, and I started the driver's litany of curses as we crawled behind the rubberneckers past the aftermath of a three-car collision. There was glittering glass on the highway, and standing by an ambulance were four small children. They were holding hands and listening intently to a patrolman kneeling in front of them.

"Look at that," I said sadly as we picked up speed. "They look like old men standing there."

Danny snapped at me: "Why did you say that?"

I was puzzled and risked a stare. Her face was pale, her hair disturbingly faded. "I don't know," I said. "They just looked like that to me."

In spite of my wit and wisdom, and my growing anger, she didn't say another word until I'd dropped her off at the boardwalk. Then she told me curtly to be at the stand after dark. I nodded and wrenched the car back on to the road, a defensive gesture to the sudden irritating mystery I thought she'd sprung on me. I hated things like that, and people who spoke in cryptic epigrams with supposedly meaningful glances only made me shed my patience. It all smacked of play-acting in an empty theatre and, especially on the heels of the funeral, an impotent way to jar me back to the land of the living.

Ten minutes later I was at my position on the porch, matching the retreating tide with the level of a pitcher filled with Southern Comfort laced with tea. Luckily this particular stretch of coastline was private, and I was spared the spectacle of sun oil gleaming off scorched bodies. Instead, I watched the waves pull away from me and wondered what the hell I'd said to make Danny draw off like that. I knew the piper had startled her, but it's a sadly beautiful thing to hear nevertheless and, coupled with what I'd been seeing lately, decidedly apropos.

I drank. Became maudlin. Dozed and dreamt: of little children with long grey hair dancing feebly beneath the image of a gigantic raven. Awoke and stared at the cloud scudding under the sun. Dozed, and the raven puffed its feathers until the entire scene hazed in shadow.

And the rhyme. That God damned rhyme!

Again I was awake, this time chilled in defiance of the sun, and gasping for air. The eyes of the raven had turned wine red, and swimming within were the faces of the world.

> *Along came the raven,*
> *Along came the bird . . .*

Simon, I thought, either you're drunk or in definite need of professional assistance.

I hurried inside, showered, dressed, decided to jog the two miles to the boardwalk. I used the wet skirt of sand as my track and spent the time recalling games I no longer saw: jumping over the snake-hiss foam, digging furiously for sandcrabs, taking imaginary potshots at wheeling gulls. The children were still there, but subdued. I also checked out a few bathing suits and the flesh they didn't cover to test my erotic stimulus level, and amazed myself by wondering why I was stalling in finding another mate.

Danny?

I refused to answer myself.

After a quick bite to eat at a pizza joint, I hurried to the dart stand. Ted saw me pushing through the crowd and lifted the counter flap to join me. Before I could pass a word to Danny, he took my arm and guided me away from the park to a bench that overlooked a slick brown jetty.

"Danny said the funeral was interesting." He scratched at his beard, then lighted a cigar butt he'd had in his pocket. "She also said something about an accident."

"Hey, look, Ted, would you mind telling me if I've offended Danny?" I reviewed our conversation for him. "And if I did hurt her somehow, why did I have to come tonight?"

He rubbed the side of his nose, crushed out the cigar with the tip of his cane. Small groups of people were passing us quickly as if they'd just realized the post-dinner sun wasn't going to do them any good. As one family huffed up the ramp not far from us, Ted pointed with his chin. "Would you say those folks are typical?"

Trying not to stare at them, I noted the towels and the toys, the umbrella, sandals, the futile swiping at sand clinging like barnacles to ankles and calves. Books, magazines, a radio and battered tennis ball. I thought I was supposed to see through the trivial to the profound, but I saw nothing out of the ordinary, and said so.

Ted nodded. "Precisely. Ordinary is the word. Right down to the premature bags under all their eyes."

"So?"

"Simon, there's no sense my being as fancy as you can be. I've been watching for years now. Seen them here, seen them in Florida, and all up the West Coast. Simon, tell me if I'm wrong, but I think they're dying."

I waited until he looked at me. "Okay. Do you know those people or something?"

"Never saw those particular ones in my life."

Another damned mystery. "Sorry, Ted, but how can you say something like that if you don't even know who they are?"

"Oh, it's not just them, Simon. It's all of them," and he covered the beach with a wave of his arm. He began lecturing even as I searched for labels from my premed psych courses, and damned if I didn't listen, caught myself nodding at figures he quoted. And as though I'd been struck in the face with a Catherine Wheel, my own half-hidden gropings meshed and blinded me.

And it was insane.

Of course it was.

In spite of the legends (and I don't even know how Ted had heard about them): stories in the Highlands of the earliest clans. Heroic men, fighting women, the prototypes for Rob Roy and the Black Douglas. And the First, with no name, known only as the Father Clan, the clan that had gone on too long, produced too many children and hunted and farmed for too many centuries. It's said that one night they vanished from the mainland, leaving behind only a hollow cairn in the keeping of a quartet of old men, all ex-chieftains. Speaking as one, reedy and faint in the Highland winter, they chanted the story of the Clan's greatest fear, and how it had sensed their longing and had come to relieve their burden, take them from the world.

Across the water to Skye. With the piper keening "The Flowers of the Forest."

And what do you think was the sound they heard?

"Simon, you're an educated man. You must have read or heard about dozens of civilizations that tried to hang on to that one extra moment, that tried to see one more sunset. Didn't you ever wonder about the historians and the smoke screens they set up to answer the unanswerable? To cover their confusion over the Atlanteans—"

"Hold it, Ted." I stood and backed away from him. "You've been playing that dart game too long. You want my professional medical opinion? Okay. I think you've spent too many years behind that counter. You watch all those folks playing so hard at resting and you're bitter because you have to work to help them along. You like to think you're an observer of the passing scene and all that crap, but in your own way, Ted, you're just as jaded as Dorian Gray."

"Is that your considered judgement, Doctor?" He didn't move, didn't look up. His shoulders lost their illusion of breadth, his arms suddenly became frail. And as the sun dripped shadows on to the low dunes, he sighed.

"Danny tried to warn you when she gave you that doll. She thought you'd understand and help try to stop it."

"Danny can take care of herself," I said angrily. "She's certainly old enough."

"Danny," the old man said, "is seventeen."

I was like a man trapped in a hall of broken mirrors, believing I saw the truth every time I turned around.

Seventeen. Like my cold in the grave cousin.

I walked away quickly, afraid I would catch the plague of his soul, dodged through the last day of vacation crowds that had become moths teasing the bulbs of coloured lights. I saw the frantic looks in parents' faces, dragging children from attraction to attraction; one last spin, one last turn, one last wheel to gain a fortune. Feet scuffling, hands clapping, laughter rising and flirting with hysteria.

As if they knew something I did not.

But it just isn't possible, I thought, that a whole race, an entire planet, would want to be carried away from the reality it had created, the only life it had known.

I passed the darts and Danny waved. She was trying to call something over the carousel music, but I heard nothing. I kept on moving, looking back only once to see her staring after me, and as though I were peering through a telescope I saw her eyes . . . the kewpie doll's . . . Avaloni's . . . the funeral . . .

I ducked into the first bar I saw and began ordering beer. There were dancers in cages, their gyrations less sexual than resigned, their costumes less provocative than functional. The music was loud, senseless, and soon enough I pushed off my stool and stumbled back to the boardwalk.

There were four children standing silently beside an overturned stroller, and I almost screamed.

Perhaps I did, because several people turned to look at me.

I hurried away, hunched against the arrows of their stares, and began wandering . . .

. . . and I wander even now. The boardwalk is deserted and my footsteps compete with the breakers to deafen me. I stand in front of the Fun House and watch the black in the giant clown's mouth twist into things that push me on; I wait at the window of the bar trying to see the ghosts of the dancers who could not now or ever arouse me; I reach out to caress the shuttered dart game stand, wincing at a splinter and in the pain evoking the talisman of Danny's smile. I don't even know when she and Ted left, but I do know they're running, speeding as fast as they can away from the sea. They wanted to help me, get me to play Paul Revere and warn the others. And God damn, but I failed them.

I may be old, Father William once said, but I'll be damned if I'm going to give in just when I'm starting to have fun.

I laugh at the notion that I can suddenly transform myself into a Lochinvar, subside to giggles when I realize the world will collapse like the slow motion fall of an empty circus tent unless I try . . . something.

I must be wild, drunk, bordering on the psychotic . . . but it stands there now, waiting to be my steed in the joust yet to be heralded.

The carousel. And the black llama.

I know nothing about the intricacies of machinery, but after pushing and pulling, jabbing and kicking, there is an explosion of light and the animals begin moving.

There are windows in houses looking out at the darkness, brittle with cold.

"Danny?"

There are sidewalks, deserted stages spawning echoes.

"Danny?"

Huddling people.

"Danny, goddamnit, look at me!"

I scramble on to the llama's saddle, using the worn leather reins to whip its rippled wooden neck.

The music . . . calliope rhyme Scottish rhyme . . .

And then there is nothing but "The Flowers of the Forest," and my bravado turns to tears as I swear in my shouting that I am not weary, clinging to the brass pole that pierces the llama's back.

And from out of the dark that envelops the ocean, over the gashes of white that push at the sand; sweeping across the trodden beach like the rhythmic slap of a sail in the wind, I can hear the truth of Ted's resigned madness, the answer to the riddle of the four old men.

The lights grow bright, the carousel spins, the clown starts to laugh, and the llama starts to buck; and relentlessly drowning the scale of my screams, the last things I hear are black wings
beating.